"So pensive, Miss?"

Lillian whirled around to find a man in shirtsleeves standing beneath the willow. A groundskeeper or stable master. She turned away without speaking.

A chuckle caused a chill to shiver up her spine. "Miss Lillian, is it not?"

"Miss O'Rourke," she corrected.

The man came around the bench and gave her an impudent smile. She felt breathless and nervous. He'd been eavesdropping.

"Well, Miss O'Rourke, you are to become a duchess. What good fortune."

She tilted her nose upward, feigning indifference.

"You can speak to me. I promise I do not bite."

She glanced at him again and noted he had an expensive jacket slung over one arm. Not a gardener. But more unsettling than she'd thought. No, he did not look suitable at all. He looked like the sort of man who would ruin a woman....

* * *

Unlacing Lilly
Harlequin® Historical #912—September 2008

Unlacing Lilly

GAIL RANSTROM

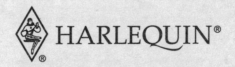

HARLEQUIN®

TORONTO • NEW YORK • LONDON
AMSTERDAM • PARIS • SYDNEY • HAMBURG
STOCKHOLM • ATHENS • TOKYO • MILAN • MADRID
PRAGUE • WARSAW • BUDAPEST • AUCKLAND

ISBN-13: 978-0-373-29512-8
ISBN-10:   0-373-29512-X

UNLACING LILLY

Copyright © 2008 by Gail Ranstrom

Printed in U.S.A.

**DON'T MISS THESE OTHER
NOVELS AVAILABLE NOW:**

#911 THE SHOCKING LORD STANDON—Louise Allen
Encountering a respectable governess in scandalizing circumstances,
Gareth Morant, Earl of Standon, demands her help. He educates
the buttoned-up Miss Jessica Gifford in the courtesan's arts.
But he hasn't bargained on such an ardent, clever pupil—
or on his passionate response to her!
*The next sensual installment of Louise Allen's
Those Scandalous Ravenhursts miniseries!*

#913 THE REBEL AND THE LADY—Kathryn Albright
Returning to an unstable Texas, Jack Dumont is determined
not to engage in the disputes brewing, wanting only to reunite
with his brother. But beholding the entrancing beauty that is
Victoria Ruiz, Jack realizes that to gain her love, he must
fight hard for her land—and for her….
Rebellion, freedom and romance—all in one passionate Texan tale!

**#914 TEMPLAR KNIGHT, FORBIDDEN BRIDE—
Lynna Banning**
Beautiful, talented Leonor de Balenguer y Hassam
is more interested in music than marriage, while
Templar Knight Reynaud is seeking his true identity.
As they travel together, both keeping secrets, attraction flares,
but Reynaud knows he can't offer Leonor what she deserves….
Travel on a thrilling journey through medieval France and Spain!

For Andrew, Connor, Lendynn, Nicholas and Sarah—
the best little buddies I could ever hope for.

Chapter One

London, July 27, 1821

This was not the first time Devlin Farrell had intruded on the grounds of Rutherford House to watch the people within. Far from it. He knew the residents almost as well as he knew himself. Knew what they liked and didn't like, who they saw, where they went and what they wanted. And he knew, too, when events would be held at Rutherford House that would allow him to watch them and, occasionally, mingle. Like tonight. There was not much, in fact, that he did not know about Lord Rutherford and his brood.

Shrouded by the branches of a sheltering willow, he went unnoticed by strolling couples and the occasional straggler. He had little fear of being discovered. There were far too many guests to keep track of tonight. With the right enticement, he might even enter the ballroom and blend. No one would recognize him, and if they did, they certainly would not give him away lest they give themselves away. Devlin was not a man people would admit to knowing.

Gay paper lanterns lit the paths and the sound of an orchestra floated from the ballroom on a summer breeze as soft as a caress to his cheek. Laughter filled the air, along with the clink of glasses, and he knew the wine would be as free-flowing as the Thames.

Devlin shrugged out of his jacket and slung it over a branch to roll his shirtsleeves up. The night was uncommonly sultry and he was not in the least concerned about how a gentleman appeared in public. He was not a gentleman.

"Oh, Lord Olney! You are beyond diverting."

Edward Manlay? Marquis of Olney and the Duke of Rutherford's heir? Devlin turned toward the voice. Coming down the path toward the bench beneath the willow were the Rutherford heir—lean and lanky Olney—and a fairylike creature whose honeyed hair was silvered by the clear moonlight. She wore a deep blue gown, turned almost black by the depth of the night, and trimmed with embroidered white birds in flight. How very appropriate for one so ethereal.

He moved behind the tree trunk and leaned against it, watching between the branches, curious to see what Olney would do next. Given that this was the cub's favorite bench for seductions, would he maul his companion as he'd done to other hapless females on countless occasions? Or yawn and make an excuse to return to the ballroom?

"Then say you'll be mine and I shall spend the rest of my days diverting you."

"Are you proposing marriage, sir, or something else?"

Olney preened, likely knowing full well a marquis, no matter his character, would be considered a good catch. "Marriage, Miss Lillian. I've never wanted anyone as desperately as I want you, m'dear. You've quite stolen my heart."

The dazzling Miss Lillian sat on the bench and the duke's heir perched beside her. "I hardly think your father would find me suitable, since I am neither titled nor the possessor of a magnificent dowry."

Olney's brow furrowed. Devlin did not know that look. Was he stringing the chit along, or was he truly vexed?

"He is anxious to see me married. I can bring him around to my way of thinking. Trust me."

The girl opened her fan and began moving it indolently, not an artifice or affectation in the sultry night, but a genuine attempt to cool herself. Devlin could easily see the girl's appeal—beauty, natural grace, self-possession and a proud bearing. Yes, she was everything Devlin could never have and that Olney would expect as his due.

"Even so," the girl said, "I think he would not like it."

Olney seized her hand and jerked her around to face him. "I must have you. I cannot countenance the way other men are watching you, courting you, sniffing around you like curs after a…"

Devlin nearly snorted his amusement. He knew the rest of that sentence and doubted the estimable Miss Lillian would appreciate being likened to a bitch in heat. But then he heard the girl's giggle and realized she knew full well what Olney had been about to say. Amused rather than insulted? Was Miss Lillian a bit saucy?

Olney straightened his lapels and continued. "The long and short of it, Miss Lillian, is that I am not willing to wait. If father does not give his blessing, we shall make a dash for Gretna Green. He will accept it after 'tis done."

Good God! The dolt meant it! He was willing to wed the girl just to bed her. Well, why not? That was as good a reason to marry as any, as far as Devlin knew. The Rutherford heir did not need a dowry, nor did he require a titled bride. If she came with connections, that would be enough. But the girl's next words dashed that conclusion.

"I can only offer you a mediocre dowry, and we have lived so long in Ireland that we have no connections but there. Indeed, we only know a handful of people in town. I have nothing to offer you."

Olney stood, gazing down his long nose at a girl he would certainly consider his social inferior. Even at this distance, his desire was clear. "Father's health is flagging. Marry me, and you will be a duchess one day soon. At the least, you will be a marchioness the moment you marry me. Grace my home, my table and my bed, and I will not ask anything more of you. But I must have you."

The old man was ailing? Then time was growing short. Drat. Devlin would have to make a move soon if he was to succeed.

Miss Lillian's pause disappointed Devlin. The prospect of being a duchess was undoubtedly more than any woman in her position could resist, but he'd hoped she would prove different. Yes, he would very much like to see Edward Manlay thwarted.

"I am mindful of the honor you have done me, Lord Olney, but good sense urges me to decline."

"I will have you, father's consent or not."

The arrogant bastard took her hand and lifted her to her feet so that he could crush her against his chest. Devlin held his breath. He would like to rescue her, but he never interfered, never gave his presence away. The coy chit would have to defend herself.

She pushed against Olney's chest with determination but she was no match for him. He subdued her quickly. Too quickly? She ceased her struggles and allowed Olney to kiss her, though he'd have wagered a good sum that she did not give him access to the full sweetness of her mouth. Clever girl. Keep him wanting more. He was liking this Miss Lillian more and more by the moment.

Satisfied with her tentative surrender, Olney loosened his

hold and she stepped back. Had she known he would release her if she granted the kiss? Canny, coy *and* saucy—a lethal combination for a man like Olney.

"I will speak with Father at once," he said, stepping backward onto the stone path. "Wait for me here, and we shall celebrate."

Devlin could guess how Olney would choose to celebrate. He wanted his Miss Lillian badly enough to defy his father and common sense to have her? This, then, would be the woman to bear the Rutherford heir? Ah, he'd waited patiently for years for something like this—and just in time, given that the old man was ailing. What a stroke of good luck this was—and one not to be squandered.

Lilly heaved a long sigh as she sank to the little stone bench again, watching Lord Olney disappear through the French windows to go find his father. He'd been most persuasive. She hadn't meant to encourage him, nor had she intended to aim as high as a marquis or a duke, but when faced with the possibility, she'd been hard-pressed to deny him. Her every instinct told her to proceed with caution, but her intellect told her that such a marriage to the Rutherford heir could be salvation for the O'Rourkes. And he certainly treated her well enough.

Life since coming to London had been such a trial. Her poor sisters! Cora dead by betrayal, Eugenia withdrawn to the point of seclusion and Isabella wed suddenly by license to the infamous "Lord Libertine" even before their mourning period was over. As Lady Vandecamp, their sponsor in London, had said, what was to become of them if something drastic was not done? That "something" had fallen to Lilly.

Her union with a marquis and future duke could be just the solution they needed to salvage what was left of the family's reputation and future. If her marriage to a duke did not stop the ton's doubts, it would certainly stop their gossip.

Although she was not wildly in love with Olney, her mother had told her that love comes with time. She supposed she could wait. But, so far, all that Lilly had been able to see was that love was just another word for treachery. It had gotten Cora killed and Bella married to an unsuitable man.

"So pensive, miss?"

She gasped and whirled around to find a man in shirt-sleeves standing beneath the willow. A groundskeeper or stable master. He'd frightened her half to death! But he was still a stranger, and if she'd learned nothing else in London, she'd learned to be wary of strangers. Especially one as wholly masculine and attractive as this one. She turned away without speaking.

A deep chuckle caused a little chill of foreboding to skitter up her spine. "Miss Lillian, is it not?"

"Miss O'Rourke," she corrected without turning.

"O'Rourke, eh? So I was right to think you have a lilt in your voice. Subtle, though, as if your tutors might have schooled you not to show your roots."

Was he suggesting that she was trying to hide her Irish blood? "I am not ashamed of my heritage, sir. No one has coached me. My mother is English and my father… But this is none of your business. I have no need to explain myself to a stranger."

The man came around the bench and gave her an impudent smile. She felt as if she'd been kicked in the stomach, all breathless and nervous. And besides, he'd been eavesdropping. How…how déclassé.

"Top of the island, I'd say. Northern and Scottish influence. Belfast?"

She gaped at him. How could he know such things? She was from Belfast, but she'd never admit it to him.

"Yes, Belfast. Well, Miss O'Rourke, you seem to be coming up in the world, eh? By design? Or serendipity?"

She tilted her nose upward, feigning sublime indifference.

"You can speak to me, Miss O'Rourke. I promise I do not bite."

She glanced at him again and noted that he had a well-cut expensive jacket slung over one arm and an intricately tied cravat at his throat. Not a gardener, then. But more unsettling than she'd thought at first. He was tall, had very dark hair, a strong jaw lined with equally dark stubble and the most astonishing blue-gray eyes she'd ever seen. And more subtle, there was a challenge veiled in those eyes. Something almost angry. Something dangerous.

"We have not been introduced," she reminded.

He looked around and shrugged. "I do not see anyone to perform that task."

And yet, she noted, he did not give his name or his business here. She glanced away again, hoping he would recognize a cut when it was given. Another time, under different circumstances, she might have ignored propriety and… No. She wouldn't have. He did not look suitable at all. He looked…like the sort of man who had ruined her sisters.

"So," he said, apparently undaunted by her snub. "You are to become a duchess. What good fortune for you."

"It is all I have dreamed of since I was a child, sir." She sniffed. "And the good fortune is all his."

He laughed outright this time. "'Tis always wise not to sell oneself short, but an inflated opinion of one's own worth might be just as bad."

Oh! Was he suggesting that she was not worthy of Edward Manlay, the Marquis of Olney? "Are you a friend of his, then, come to save him from my social-climbing grasp?"

"No friend of his, Miss O'Rourke, and thus I suppose I ought just to leave him to you."

Heat swept up from her toes. Could she even count the

number of veiled—and not so veiled—insults he'd delivered in the course of scant minutes?

"Denial, eh?" He posed a thoughtful look. "Is that what makes the heart grow fonder? Have you considered if he would propose if you had given him what he wanted?"

"I am not certain I will give him what he wants even after we are wed." She lifted her nose in the air and turned away, dismissing him once and for all.

The insufferable man roared with laughter this time. "Dear Lord! You are so pitifully naive, Miss O'Rourke. Do you know what kind of man Olney really is? Not the eager oaf who just pawed you, but the man he is when there is nothing to stop him? And, alas, when you wed him, there will be, quite literally, nothing to stop him."

"How dare you presume to know his mind, or his nature!"

"As you say, Miss O'Rourke." He bowed, an elegant and graceful move for one so large. "We shall meet again, and I shall look forward to hearing your experience in dealing with Olney. No doubt you will be sadder, but wiser."

"Is that a threat, sir?"

"Take it as you will, miss, but take it you will." And with those words, he departed, merging with the shadows and leaving her quite unsettled.

A glimpse of Olney returning along the garden path ended Devlin's interview of Miss Lillian O'Rourke rather abruptly. Alas, it would never do to run into the cub. As doubtful as it was that Olney would remember Devlin after twenty years, it was a risk Devlin was not willing to take.

A pity his interview had been cut short, though, since he'd been quite amused by his conversation with Miss O'Rourke. And quite drawn by her natural appeal. There was something compelling in those unusual blue-green eyes of hers. Something hidden and mysterious. Alas, that had to be his imagination. Miss O'Rourke was far too young and far too gently born to have a "past."

He resumed his position behind the ancient willow, wondering what verdict Rutherford had given. Yea? Or nay? Was the lovely Miss Lillian about to become the Marchioness of Olney? Soon, if Olney had been telling the truth, to be the Duchess of Rutherford? Though she couldn't know it, Devlin's own future hinged on the answer.

"I am to ask you if you wouldn't be content with a generous sum settled upon you and your family to make yourself available to me for as long as I pleased."

A mistress? How would the proud minx answer that?

She blinked. Several times. "Lord Olney, you cannot mean what I think you meant. You cannot be suggesting…"

Olney shrugged. "I told him you would not consent, but I promised I'd put the proposition to you."

So, Olney considered Miss O'Rourke inferior, but knew she would not consent to an illicit liaison. And he obviously wanted her for more than his usual single conquest, else he'd have forced her, as he'd forced others against their will, if the whispers were true. Better and better. A plan so devious that it would pierce Olney's pride for the rest of his life and embarrass Rutherford began to take shape in Devlin's mind.

"You may tell him that you made that insulting offer, and that I refused. In fact, I refuse *you,* your lordship."

"What? But why?"

"That you could even make such an offer tells me that the 'tender regard' you have professed does not extend to my best interests. Only yours."

"Here now, Miss Lillian! Did I not say that my father bade me to ask? Have I not been willing to wed you all along?" Olney's smile betrayed his father's verdict. He sat beside

Miss O'Rourke and took her hand. "I will not say that my father was pleased, my dear, but pending your refusal to what he termed 'a more suitable arrangement,' he gave his consent."

"Then…then he was disappointed in my dowry?"

The cub laughed. "My dear, the dowry was less a consideration than your…ah, humble origins. Father had pinned his hopes on a merger with a more prominent family."

Even from his position, Devlin could see Miss O'Rourke's deep flush. That, at least, he could understand and sympathize with. He'd spent a lifetime with an even worse taunt than "humble origins."

Devlin grinned when Miss Lillian contrived to look mollified, though the outcome had never been in doubt. No chit would refuse a marriage offer from the Rutherford heir. In fact, he was considered by those who did not know his true nature to be a stellar catch for any ambitious miss.

"What else did your father say?"

"Come, Miss Lillian. You may call me Edward now that we are betrothed."

"*Are* we betrothed?"

"We shall be on the morrow. Lord and Lady Vandecamp are shut in the library with Father at the moment, discussing the details. They are your sponsors, are they not? Lady Vandecamp said she would put the offer to your mother tomorrow. And, if all is agreeable, the first banns will be read as soon as can be. Just think! We should be married by the eighteenth of next month."

"S-so soon?"

"Come. Do not go all missish on me now, Miss Lillian. In just over three weeks' time, you will be the Marchioness of Olney. We shall have such a wedding night as the gods would envy. You will lack for nothing, my dear."

Then why did she not look happier, Devlin wondered. She

had dropped her gaze and would not meet the cub's eyes. More coyness? No doubt Olney had expected her to sigh and swoon into his arms to seal their bargain with a kiss. Miss Lillian, it would seem, knew how to keep her suitor eager to advance.

"Yes. Yes, of course…Edward."

"Three endless weeks. How shall I wait that long, Lillian?"

And before she could answer, Olney took matters into his own hands. He pulled her against his chest and crushed her to him, pressing his lips to hers in an even more forceful manner than he had earlier. Miss Lillian twisted, her arms caught between them. Olney was more determined than last time and did not release her. The kiss deepened.

Devlin's hands twitched. He longed to wrap them around the cub's throat and squeeze. He'd heard of Olney's cruelty to women from the demireps and courtesans who served the elite. Olney and his father were both infamous in those circles.

"Come now, have I not paid the price for a kiss? Give me another taste of what I might expect."

She pushed herself backward, opening a gap between them. Olney, however, used the maneuver to his advantage. Tightening one arm around her waist, he used the other to cup her breast and squeeze. Devlin could hear the terror in her outraged squeal. His fingers curled into fists and he tensed to go forward.

Miss Lillian countered Olney's ploy by bringing her slipper down sharply on his foot. "Release me! How dare you presume such familiarity?"

"'Twill not soon matter. Give over, Lillian."

"If several weeks will not matter, then you can wait, my lord."

"Or what?" He pulled her waist against him and pressed her hips into his groin. "Will you cut me? Refuse to marry me?"

Would she denounce him for his boorish behavior? Would she vow not to marry such a rough-handed brute? Could she even begin to see what life with Olney would be? A part of Devlin hoped she would recant, even though that would confound his own plan to use her. But a part of him was still disappointed when she answered.

"I...I only wish to do what is proper. We should wait until we are married for such intimacies."

Olney leaned toward her, his hand still on her breast. "Very well, Lillian. I value your purity, so I will wait. But I expect you to be pristine on our wedding night."

He released her and straightened the lapels of his jacket before offering his arm to take her back to the ball. With only the slightest hesitation, she took it.

Devlin watched them go, the clue into Olney's thinking giving rise to a new and better plan in his mind. He'd need a bit of time to make the arrangements, but he could accomplish it all before the wedding. Oh, this rough justice would be everything he'd waited for, planned for. His game had begun at last.

Chapter Two

August 15, 1821

"Devlin Farrell! Just the man I wanted to see."

Devlin heaved a deep sigh and looked to the side to find James Hunter had occupied a chair at the table next to his. This could not be good. Whenever a Hunter came to see him, it meant problems. "What is it, Jamie?"

"Good to see you, too, Dev." Jamie took a deep drink of ale from his tankard before he spoke again, scanning the barroom as if looking for trouble. "But as it happens, I do need something from you."

Devlin stood and tilted his head toward the back passageway. After he unlocked his office door, he left it ajar for Hunter, who he knew would follow in another minute or two. Hunter, it seemed, was no more anxious for people to know that he associated with Devlin than Devlin was. He took two glasses and a bottle of excellent rye whiskey from the cabinet behind him, poured a measure in each glass, then sat back to wait.

A few minutes later, Hunter slipped through the office

door and closed it behind him. "You're a complicated man to see," he said. "I meet most of my contacts at their club."

Devlin snorted. "I doubt I'd be admitted to one of your clubs unless I was carrying the coal scuttle. You have to go slumming if you want to see me, Hunter."

Despite his excellent instincts for survival, Devlin liked James Hunter. The man worked for the Home Office as a clandestine operative, he was honest and straightforward, and he never interfered with Devlin's business. But, as a younger son of an earl, he was certainly a member of the ton, and consorting with society could give Devlin a bad name in Whitechapel.

"Farrell's is the best of the Whitechapel gin houses, Dev. At least I know I won't go blind drinking what you serve. In fact, if it was in Holborn or Mayfair, it would be quite a respectable place."

"Aye? Well, it's not in Mayfair. And neither am I. I'm a Whitechapel gutter rat, and here I'll stay. But did you not see the sign outside? I've changed the name to The Crown and Bear."

Hunter shrugged. "It's your business and your life."

"What do you need, Hunter?"

His guest sipped his whiskey and looked thoughtful. "I've been meaning to thank you for your assistance last month at the chapel on the old Ballinger estate. We could never have stopped the Blood Wyvern Brotherhood without your assistance, and my brother would be dead without your help."

Devlin sipped again, remembering the incident. A degenerate group of peers looking for excitement had made a game of human sacrifice and Devlin had been drawn into the scheme by those trying to stop it—James Hunter and his brothers. "It wasn't a fair fight. If I hadn't thrown him a sword, someone else would have."

"No one else had one," Hunter reminded him.

"I am no hero, Hunter. Don't try to pretend otherwise."

Jamie gave him a wry grin. "If you say so, Dev. But you didn't have to be there. Did you?"

"I felt some complicity since I told you where to find the bastards."

"If I recall correctly, you mentioned that you had your own reasons for being there."

Damn! He knew he would live to regret those unguarded words. "That's my business, Hunter."

"And I won't interfere. But my investigation is not finished. We disbanded the bloody Brotherhood, but we did not capture them all. Since they were disguised by their robes, we cannot be certain we even know everyone involved."

"They scattered like cockroaches in the sunlight." Devlin chuckled. "They won't surface again for a very long time."

"And that is why I've come."

"You want me to flush them out?"

"Aye. The problem is in bringing them in. We know some of those involved, but they are lying low until the affair blows over. It will *not* blow over. These men are murderers and must be dealt with. We suspect some of them may be hiding in the rookeries. Thieves Kitchen. And that's where you come in. You know things, Dev. You hear things. People will talk to you because they trust you. See what you can learn."

Devlin shook his head. "I've grown accustomed to my neck the way it is. I do not need it broken."

"Does it not bother you that Henley got away? Or that Lord Elwood and Percy Throckmorton are continuing on as if nothing has happened? There were others, Dev. If stopping them was not your reason for being there, what was?"

Revenge. Rough justice. He'd waited for an opportunity like that, only to watch it disappear in an instant when he stopped to throw a sword to Hunter's brother. "'Twas none of my business. I owed your brother a favor, and now it's paid."

"There are some compelling reasons why you should help, Dev. Self-interest, chief among them."

"How is it in my own interest to assist the Home Office in anything?"

Hunter's dark purple eyes narrowed, and he took a deep breath before speaking. "Your…cooperation with the Home Office keeps the charleys from your door. If you didn't cooperate, their frequent visits at The Crown and Bear could be bad for business."

Ah, blackmail. Devlin seethed beneath the surface. Hunter must be desperate, indeed, to resort to that. He took another long drink from his glass and considered his options. Refusing Hunter's request would gain him nothing. Nor would granting it cost him anything. He did not respond favorably to threats. Nor did he think the charleys would be particularly bad for business. The crowd that frequented The Crown and Bear were a cut above the usual gin-house rowdies. He and Mick Haddon kept a superficial peace. And, to tell the truth, he didn't give a damn about Henley or the others.

No, he'd only wanted to know if Olney or Rutherford were at the sacrifice. And he'd wanted to use that information against them. But perhaps he could still uncover that information. If he and Hunter tracked the Brotherhood down one by one, he might get lucky and discover a stray duke or marquis in the lot. Now wouldn't that be delicious? Yes, that would make an excellent backup if his first plan failed.

"I have pressing business for the next week, Hunter, and may have to go away for a short while. A week, at most. After that…I might find some time."

"The sooner, the better," Hunter urged. "A month has passed already, and I fear the blackguards may be making plans to leave the country until the scandal blows over."

Devlin laughed. "I disagree, Hunter. A month is just enough

time for them to get cocky and think they've escaped unnoticed. Give them another week, and they won't even be looking for us. We shall take them by surprise."

Hunter raised his glass in a salute and Devlin returned it. Yes, things were coming together nicely.

Lilly sipped her tea, affecting a serene countenance as all about her was in turmoil. Isabella and her new husband were gently entreating her mother. Gina sat in a corner, applying herself to her needlework and ignoring the conversation. Lilly wished she could, but since she was the subject of it, that was not possible.

"I really think—" Isabella began.

Their mother waved her hand to silence her sister. "Good heavens, Bella, I cannot believe you want us to remove to your home. That would be so disruptive when I am still in mourning for poor Cora. Why can we not stay on here? The lease is paid through September."

Andrew Hunter, her sister's new husband, placed his hand on Bella's shoulder in a show of support, an expression of profound patience etched on his face. "Because, Mrs. O'Rourke, we wish to see to your needs and to offer you the protection of our home. When Miss Lilly is married, I am certain you would not want to intrude upon the newlyweds. Your house will be nearly empty with only you and Miss Gina left."

"I suppose it will be very lonely and quiet here when Lilly is gone." Mama glanced over her shoulder at Gina and lowered her voice. "I cannot think what has got into Gina. She used to be so lively."

Lilly and Bella exchanged a quick glance but said nothing. Only they knew of the night barely a month ago when a brotherhood of murderous villains had kidnapped Gina intending to make her their next victim. If Mama ever found out how close Gina had come to death, she'd never allow her to leave the house again.

Bella tried again. "Lilly and Lord Olney will be away on their wedding trip for a month or more, and by then you will be settled in with us. We have room enough, and Andrew has said he'd rather have you with us than with Olney."

"But why?" Her mother's tone was querulous. "I am certain the *marquis*—" she paused for emphasis "—would be delighted to make room for us. When we went to his home for tea last week, he was quite accommodating."

Lilly was not as certain as her mother that her new husband would welcome her family. In the two months Olney had been courting her, he had given her dozens of costly trinkets as if to prove his generosity. He had sent her poems and letters on the days when they had not met in person. He'd been her most ardent suitor by far—almost inappropriately so. But never once had he indicated that Mama and Gina would be welcome to stay in their home once they were wed, and though her mother was delighted that Lilly would be a duchess someday, Olney's parents could not forget that her family came from "humble origins." Which always begged the question—why had he stooped so low as to propose marriage to her?

That odious man in the garden the night of Olney's proposal was likely right. Olney would marry her to have what he otherwise could not. Well, as far as she was concerned, it was a fair trade. He would have access to her body, and she would have social and financial security for Mama and Gina. Even Mr. Hunter and Bella would benefit from that association, though it was clear to her that Mr. Hunter did not like Olney in the least.

"Perhaps later you could join Lilly and Olney," Bella was suggesting. "When they are settled."

"You are a fine one to talk, Bella. You and Mr. Hunter have

been married, what, a month today? Are you not newlyweds yourselves?"

"Andrew feels—"

"That you need the protection and presence of a man," Andrew finished for her. "Surely you can see the benefit to Miss Gina and yourself in having a male presence to protect you from unscrupulous tradesmen and other bothersome details, not to mention the troublesome events surrounding the disgraced queen's funeral procession yesterday? People were hurt in those riots, Mrs. O'Rourke. My servants are more than adequate for your needs. And, of course, you will bring Nancy with you, and Cook if you wish."

Her mother looked mildly surprised. "So this is your idea, is it, Mr. Hunter?"

"Bella and I have discussed it at length and believe that it is the best possible place for you. Once you are out of mourning, you will require a safe place to entertain Miss Gina's callers and freedom from the cares of running your own household. Surely you can see the attention that two attractive women alone would draw from scoundrels."

Mama gave him a little smile, almost flirtatious. "And who better to recognize them than another scoundrel?"

"Precisely," Mr. Hunter replied, not in the least put off by Mama's veiled barb.

"Well, in that case…I suppose I could always go to Lilly after she and Olney have settled and are accustomed to one another."

Mr. Hunter gave Lilly a quick glance, and she was surprised by the concern she saw in his eyes. "Yes, you could. And, of course, Miss Lilly will always be welcome in my home, as well."

What an odd way of phrasing such a sentiment. Lilly wondered if he was hinting that Olney would *not* be welcome. He and Bella had tried to talk to her about her impending nuptials several times, but she had changed the subject. She really did not want them planting doubts in her mind. Why could they not see that Olney was a dear in so many ways? Yes, she knew that he would be a challenge to handle, but she was certain she could manage. And the benefit of the lofty connection for Mama and Gina was immense.

"Gina? What do you say? Shall we remove to Mr. Hunter's house?" Mama asked.

Gina looked up from her needlework and swept a stray strand of dark hair back. "Will there be servants about? And locks on the doors?"

Bella smiled encouragingly. "Yes, Gina. And you shall have your own room. I picked a bright and sunny one for you, with a sitting area where you can do your needlework or read."

"Then, yes. I should like that very much. I have missed having you about, Bella."

"Then it is agreed!" Mr. Hunter rubbed his hands together. "I shall send servants to pack you up this very afternoon. No sense putting it off. You shall be settled before the wedding, Mrs. O'Rourke."

"But Lilly has her last fitting for her wedding gown this afternoon. And I had hoped to shop the stalls at Covent Garden for ribbon."

"By all means, do your chores. Bella tells me there is not much to be done since you leased this place fully furnished. Your Nancy can supervise the packing of your personal belongings."

"This is so sudden...."

Lilly touched her mother's arm. "I think this is for the best, Mama. I do not mind in the least, and I shall feel better leaving knowing that you will have someone to look after your needs and that you will have the protection of family."

Mama's eyes grew sad and Lilly knew she was thinking of Cora, and how she might still be alive if there had been more people about to see what she'd been doing. Mama took a deep breath before speaking. "Yes, then. Thank you, Mr. Hunter. We shall be delighted to accept your hospitality."

"Miss Lilly, may I go look at the gewgaws? I'd like to find some little trinket to send my sister. I shall be right behind you."

Lilly glanced at her rosy-cheeked, plump maid, Nancy, then down the row of stalls at Covent Garden and nodded. "I shall be looking at the ribbons. Mama asked me to find some greens and lavenders. Stay within calling distance."

Nancy nodded and disappeared into a stall selling fairings and Lilly continued down the row, feeling wilted in the late-afternoon heat. Even Mama had decided to stay at home to supervise the packing and sent Nancy to the fitting as her escort instead. It was just as well. Her fitting had taken more time than she'd planned. It seemed she'd lost weight since the first measurements had been taken—enough weight to warrant alterations to the nearly finished wedding gown.

She hated the garment. It was heavy with the frills, flounces, lace and bows reminiscent of court gowns of old, and made her look like a parody of a bride. Olney's parents had chosen the pattern, saying it was the only design befitting their wealth and consequence.

In fact, she had not been allowed to choose anything for her wedding. The duchess had decreed that, since the O'Rourkes were new to town, they would not have the slightest idea about who should be invited, what to do or how to proceed. The duchess had handled it all. Mama had been relieved. Lilly, however, was growing very tired of their interference and the constant harping on their consequence in society and wondered if she was cut out to be a marchioness, let alone a duchess.

But it was too late to turn back now. Her future in-laws

would just have to accept her as she was. She was committed to her course and nothing could change that. She had remained resolute in the whirlwind of the past three weeks because of Mama's delight in such a good match and the thought that Gina would have her pick of men. That was all she cared about.

Of course, she could find happiness with Olney.

She blew a drooping strand of hair away from her face as she looked down to inspect a row of rainbow-colored ribbons. She found the exact shade of lavender her mother wanted and asked the merchant to cut a length. The green she found was near to Mama's shade, but a bit lighter. Still, rather than shopping in the heat, she ordered a length of that, too. The merchant announced, "Sixpence, if you please. Three for each."

When she opened the drawstrings of her silk reticule, she was confounded. She could have sworn she had taken a one-pound banknote before she left the house. "Sir, if you will hold those ribbons for me, I shall return with payment."

The man narrowed his eyes as if he suspected trickery. "Tryin' to cheat an old man, are ye?" he asked in a loud voice.

"No!" The heat of a deep blush stole up Lilly's cheeks. "I promise I will be back. I must find my maid. She will lend me what I need."

"Yer maid? She's got money when you don't? The ribbon is cut, Miss Hoity-toity. Ye'll pay fer it or I'll call the charleys."

"I will advance her the money," a voice from behind her offered.

She turned and was both dismayed and relieved to find the man from Olney's garden. "Thank you, Mr.…ah, but I cannot accept. I barely know you, and it wouldn't be proper."

"It is only a length of ribbon, Miss O'Rourke. 'Twill not bankrupt me. I warrant you are good for it."

The merchant crowded forward and put his hand out.

"But I do not even know your name, sir."

"Devlin." And he gave her that crooked devil-may-care smile she had not been able to forget.

"Mr. Devlin? Very well. I am indebted to you."

With her nod, the man dropped sixpence into the merchant's palm. She stuffed the ribbons into her reticule and stepped away from the stall, anxious to disassociate herself from the scene.

"Thank you so much, Mr. Devlin. I fear that man was about to turn me over to the police. I cannot even begin to imagine what my mother would have done. Or Olney."

He laughed and she had to smile, too. The very thought of Olney trying to explain that the woman he was going to marry in three days' time had been arrested for theft was completely absurd. He would be certain to cancel the wedding.

"Alas, we shall never know," he said. "And I swear I shall never breathe a word of this to anyone. Now, tell me. Is your maid really about? And will she stand you the sixpence?"

"She is, sir. She is trying to find a trinket for her sister. She should be along any moment."

He reached out and brushed the loosened curl back from her face. The gesture was innocent, but somehow so intimate that it left her breathless, and she could not think of anything to say.

"I am not worried over my sixpence, Miss O'Rourke. I was merely wondering if you were trying to stall the merchant."

"It is true, sir. If Mama had not asked for ribbons, I would be home now."

"Ah, they are for your mother? I thought the green to be a perfect shade for you." He took her arm. "Come, let's stroll along until your maid comes. I'd prefer to be away from that man's stall."

"Yes!" She breathed a sigh of relief and did not even glance back as they left the merchant behind. "I promise you, I have never had anything like that happen to me before. I was certain I had a banknote in my reticule. I must have forgotten to put it in before I left the house."

"Or you put it in and some enterprising street urchin relieved you of it."

The thought of such a thing made her indignant. "Oh, that cannot be. My reticule has been over my wrist the whole time."

"Allow me." He slipped behind her and loosened the drawstrings with a touch so light she couldn't feel it. In a fluid movement, he dipped two fingers in, withdrew a glove and turned away, all without a single sign that he had violated her property.

She was astonished. "How did you do that?"

"Years and years of experience, Miss O'Rourke. Accomplished thieves are not heavy-handed. Nor do the good ones have to resort to being a cutpurse."

"You are a thief?"

"*Was,* Miss O'Rourke, in my misspent youth. I am reformed now." He tucked the glove back in her reticule and gave her an impudent smile. "Well, from thieving, anyway."

A thief? Did Olney really invite such people to his fetes? "Then what do you do now?"

"Oh, a number of things. Look after my investments. Manage my employees. Look for new opportunities. But I am a dull subject, Miss O'Rourke. I am more interested, instead, about why you are wandering London streets without a groom or male servant in view of the Queenite disturbances yesterday."

She shrugged. "Perhaps I am a Queenite."

He laughed and gave her a friendly nudge. "Now that would surprise me. No respectable young miss with an eye to her reputation and standing in society would admit to being a supporter of the queen. Risk the displeasure of the king? No."

"You have made the rather sweeping assumption that I am respectable, Mr. Devlin. Perhaps I am not."

"If you were not, Olney would not be marrying you."

"Oh, dear. You've caught me out." She gave him a sideways glance and a tingle of pleasure went through her when she saw his wide grin.

"You are a bit of a tease, are you not, Miss O'Rourke? I hope Olney appreciates that."

She rather doubted he did. He never seemed to know the differences between teasing and serious discourse. But there were worse things in a man than a lack of humor. She shrugged. "He will become accustomed to my little quirks."

"I shall pray he does."

Lilly was about to respond when she was distracted by a small dirty child who came running toward them, looked up, saw Mr. Devlin's face and came to an abrupt halt. His mouth formed an O and his eyes grew wide.

"Sorry, sir. I didn't mean no 'arm. I didn't know she was yer lady." He stuck one grimy hand into his pocket, withdrew a one-pound note and offered it to Mr. Devlin.

Mr. Devlin took the banknote and gave the boy a stern look. "Next time, Ned, keep going. Returning invites recognition and being caught."

"Aye, sir." Ned turned and ran back the way he'd come.

Lilly looked at him in amazement. "Is that my banknote? Are you teaching the boy to steal, Mr. Devlin?"

"No. I was teaching him not to get caught."

"Perhaps he should be, if he is taking other people's belongings."

"I might agree with you, Miss O'Rourke, if I did not know that he will not eat tonight if he does not steal. Nor will he have a place to lay his head."

"Surely his parents—"

"He does not know his father, and his mother…well, shall we say she is not interested in her son?"

"But she is responsible for him."

"She believes her first responsibility is to her addiction. Blue ruin, Miss O'Rourke. Everything she can manage to scrape together goes to feed that need."

Blue ruin. Gin. Lilly shuddered. She could not even imagine such a life. "I am sorry for him, but would he not be better off in an orphanage? There, at least, he would be fed and have a place to sleep. Perhaps he would learn his letters and ciphers, and certainly the difference between right and wrong."

Mr. Devlin gave her such a look of profound disbelief that she began to question her conclusion. "The street is often a better place than an orphanage." He presented her with her banknote and a small bow. "I pray you do not think less of me for assisting your villain."

In truth, she didn't know what to think of him. His physical presence was nearly intoxicating, and she'd never met a man who admitted to having been a thief. Nor one who commanded the respect of a small pickpocket—a very good one, at that.

She took her banknote and pushed it back in her reticule. "The note is all I have. Can you make change for it?"

He shook his head. "You may pay me the next time we meet, Miss O'Rourke. Meantime…" He tossed another coin to a flower vendor they were passing and plucked a dewy pink rose from a bucket with a natural grace that belied his size.

When he presented the rose to her, she knew she should refuse, but she found she couldn't. The hypnotic hold of his eyes compelled her to accept. Their fingers brushed when she accepted the flower, and the heat of his touch spread up her arm to make her cheeks burn.

"Thank you, Mr. Devlin. If you will give me your address, I shall send payment once I am home."

He seemed almost as unsettled as she had been. He waved one hand in a gesture of dismissal as he backed away. "Never mind, Miss O'Rourke. I can wait until we meet again." He turned and wove rapidly through the crowds.

Nancy tapped her shoulder. "I say, Miss Lilly! Who was that? A real looker, he is."

"His name is Mr. Devlin. I barely know him, Nancy. I met him a few weeks ago at Lord Olney's ball."

Nancy gave her guarded look. "We had better get you married soon or 'twill not be the last we see of him, I warrant. He looked at you like you were a cherry tart, miss, and he had a very big spoon."

Cherry tart? Nancy's assessment was unnerving. In truth, Lilly did not know what to make of Mr. Devlin. Why, she had recently thought of him as an "odious man," and mere moments ago she had thought him quite gallant to come to her rescue. But perhaps Nancy was right. She had better marry Olney soon, before her vague misgivings took root.

Chapter Three

Devlin separated his papers into stacks. One for his bar-keeper, one for his solicitor, one for his valet and his own private list. Within a day or two he'd be ready to put his plan in action, and just in time.

A soft knock at his study door as the clock chimed eleven drew his attention. This would be Basil Albright, his solicitor, prompt to a fault.

The door opened a crack, and Knowles, his valet, announced, "Mr. Albright, sir."

Devlin nodded and Knowles widened the gap to allow the solicitor through, then closed them inside. A smallish, balding man, Albright looked meek and ineffectual, but in reality, he was a shark. Nothing got past the man, and he was ruthless in dealing with his opponents.

"Mr. Farrell, what is this nonsense about drawing up a will? Has someone challenged you?"

How interesting that Albright would think in those terms. And yes, it was a very distinct possibility someone would, considering what he was about to do. Nonetheless, Albright's impertinence should not be indulged. "I am simply trying to tie up loose strings before I turn my attention to other matters." He gestured to the chair across the desk from him.

Albright gave him a sharp look as he sat down, opened his portfolio and withdrew a lead pencil. "Give me the particulars and I shall have it drawn up immediately. If it is not complicated, I should have it ready for signature tomorrow."

"Not in the least complicated. First, I wish to leave the gin house, both business and building, to Knowles."

"The valet? But what does he know of running a gin house?"

"We've lived above it for five years now, Albright. Do you think he's absorbed nothing?"

Albright looked around and Devlin knew he was assessing his apartments above The Crown and Bear. He'd said on more than one occasion that he found Mayfair quality above a Whitechapel slum to be a poor investment. But Devlin liked living above his business. He hadn't acquired wealth by delegating responsibility to others. No, he'd learned early to cling tight to what was his.

"The contents, as well?" Albright asked.

"Everything as it stands at the moment I cease to breathe."

"Mr. Farrell, the furnishings alone must be worth—"

"As it stands," Devlin repeated.

He waited until Albright finished making his notes, then continued. "My investment portfolio to Mick Hadden."

"Why, that's—"

"He wasn't always a barkeeper, Albright. Michael Haddon. M-i-c-h—"

"I can spell Michael, sir. And what of your cash accounts?"

Devlin turned in his chair and gazed out his window to the teeming street below. He lived in the midst of poverty and squalor. There was no way to end it, and he hadn't enough to make a scintilla of difference to the inhabitants of Whitechapel. He was not even certain most of them wanted a better life. But a few did. And he'd already made provisions for them.

Had his own mother had the wherewithal, she'd have gone back to Wiltshire when she'd found she was expecting him. Instead she'd been discharged into the Whitechapel rookeries to make her way the best she could. At first that had meant sewing and mending for a bawdy house, and when her eyesight began to fail when Devlin had been merely eight, she'd done whatever had come her way to put food in his mouth. Yes, even *that*.

"I want you to look into establishing a fund—a foundation, if you will—to assist women who wish to leave a dissolute life."

Albright coughed and glanced up from his writing. "Surely I did not hear you correctly."

"Surely you did."

"But you…"

He raised an eyebrow, daring Albright to continue. After escaping the orphanage when he was eleven, he'd done many things to build his fortune, most of them illegal, some of them immoral, but he'd never made money off women's backs. That one sin, at least, was foreign to him.

Albright wisely bent his head to his notes again. When he was finished writing, Devlin continued.

"Open a separate account at my bank for a thousand pounds under the name of Mr. Carson. I shall be making withdrawals over the next few weeks and I do not want them traced. During that time, you will not be able to reach me. If you need clarification or direction, meet with Haddon."

"He will know how to reach you?"

"Aye, and he'll be the only one."

"And meantime?"

Devlin stood and went to the door. "Meantime, I have long-overdue business to take care of."

* * *

"Farrell! Here you are. I'd have come sooner, but I was tying up some loose ends on a case."

Devlin heaved a deep sigh and looked to the side to find that Jack Higgins had occupied a chair at the table next to his. He'd sent word this morning before his solicitor arrived that he wanted to see the investigator this evening. "About time, Jack."

Jack signaled the barkeeper to bring a tankard before he spoke again, scanning the barroom as if looking for trouble. "And as it happens, if you are about to offer me work, I have just had an opening."

Jack had been one of the best of the Bow Street Runners, knew the rules of the Home Office and knew how to break them. Too bad he hadn't known how to avoid getting caught breaking them. Thus, Jack Higgins was no longer employed by the Home Office—he was a disgraced police investigator who now hired out to any man with the price. Men like Devlin.

He stood and tilted his head toward the back passageway. After he unlocked his office door, he left it ajar for Jack. He sat at his desk, took two glasses and a bottle of port from the cabinet behind him, poured a measure in each glass, then sat back to wait.

A few minutes later, Jack slipped through the office door and closed it behind him. "So, what do you need, Farrell? I know you didn't ask me here just to pass the time of day."

Devlin shrugged, hoping the gesture would belie the importance of the errand. "I need you to do a little snooping for me."

Jack's right eyebrow went up. "This is interesting. I thought you knew everything that went on in the rookeries. Why do you need me?"

"Because this has nothing to do with the rookeries. It has to do with the ton."

"You could still find out whatever you wanted. Put one of your snitches on the case."

"I need finesse, Jack. I can't have a heavy-handed gutter rat making a muddle of this. Or even getting himself noticed, for that matter."

"Ah, finesse. Discretion." Jack grinned. "This has to do with a woman, does it not?"

Devlin nodded and endured Jack's inevitable chortling.

"At last," Jack said when he'd controlled his laughter. "Pierced by Cupid's arrow. Oh, this will be the talk of the town. Well, certain parts of it, at least."

"Cupid has nothing to do with this."

"Do tell?"

"I am offering you a job. I need to find someone."

"Then give me the particulars of the search."

"The family name is O'Rourke. They are from Belfast. A mother and her daughters. I believe they have been in town since May. Their lodgings will be a good address, but not extravagant. They are gentry, not nobility."

"Hmm. Not much to go on. When do you need the information?"

"Tomorrow night."

Jack laughed.

"Tomorrow night," he repeated. "Twenty-four hours. And I have one other piece of information that should help you."

Sitting forward in his chair, Jack nodded. "Spill it, then."

"One of the daughters is betrothed to the Marquis of Olney."

The smile faded from Jack's face. "Rutherford's heir? Tell me you are not dallying with the fiancée."

"I am not dallying," Devlin confirmed, wondering if Jack would see through the subtlety.

"Rutherford. This puts a different light on the matter. He's a nasty one. I wouldn't put much past him. And if his cub follows in his footsteps, I'd watch Olney, too."

"Scared?" Devlin asked.

The pause was just long enough to confirm the charge. "Why do you need the information so soon?"

"Because the wedding is set for day after tomorrow."

"Do you think you're going to rescue the girl?"

Rescue? It hadn't even occurred to him to use such a label, but he supposed his plan could have that effect. "This actually has very little, if anything, to do with the O'Rourkes."

"Then—"

"A means to an end, Jack. And that's all you need to know." He removed a small stack of banknotes from his drawer and laid it on the desk. "Will you do it?"

He nodded. "I'll be back tonight with what I've uncovered."

Lilly stood at the French windows looking out on Rutherford's back gardens, remembering her odd conversation there with Mr. Devlin. A shiver passed through her, and she had a sudden fear that she would never marry Lord Olney. That something would happen to tear them apart. What silliness. All Mr. Devlin had done was tease about improving her fortunes and wanting to marry a duke. He'd certainly meant nothing sinister.

What an odd man Mr. Devlin was, a quixotic mix of brash impudence and unexpected chivalry. And certainly more complex than any of the men she'd met in London so far. Of course, she hadn't met many. She'd only mixed in small groups for the past six weeks since her family had been in half-mourning.

And tomorrow would mark three months since her oldest sister's death, and official mourning would end. Her wedding was scheduled for the day after—the soonest Mama and Lady Vandecamp would hear of allowing the ceremony. And not a moment too soon! As the day approached, Lilly grew more and more anxious to have it done with. She grew increasingly worried that something would happen to ruin her dream.

"So pensive, Miss Lillian?"

Olney had come to stand behind her and his breath was hot on her neck. A little frisson of excitement passed through her with the sudden realization that her wedding night loomed ahead. "Just thinking," she answered.

"About the wedding?"

She nodded, unwilling to turn and face him when she was certain she must be blushing. "Actually about Mr. Devlin."

"Who?"

"Your friend. The one I met in the garden the night you proposed."

She noted Olney's frown in his reflection in the window. "I do not believe I know a Mr. Devlin. Did you tell me about him?"

"You returned with your father's answer and I forgot all about meeting anyone."

He tilted his head, and his breath tickled her ear. "Ah, well. Never mind, m'dear. He could be a friend of my father's. Perhaps he was invited to the wedding. If you see him, you must introduce us."

The wedding! Since the duchess had taken over, Lilly couldn't even be sure who had been invited and who hadn't. "Yes, I shall look for the opportunity."

"Thank heavens Lady Vandecamp backed down from the duchess. Though your side was in favor of a small, discreet affair, my mother has been determined to make a lavish splash with the event. I vow she has invited half the ton—even those who have removed from London for the country."

"My sister…"

"Yes, my dear, we've all heard about Cora. And, to be perfectly honest, just the mention of her casts a pall over the occasion. Is it not time to put it behind you? After all, it has been three months."

She turned to look up at him. Olney had led a charmed life

if he hadn't lost anyone dear to him. He chucked her under the chin as he might a child. "Chin up, m'dear. Better days ahead. Soon you will be mine."

She forced a smile, pretending that the mere thought of such a thing cheered her. And, in truth, it did. Marriage to Olney would brighten her life once they settled in together.

"My dears, come join us," the duchess called in her imperious voice. "There will be time for sneaking away together after the wedding."

Olney cupped her elbow and turned her toward the grouping of chairs around the low table bearing a silver tea service. He sat her on the divan and went to stand behind her, resting one hand on her shoulder.

"The *most* exciting news, my dears. Rutherford believes the king will grant permission to proceed with the wedding."

Lilly's heart stopped. "I was not aware that was in question." She twisted to look around at her betrothed. "Olney, did you not say you had acquired a license so that we would not have to wait for my parish in Belfast to forward the declaration of banns there?"

He nodded. "Yes, but then Queen Caroline died and that has muddied the waters."

"A delay would be terribly inconvenient," the duchess declared. "The invitations had already gone out when Caroline died. Why, the flowers, the food, the church—all are in readiness."

Mama put her teacup down with a sharp crack. "Mourning is a most serious matter, madam. I, for one, would never have cut short our mourning for Cora, and—"

Behind her, Olney cleared his throat. Yes, Cora was not supposed to be mentioned. She sighed and looked down at her lap waiting for the inevitable rebuke from the duchess.

"Are you correcting me, Mrs. O'Rourke?"

"Oh, I am certain my mother would do nothing of the sort," Lilly hastened to explain with a quick glance at her mother.

The duchess nodded. "Well, dear Lillian, the wedding of a future duke takes precedence over some things. The acceptances to the wedding and the supper following have been pouring in. Evidently most of the ton does not think it in poor taste to continue with one's obligations. There may be a somber tone and a surfeit of drab colors, but there will be a large attendance."

"I suppose there will be time to mourn the poor queen afterward," Mama allowed with a conciliatory smile.

Olney's mother, always conscious of being a duchess and superior in all ways to her son's future in-laws, sniffed impatiently. "Mrs. O'Rourke, it is unlikely that any but commoners will truly mourn Caroline for long."

Lilly stiffened. The duchess could not have been clearer in her meaning. Mama was a commoner—one of the unwashed masses who would mourn the queen.

As if sensing her rising protest, Olney's hand squeezed her shoulder, warning her to silence. "Yes, yes, Mother. But can we not talk of something else? That topic is growing old," he said.

Lilly sighed gratefully for Olney's attempt to defuse the situation and glanced at her mother, praying she would let the comment pass. Unfortunately, that was not to be.

Mama drew a deep breath. "If you cannot mourn the queen, surely you can respect the dignity of her station."

The duchess's mouth worked but no sound issued forth. Mama had rendered the woman speechless! Oh, dear Lord! She glanced up at Olney again, hoping he would smooth things over, or at least change the subject, but the duke returned from his brandy in the library and provided the needed distraction.

"Rutherford, come join our little group," the duchess said,

still flushed from Mama's impertinence. "You will never guess. Mrs. O'Rourke is a Queenite. Is that not amusing?"

Lilly shot a glance at her mother to see a deep crimson flush her cheeks. If something were not done quickly, disaster would ensue. What if Olney's parents withdrew their approval of the marriage? Olney had already told her that they were less than pleased. Still, to insult her mother by suggesting that she supported the scandalous queen! Insult? No, humiliate. She started to rise, but again Olney's comforting hand on her shoulder held her back.

The Duke of Rutherford took a seat next to the duchess and looked down his long aristocratic nose at her mother. "Is that so? Well, I pray you have enough good sense to keep your opinions to yourself, madam. Yours is not a sentiment common in our circle."

"I believe your wife misunderstood my mother, your grace. She is not a Queenite."

"Hmm," was his only comment to that. "Well, the queen's body has left English soil to return her to Brunswick today, and we are well quit of her. She has proved to be as much trouble dead as she was alive. Such disgraceful goings-on! And now…well, the timing of her death is damned inconvenient."

Good heavens. Was the duke so arrogant that he suspected the queen of choosing a date to die that would inconvenience *him?* Olney cleared his throat and turned the conversation to the impending wedding. Lilly merely sat with a stiff back and allowed the chatter to wash over her as she studied the duke and his duchess.

Graying, and heavy through the bosom, the duchess was also possessed of a pinched mouth for pursing in disapproval. Apart from that, she was fairly unremarkable. It was the duke who really interested her. Dark hair with silver-gray streaks lent him distinction, cold blue eyes regarded all around him with suspicion and superiority, and a rod-stiff posture made him look as if he'd been carved from stone.

Still, there was something vaguely appealing about him. Perhaps the part Olney had inherited. Yes, the similarity was in the looks, not the bearing. Thank heavens! Then Olney would age well and she prayed her influence would save him from the insufferable arrogance displayed by his parents.

"Are we to be treated to the presence of your sister, Miss Eugenia, at the wedding? I must say that I find her absence to be unseemly." The duchess put her teacup down on the low table. "Why, any ordinary girl would be indulging in the rare opportunity to shine in society. What illness keeps her at home?"

"She took a bit of a spill not long ago," her mother answered for Lilly. "She knocked her head and has headaches since. Our physician says they will improve given time. And she has promised to stand up with Lilly on her wedding day."

"Then we shall not meet her until then?"

"There is only tomorrow," Lilly interjected, praying that was so, and that they would not call off the wedding now that they knew how "unsuitable" the common O'Rourkes were. "I shall be needing her to assist me in preparing to remove to Olney's apartments here." In truth, she did not need her sister's help; she only wanted to spare her the duchess's scrutiny and judgment.

At the moment, she only wanted to end the uncomfortable situation and the possibility of further disaster. Alas, the duchess had one last reminder of the O'Rourke's unsuitability.

"Well." She sighed deeply as she put her cup down. "Rutherford and I are just relieved Edward has finally proposed to *someone*. We began to despair of ever seeing grandchildren."

"Though we could have wished for someone…"

"Exactly like you, my dear," Olney finished for his father.

But it was too late. The unspoken words *more suitable* hung in the air like a dark cloud. She stood and gave the Duke of Rutherford the barest possible curtsy. "Thank you for a most enjoyable evening, but Mama and I should be returning home. I do not want to come to the wedding exhausted."

"If," the duchess emphasized with a glance at Mama, "there is to be a wedding."

Oh! What else could possibly go wrong? Surely Olney's parents would not withdraw their consent? A cold dread invaded Lilly's vitals.

Chapter Four

"All I asked was that you locate where the O'Rourkes from Belfast are living." Devlin took a breath and tried to curb his impatience. He was never at his best in the morning.

Jack Higgins sat across the desk from him, his rugged face furrowed in concern. "And I did. But they are gone."

"That doesn't make sense, Jack. Where in blazes would the family go when Miss O'Rourke is about to marry a marquis?"

"That appears to be the problem. The logical conclusion was that they had removed to other lodgings. But I was stymied. London is too large to go knocking door to door."

"Are you certain they are gone?"

"When there was no sign of a light or life within, I picked the lock on the garden door. They must have let the place furnished because all the furniture remains, but there's not a single personal item to be found."

Devlin gritted his teeth. No, damn it! He was too close to let this opportunity slip away. He had to find her. Had to know where she would be at the precise moment he was ready. "The neighbors would know something."

"I already queried them, Farrell. Let me tell you, they were not pleased to be called from their beds at midnight to answer questions about the O'Rourkes."

"What did you tell them?"

"That it was a Home Office matter. And that cooperation was in their best interests."

Yes, Jack could make that believable. "Then what did the neighbors have to say?"

Jack sat back in his chair and took a deep swallow of raw whiskey. He'd refused coffee, saying it might be morning for Devlin, but that he hadn't been to bed yet. "Said they were a quiet family. Confirmed that there were four girls when they moved in, and one met with some sort of unfortunate end not long after they arrived. One recently married, and there were two still at home. The mother is widowed and, from all accounts, a bit vague and wholly incompetent."

Devlin tamped down the quick flash of sympathy. Perhaps Miss O'Rourke was not as pampered as she had seemed. She had been wearing darker colors fit for mourning whenever he'd seen her. The neighbors could have the truth of it.

"What of their friends? People who came to call?"

"The neighbors all say they did not notice anyone or anything remarkable. Very few callers, they said. A coach or two just before the one sister married. Then, of a sudden, two coaches appeared yesterday afternoon, trunks and bandboxes were carried out and stuffed in the coaches, and the household departed, servants and all. If I didn't know better, I'd suspect chicanery of some sort."

"What? Kidnapping?" Devlin's stomach clenched. The wedding was tomorrow. If anyone got to Miss O'Rourke before he did, there'd be hell to pay.

"No. Who takes the servants on a kidnapping?" Jack gave him a canny grin. "And what's your interest in the O'Rourkes, Farrell? You said you had no plans to court one."

Ah, here was the ever present specter of his birth. Devlin
Farrell was not even good enough to court an obscure miss
with neither fortune nor title. No, he was about as low as a
man could be. A hundred years ago, his hand would have been
lopped off for even touching the hem of Miss O'Rourke's
gown. He gave Jack a snort, warning him to drop the subject.

"How do you want me to proceed?" he asked.

"Find the estate agent who is handling the property, and ask
him for forwarding information. He should know where
they've got to." Meantime, Devlin had his own idea to find her.

"What's so deuced important about a batch of females
from Belfast?"

"It is not about them, Jack. It is about something else entirely."

"I think you are looking for trouble, lad."

"When have I not been looking for trouble? Just find them.
Before tonight."

Edwards, her brother-in-law's valet, presented Lilly with
a silver salver bearing a letter with the Rutherford seal. "For
you, Miss Lillian. Urgent, I was told."

Lilly looked around the breakfast table. Of all of them, only
Andrew did not look surprised. "Go ahead," he told her.

She put her teacup down, took the letter, broke the seal,
scanned the first lines and felt a warm flush wash through her.

Mama gasped. "What is it?" She leaned forward in anticipation, her hand going to her throat.

"I…I am to be married tomorrow at eleven o'clock."

Bella and Gina both drew in long breaths and Mama
squealed with delight.

Only Andrew maintained a steady composure. "Is that
all it says?"

"No. It says that—" She paused to scan the lines again.
"That the king has sent his permission for the wedding to

proceed as scheduled and that he could not see any reason for general mourning—not even the shortest period, though he has agreed to a short court mourning. The duke further says that I should arrive at their church no later than half past ten tomorrow, and that he has arranged for me to wait in the vestry until all the guests have arrived. He says that the duchess will attend me there. My only duty is to claim my wedding gown at the dressmaker's this afternoon and ensure that it fits me well."

"How very thoughtful of the duchess to take on the burden of all the preparations. She is most considerate of our mourning, is she not?" Mama asked.

Lilly did not have the heart to tell her that the duchess had no patience at all with their mourning. She bit her tongue, though, thinking it better for Mama to believe the best of the duchess, as they would all soon be family.

Mama stood and dropped her napkin on her chair. "Mr. Hunter, would it be permissible for me to use your library for a private word with my daughter?"

Andrew had stood when Mama rose and gave a little bow. "Of course, Mrs. O'Rourke."

Lilly followed Mama down the corridor to Mr. Hunter's private sanctuary—the only place he'd found peace since the O'Rourkes had moved in, no doubt. What on earth had gotten into her mother?

As soon as Lilly entered the room, her mother pushed the door closed, turned a vivid shade of crimson and began to wring her hands. "I know I have been remiss these past few months, Lilly. But you are my baby, my dear sweet girl. I must pull myself together now, for your sake."

She drew Mama over to a chair and sat her down. "What is it? Is something wrong with my dowry? Oh, say we have not lost it in investments!"

"No. No, nothing amiss with your dowry, my dear. But…
but lacking in your education. I have put this off, thinking it
unnecessary should the king deny permission and unless you
are truly to be wed. Now that it is final, it is my obligation to
inform you of your duties as a wife."

"Oh, this is not necessary, Mama. You have been a pattern
for me in your devotion to Papa. I do not believe you ever
failed him."

"Yes, but…there are other duties that you would not have
known about."

"I really—"

"Duties to be performed only, um, behind closed doors.
The bedroom door, to be precise."

Heat burned her cheeks and Lilly imagined herself every
bit as crimson as her mother. Heavens! In all the excitement
of the wedding, she had not given much thought to the
wedding night. Each time her mind had wandered in that
direction, she had quickly thought of something else—her
gown, the flowers, her mother's delight.

"Now sit down, dear, and I shall have to educate you to a
woman's duty."

Lilly was mortified. She'd been raised around animals and
had a fairly good working knowledge of the harsh reality. She
further knew that the law required her to submit. As an ex-
periment, she'd even kissed two different boys before leaving
Ireland. Surely there was little further she had to know? But
she knew her mother, and she knew she would forge ahead,
regardless of Lilly's wishes. Perhaps a little lie?

"Completely unnecessary, Mama. Bella and I had a chat
yesterday. She has brought my education up to snuff."

"Oh." Looking disconcerted, her mother stood. "Well, then.
I suppose there's nothing more for me to say. I hope she did
not neglect to tell you about—"

"I promise, Mama. She neglected nothing."

"And that you cannot refuse, however much you might want?"

That caused her heart to skip a beat. "Yes, Mama. Even that." But she had seen the way Bella and Andrew looked at one another and she had to doubt that Bella would ever refuse anything Andrew wanted. Or that he would refuse her.

"I shall have to remember to thank Bella." And with a monumental sigh of relief, Mama stood and hurried to the door. When she opened it, Gina edged past her and closed her out.

She turned to Lilly and began giggling. "Did she give you the talk?"

Lilly covered her mouth to contain her own giggles as she nodded. She was relieved to see that Gina was becoming more like her old self now that they'd relocated to Mr. Hunter's house. Perhaps all she'd needed was to feel secure once again.

Gina crossed the room to the bookcases and trailed one finger along the spines. "I wanted to catch you alone, Lilly, and I am afraid there will be little opportunity between now and when you become the Marchioness of Olney. Shall I have to call you Lady Lillian?"

"Of course not."

When she turned back to Lilly, her expression was serious. "I shall miss you terribly. You realize, do you not, that now I will be all alone with Mama."

They both began giggling again. "Not entirely," Lilly reminded. "Mr. Hunter said you and Mama may stay here as long as you wish. And I hope you and Mama will come to stay with me, too, once Olney and I are out of Rutherford and settled in our own place."

Gina shook her head. "Mama may have missed it, but I have noted how both Olney and his parents look at us. We are beneath them, and they know it. I doubt they will ever let Olney forget it. Mama and I would only be a constant reminder."

She wanted to refute Gina's words, but she could not. It was true, and Gina was intelligent enough to have seen it. But the thought of never sharing a room or even the same house with her sisters again brought tears to her eyes. And then a rogue thought occurred to her—did she want to marry a man who would alienate her from her family?

Before she could think further, Gina gave her a fierce hug and dashed out the door. She dabbed at her eyes with a corner of her long sleeve, glad that she had an errand to do. The fresh air and the walk to the modiste would clear her mind and restore her balance.

Devlin watched as Miss O'Rourke huddled beneath the canopy of a sheltering elm in Green Park, her straw bonnet dripping from the sudden rainstorm. She clutched a box against her chest and seemed to be arguing with her maid. A moment later, the maid dashed into the rain and ran along the path. She would likely be going to summon a coach.

This was the opportunity he'd been waiting for. It had been easy enough to find out which fashionable modiste had been employed to make the Rutherford wedding gown. He could not imagine the Duchess of Rutherford using an ordinary modiste. And it had been just as easy to discover that the finishing touches were just being made and that the gown would be retrieved before tea.

So he'd waited patiently in his coach across the street from the modiste. It had not mattered to him who came to fetch the frippery, only that whoever it was would lead him back to Miss O'Rourke's home. And thus he would know where to find her when he was ready.

But this was even better. Miss O'Rourke herself had come

to claim her gown. And better still, the storm had broken as his coach was following her home, and she was now alone and vulnerable—an opportunity not to be squandered. While he watched, she fished through her reticule to find a handkerchief to dab the rain from her face and the action dislodged a scrap of paper that fluttered to the ground without her noticing. He gave his driver instructions to wait, hopped down into the rain and crossed the street to the park at a run.

The storm did not let up, but rather increased in intensity. People scattered, running for protection or for the doorways of houses across the street. Even better. They'd be as good as alone. Her back was turned to him and he swept up the small scrap of paper and secreted it in his waistcoat pocket before speaking.

"Miss O'Rourke!"

She spun in his direction, looked momentarily pleased, then covered it quickly. He arrived beside her and removed his hat to shake the rain from the brim.

"Mr. Devlin," she answered. She brushed the strands of wet hair peeking beneath her bonnet out of her eyes and gave him the tiniest of smiles. "Good heavens! You should not have gotten out of your coach. Now you are all wet."

"A small price to pay to rescue a pretty girl." He removed his jacket and made a canopy over her with his arms. "Come, I shall give you a ride home."

"Oh, thank you, but no. My maid will be returning with an umbrella any moment. She would be terrified to find me gone."

"We could watch for her along the way. Truly, an umbrella could not give you the protection of a coach."

"Thank you again, but no. I would not like to do anything that could look improper. Perhaps when Nancy comes back, you could give us both a ride?"

Drat! He could not drag her across the street and toss her into his coach in broad daylight, even if it was in the middle of a drenching thunderstorm. "Properly chaperoned, you mean. Is that because you are to say your vows tomorrow?"

She looked down at her box she clutched to her chest, then back up at him. "Yes. We just heard this morning that the king has given his permission, if not his approval."

"You look a bit disconcerted about that."

"I…was not certain it would arrive in time. I really thought there would be a delay."

"Did you want a delay? Are you having second thoughts, Miss O'Rourke?"

"No!" Her quick denial belied her words. "I mean, of course not. It will be lovely to be a marchioness, and then a duchess."

She blushed. How charming. He could not resist teasing. "Ah, is *that* what you are looking forward to?"

A mutinous light filled her eyes. "But of course. How perfectly exquisite to have people defer to me, ape my words and actions, regard me with fear and awe. I cannot think of anything more divine. I would have to be mad to not want it, Mr. Devlin. Of course I want it."

Tears welled in her eyes and she turned away. Good God! What was wrong with her? "Miss O'Rourke, are you quite all right?"

"Yes!" She gasped and looked at him with a horrified expression. He would wager she had not meant to say any of that aloud, let alone to have betrayed her misgivings.

Devlin chuckled. "If you say so. Just as well that you are not having second thoughts, though. With everything set for tomorrow, it would be a shame to delay or cancel."

She nodded. "*I* shan't. I cannot speak for Olney or his family."

"He'd be mad to let one more day pass with you not his wife."

She looked up at him and he was drawn into the raw emotion in her eyes—eyes as clear and seductive as a lazy summer afternoon. The rain had eased somewhat and Devlin slipped his jacket on before he cupped her chin, removed his handkerchief from his waistcoat pocket and dabbed at her tears. She sighed and swayed toward him.

Unable to resist, he bent his head until his lips were mere inches away from hers. "You are too damned tempting, Miss O'Rourke."

She did not move, did not even breathe. Then, as powerless to stop himself as he was to fly, he brushed his lips over hers and groaned. A quick jolt of desire shot through him. Damn! He had not meant for this to happen. He could ill afford any sentiment now. He released her and stepped back. "Olney is a lucky man. I hope he knows that."

She blinked. "I…I think he would not feel so lucky if he had seen that." She glanced around, but no one had noticed.

He cleared his throat. "I apologize for my familiarity. I shouldn't have done that."

"No, you shouldn't. And I cannot believe…I allowed you that liberty."

"Believe me, Miss O'Rourke, I am as surprised as you. Shall we forget it? I swear I shall never mention it again."

She bobbed her head in agreement and glanced away. Her embarrassment was painfully obvious. "Where has Nancy got to?"

That question was concerning him, as well. She would be back soon, and Devlin did not want to give her any chance to ask questions or be able to describe him later. "I think we can safely assume that Nancy will wait for the worst of this to pass before she comes after you. I am afraid you shall have to come with me or wait beneath a dripping tree."

"It is not necessary for you to wait with me, sir. There is nothing you can possibly do for me that I cannot do for myself."

He could not help but grin at the wide opening she had left him. "Oh, I think there may be a few things."

The remark was lost on her and she fussed with the box she'd been holding, straightening it and holding it closer.

"What do you have in the box that you are protecting so fiercely, Miss O'Rourke?"

She glanced down at the package she was now crushing against her chest. "My wedding gown."

"Ah. I wager it is a stunning creation."

She emitted an unladylike snort. "Are you coming to the wedding, Mr. Devlin?"

He nodded.

"You must tell me what you think of it."

"At the first opportunity." He glanced over his shoulder and sighed. The maid, still a block away, was returning with an umbrella. One last try. "Are you certain I cannot take you home, Miss O'Rourke? I hate to leave you alone out here in the weather."

"I am certain," she confirmed.

He put his hat on and took a step back. "Tomorrow, then."

"Oh, I had forgot! I owe you for the ribbons, Mr. Devlin. Here, if you will hold my box, I shall get the sum from my reticule."

"Never mind, Miss O'Rourke. I shall collect it from your new husband tomorrow. In full."

Devlin stared at the piece of paper Jack dropped on his desk. The address, written in scrawled numbers, was vaguely familiar. It was also close to the park where he'd left Lillian O'Rourke earlier today.

"You're certain?"

"No doubt. It appears he is her brother-in-law. Logical for him to take them in, under the circumstances."

"Logical, but damned inconvenient," Devlin murmured. "Too bad. I have no quarrel with the Hunter brothers but this will certainly start one."

"This? What? Is it not time you told me what you are up to, Farrell?"

"It is not. In fact, I think it will be a greater benefit to you if you haven't any idea what is afoot."

"Your game is afoot, that much is clear." Jack sat back in his chair and rocked on the rear legs. "But it is the nature of the game that troubles me. I begin to regret having any involvement in this at all. The Hunters are not ones a sane man would wish to cross. You've said you do not have a grudge with Miss O'Rourke, and that she is merely a means to an end, but I have misgivings as to the way you intend to use her."

So did Devlin, but he merely regarded Jack with an even expression. He could not afford to give anything more away. Not that Jack could stop him if he knew the whole plan, but Devlin had no stomach for a quarrel with no purpose. Quite simply, there was no way to turn him back now.

Jack was studying him and Devlin could almost see the wheels turning in his mind. He was quick and could put clues together faster than anyone Devlin had ever known, but pray he did not put this scheme together.

Yes, there would be adjustments he would have to make, and consequences to pay, but that was unavoidable. It was the greater risk of failure that troubled him. His original plan had been straightforward, clean and sure to succeed, but now it was fraught with possible disaster. If he failed…well, he'd lose his life. To target so powerful a family as Rutherford's was foolhardy. He'd known that from the beginning.

Apparently tired of waiting for Devlin to tell him more, Jack finally rocked forward in his chair and stood. He headed toward the door, shaking his head. "I'd appreciate it if you never mention my name or my involvement with this, Dev."

"Done." But he had one last chore for Jack, and he knew he could persuade him. He reached into his waistcoat pocket and withdrew the scrap of paper that had dropped from Miss O'Rourke's reticule. Her list of things to do and items to fetch. It would be enough.

Fricke was a dab hand at such things. "Take this to Fricke, will you? He will know what to do with it."

Jack came back for the paper and pushed it in his pocket. "A forger? Deeper and deeper," he said in mock despair before he closed the door behind him.

Devlin stood and went to his window to look down on the teeming Whitechapel street. Especially after dark it swarmed with men seeking strong drink and an easy mark, and women seeking the same. This was not a place for the timid, and he wondered how Miss O'Rourke would have fared here. Most likely she'd have hidden in corners and avoided the citizens. She was far too well-bred to even understand the misery in such places.

He remembered her as she'd been this afternoon, a bit bedraggled from the storm, smelling of starch and wet straw bonnet. Even that could not douse the fire she'd kindled in his groin. She'd been so completely lovely, so blissfully unaware of her appeal, that he'd been tempted to tell her. But she'd have run from him, and rightly so. His intentions were about as far from honorable as they could be.

He was still a bit bemused by the brush of their lips. He could not call it a kiss, at least none like he'd had before. Their lips had barely met, and yet he'd felt a surge of heat he hadn't experienced since his first time at fifteen years old when he'd lain with one of the prostitutes who had been a friend of his mother. In the countless encounters and women since, he'd never found anything remotely as exciting.

And, curse the luck, she was Andrew Hunter's sister-in-law. Hunter was a man of his word, and he respected that. In fact, Hunter had intervened to keep Devlin out of gaol once.

And Devlin had repaid the debt only a month ago by helping Andrew stop the brotherhood of sacrificial killers his brother James was now seeking. If he recalled correctly, Miss O'Rourke's sister was to have been the last sacrifice, but Hunter had arrived in time to foil their plans and disband the treacherous group.

What a quagmire of conflicting loyalties he'd fallen into. Honor his friendship? Be the gentleman to Miss O'Rourke? Or achieve the very thing he'd lived for since his mother's death twenty years ago?

He experienced a quick flash of sympathy for the O'Rourkes. They deserved a respite. They deserved a bit of peace.

They deserved better than they were going to get.

Yes, Devlin was the proverbial ill wind for Miss Lillian O'Rourke, and within twelve hours, her life would be changed forever.

Chapter Five

L illy tucked a strand of hair beneath her ivory silk bonnet. She had trimmed it with fresh pink and white roses, praying that would draw attention away from the hideous wedding gown. Yes, it fit her perfectly, but the multiple bands of ruffles around the skirt combined with the flounce at her neckline and the ridiculous bows on her sleeves and down her back made her look as if a milliner's shop had exploded on top of her. And the veil attached to the back of her bonnet was just too much. She could not wait for the wedding to be over so she could take the horrid thing off.

The murmur of voices from the church nave made her nervous since it was an indication of the growing crowd who'd come to witness the nuptials. She couldn't see a thing since the vestry, an interior room, opened off a side passageway and had no windows and only one door. The minister would come in from an outside door just across from the vestry so he could enter the church and change unseen. He had already done so, leaving the vestry for Lilly's use.

She glanced at the small clock on the console table beneath the oval mirror. Only a quarter of an hour before she would become the Marchioness of Olney. Her heart skipped a beat at that realization. Heavens, she only wanted it over.

A soft knock and a muffled, "Miss Lilly?" told her that her brother-in-law was outside. Was it already time to walk down the aisle? Her hands shook as she opened the door and let him in.

Andrew Hunter was ungodly handsome in his dark jacket and trousers. As he took off his hat, only the expression on his face betrayed his concern. "May I have a word with you, Miss Lilly?"

"Of course." She stepped back to give him room to enter.

He shut the door behind him and looked uncomfortable. He studied her for a moment before he began.

"Miss Lilly, are you having second thoughts? Any misgivings at all?"

"N-no. Why would you think that, sir?"

"It would be natural at this point. And completely understandable."

"The excitement…"

He nodded. "This must be a very…confusing time for you. I wanted to take this opportunity to assure you that there will always be a place for you at my home—Bella's home. Whatever is to come, I will give you sanctuary."

Sanctuary? Lilly studied Andrew's dark eyes and wondered what he could be hinting at to warrant such an odd declaration. "Do you anticipate a problem, sir?"

He glanced down at his highly polished shoes. "I, ah, hardly know how to answer that, Miss Lilly. Anything can happen. Olney is a man who has varied and exotic interests. You are innocent of society and may take issue with…well, something."

"What in heaven's name are you trying to tell me? That you do not like Olney and would rather I did not marry him?"

He combed his fingers through his dark hair and frowned as if that were a complicated question to answer. "Until recently, Miss Lilly, I was shoulder to shoulder with him in interests. Just as anyone who cared for your sister would not have chosen me for her, I would not have chosen Olney for you. But Bella has proved to be my salvation, and if Olney is likewise inclined to change, then I would not stand in the way. If he is not…"

"If not? Then you would give me *sanctuary* from my lawful husband? Is this why you and Bella insisted that we move to your house?"

Andrew's jaw tightened and he gripped her shoulders in his earnestness. "Lilly, try to understand. I wanted your family, including you, to have my protection should anything untoward occur."

"Untoward?"

"Should you decide not to marry Olney after all. Or should you decide to leave him afterward."

"What do you think he would do?"

She saw the defeat in his posture. "I can see that you are determined to proceed. I will respect your wishes, my dear. I will go inform Bella, and I'll be back for you as soon as the last of Rutherford's guests have arrived."

Lilly frowned as he turned and opened the door. She was about to call him back and demand an explanation for his odd offer, but the Duchess of Rutherford was standing there with her hand raised to knock.

She pushed past Mr. Hunter carrying a small deep blue lacquer case with a jeweled clasp. "Oh! My goodness. I hope I am not interrupting. I must speak with Lillian immediately."

"I was just leaving," Andrew said with a stiff bow and a reassuring glance back at Lilly.

The door closed again and the duchess sighed heavily.

"Well, as it appears this wedding is to go forward, I have come to do the proper thing."

"The proper thing?" Lilly was bemused. She could not imagine what the duchess meant. This was certainly a day for out-of-the-ordinary behavior.

"It does not surprise me that you do not know of these things, Lillian. I believe we shall have quite a chore in bringing you up to snuff."

Torn between embarrassment and indignation, Lilly bit her tongue. She did not want to quarrel with her future mother-in-law mere minutes before the vows.

The duchess put the lacquer case on the console table beside Lilly's bouquet and turned Lilly to the mirror. "Does nothing occur to you, girl?"

She could see nothing in her reflection that needed fixing, except, perhaps, the duchess's proximity. "Nothing," she answered cheerfully.

"What would people say if you walked down the aisle like that?"

"Here comes Miss Lilly?"

"Do not be impertinent with me, chit!"

She sighed and reminded herself that she and Olney would be living at Rutherford House until they could find a suitable place of their own. It would be much better if she could find a way to be at peace with her.

She took a deep breath. "I apologize, your grace. I did not mean to upset you. But I really have no idea what is wrong. You designed the dress. You selected the modiste and milliner. You have made the preparations here at your own parish church and selected the refreshments for the reception following. I have only chosen the flowers. Are they not suitable?"

The duchess surveyed her bonnet and the bouquet with

narrowed eyes. "They are nice enough, though I wish you had chosen something a bit more colorful. Something blue, perhaps."

Lilly gritted her teeth. Had she chosen blue, the duchess would have wanted pink.

The duchess opened the lacquer box to reveal a stunningly elaborate necklace of flawless clear blue sapphires between two rows of smaller glittering diamonds. Lilly had never seen anything even remotely like it. Her astonishment must have shown, because the duchess smiled with satisfaction.

"Yes, I thought you might be impressed," she said. "And there are earrings to go with it."

"But…it is too much."

"They are not a wedding gift, Lillian. They are the Rutherford Sapphires, the very best of the Rutherford collection. I have decided to loan them to you for this very special day. People will see them and recognize that you are one of us now. It is important that they believe we have approved of you."

Believe they approved of her? Lilly smiled before she realized that the duke and duchess were only putting a good face on a poor choice. They did not approve of her, but they wanted their friends to *believe* they did. She nearly refused to wear the jewels, but she remained silent again as the duchess turned her back toward the mirror, lifted her veil out of the way and fastened the clasp of the stunning necklace at her nape. She had to remove her bonnet to attach the earrings, clusters of diamonds surrounding large sapphires.

She didn't know what to say as she looked at herself in the mirror. She loved them. She hated them. She would wear them for Olney's sake. "Th-thank you, your grace. I promise I will take good care of them."

"See that you do. You and Olney will not be attending the reception as it would be improper of you to appear publicly for the next month, so I will expect you to return them before you leave the church. Rutherford or I shall come while you and Olney are signing your marriage lines afterward."

"Yes, your grace. Of course."

"Now I must return to Rutherford. We shall begin the wedding immediately after Rutherford's brother arrives. I believe your brother-in-law is escorting you down the aisle?"

She nodded.

"Very well, then. And do not forget to pinch your cheeks before you leave the vestry. You need color, child."

It was true. She'd gone quite pale. She turned away from her reflection and watched the door close.

Alone now in the small room, she shivered with a moment of panic. The next knock on that door would be her summons to walk down an aisle and then say two words that would forever tie her to a man she barely knew. Before she left this church, she would be Lillian Manlay, the Marchioness of Olney.

And with those two little words—*I do*—her whole life would become a lie. What she wanted would be hidden, what she thought would remain unspoken, what she said would have to be a polite evasion of truth, and what she felt would be denied. Her hands began to shake. Oh, dear Lord! Why had she not realized this before now? Could she do it? Could she commit her life to Olney, submit herself to him, knowing it was all a lie?

She lifted her massive bouquet from the console table and watched the delicate pink rose petals tremble as if in a wind. Then she remembered another pink rose, the single stem still fresh but now fully opened and lush, in a small vase on the dressing table in her room at Mr. Hunter's house—the rose Mr. Devlin had given her at Covent Garden. At the moment she'd rather have that one rose given in honesty than her elaborate wedding bouquet as a symbol of the lie she was entering into.

That single rose… She'd held it to her lips this morning, remembering the brush of Mr. Devlin's lips against hers. How could such a gesture cause her heart to skip and awaken such a sinful yearning for more? Certainly Olney's forceful, almost brutish, kisses had evoked none of those forbidden desires. And if Olney was brutish in that much, would he be brutish in more?

The consummation loomed ahead. She had dismissed her misgivings before, preferring not to think of what was coming. And now she would finally know what he meant when he cast her hot glances and promised her an experience she would never forget. The sudden overwhelming urge to beg off washed over her and she fought it back, reminding herself over and over how much this marriage would mean to her family.

The next knock caught her unawares and she jumped. Mr. Hunter had come so soon? She tried to squeak out an invitation to come in, but her voice failed her. Instead, she reached out and opened the door herself.

"Mr. Devlin!"

He pushed his way in and closed the door. "Miss O'Rourke." He surveyed her from the top of her bonnet to the tips of her slippers. His lips twitched and she couldn't tell if he was amused or pleased. "You quite take my breath away."

She tore her gaze away from his full, perfect lips—the ones she had just been thinking of. But he must have lost his way. "If you will go down the passageway and turn to your right, you will find the nave. I believe everyone is gathered there."

He nodded. "I do not believe I will stay for the wedding, Miss O'Rourke."

He was dressed in elegant formal clothes, as if he'd come for the event, but if he had not come for that, why was he here? "Your…your loan? But, as you can see, I do not have my reticule. Did you not say that you would collect from Olney?"

His lopsided smile almost undid her. "I shall. It is, in fact, the very reason I have come."

"Then why are you here? I mean, in the vestry?"

He shrugged. "I am wondering if you are having second thoughts about walking down that aisle."

"Heavens! What has gotten into everyone? Why is everyone asking that question? Have I done something to give people that impression?"

He laughed. "How many of us are having that same thought?"

"Aside from my sister, Mr. Hunter and you."

"Hmm. Well, it may be that we are more perceptive than the others."

"What is it that everyone is afraid of? Olney has been nothing but kind to me. He has stood by his proposal to me even when his parents were less than pleased. Does that not prove he loves me?"

"It proves that he wants you, Miss O'Rourke, and is willing to pay the price to have you. But it pleases me to hear how much he is looking forward to tonight."

Heat scorched her cheeks and she was slightly dizzy. What possible interest could Mr. Devlin have in how much Olney wanted her? The way his gaze swept slowly up her body until he met her eyes was unsettling, to say the least. Not insulting, but far too familiar. Far too knowledgeable.

He walked in a circle around her and then stopped in front of her again. "As for the wedding dress, I confess it is quite unpleasant. You'd have done better to leave it in the rain yesterday."

She laughed, surprised by his bald honesty. "I fear you and I are the only ones who think so, Mr. Devlin. I suppose I shall know what the general consensus is by the gasps of astonishment or murmurs of appreciation as I walk down the aisle."

"I'd prepare for gasps, Miss O'Rourke."

The faint strains of music carried to them, and Lilly knew Mr. Hunter would be coming for her momentarily. "You had better go now. The moment is at hand and my brother-in-law will be coming for me."

"Yes, indeed. The moment *is* at hand." He took a sealed envelope from the inside of his jacket and placed it on the console table, then reached out and ran his finger over the sapphire necklace at her throat, his finger leaving a wake of heat to contrast with the cold stones.

The gesture was uncomfortably familiar and she looked up into his eyes. They were somehow colder than before, and quite calculating. "I think you should go, sir."

"I think we both should."

His large hand circled her throat and she felt a moment of pressure behind her ear before darkness descended.

Devlin caught her before she fell. He lifted her so quickly that her bouquet was caught between them. He had to dip slightly to reach the knob and open the vestry door, then a quick peek into the passageway revealed that he had a clear path to the exterior door. From there, it was only a few steps to the street and his coach, an anonymous black hackney. He lifted Miss O'Rourke onto the seat, gathered the veil into the coach and got in opposite her. A quick rap on the roof set the driver off at a gallop.

He drew a deep sigh and resisted the impulse to look back and see if they were being pursued. Once Andrew Hunter found his sister-in-law missing, there would be no safe place for them in London.

He braced his boot on the opposite seat as a barrier to keep Miss O'Rourke from being tossed to the floor as they rounded a corner on two wheels. Her bonnet fell off, revealing the soft curls of her honey-blond hair secured with white ribbons. He leaned forward to brush one wayward strand back from her cheek and was surprised when it curled around his finger. The feel of the cool silken lengths beckoned him closer to smell her shampoo, a mixture of rain and faint meadow flowers. A womanly smell. No, more than that—a *gentlewoman's* scent.

Devlin had never smelled anything quite like it. The women he'd lain with, who had fostered him after his mother's death and who had since escaped Whitechapel or had been destroyed by the iniquity, had not had the luxury of baths and fine shampoos. They'd been lucky to find a sliver of soap. He inhaled deeply, savoring the clean wholesomeness so foreign to him. So foreign, in fact, to everything he had ever known of life.

His success with The Crown and Bear and his investments abroad had made him a wealthy man. He had a valet and fashionable clothes. He bathed and aped the manners of his betters. But that did not make him one of them. Nor did it make him acceptable to their women. Not a one of them who knew who he was, including Miss O'Rourke, would have stopped to glance at him if he'd been on fire. Here, this very moment, leaning over her and inhaling her scent, was the closest he'd ever been to a woman of Lillian O'Rourke's class and quality.

Oh, yes, he rubbed elbows with their husbands nearly every night as they came to *his* part of town to gamble, drink and whore, but that was not the same. He catered to their sins, and they hated him for it. And hated him because they were afraid of him—afraid because he knew their secrets and afraid of what would happen if he exposed them. And now she, too, would hate him—for those and so many more reasons to come.

Devlin released that sun-burnished curl but remained bent over her, resting his forearms on his knees. He marveled at her flawless complexion and the faint variation of color from her cheeks, flushed with the heat of the summer afternoon, and the ivory smoothness of her forehead and chin. And how her dark lashes—those absurdly long lashes—lay in a perfect sweep against her cheeks. Her lips, bowed and plump, beckoned him and he grew relentlessly hard as he remembered how they'd felt brushing against his yesterday. But he hadn't tasted them. Not yet. Would they be as tart as her words? Or as sweet as her smiles?

He did not know how long he remained thus, studying her, memorizing her, but he'd been unable to stop until the coach rocked as the driver got down and opened the door.

"There's a special place in hell for me now," Jack Higgins said, doffing the driver's cap. "Kidnapping, for God's sake! I do not know how I let you talk me into this."

Devlin grinned at the man and sat back against the squabs. "I gather we're well out of town."

"Aye. A good piece. How's the little miss?"

"She'll be coming around before long."

"Are you sure you don't want me to drive you the rest of the way?"

"Wouldn't want to put you in that position, Jack. If you're asked, you'll be able to say with complete honesty that you haven't the faintest notion where I am."

Jack heaved a deep sigh. "Considerate of you to attend my conscience. Don't you think you ought to tie her up? If she wakes while you're driving, she could try to jump out."

Would she? Aye, she would. He'd seen that hint of steel and that flash of defiance in her. She was not going to take this lightly. "You've got us past St. Elmo. There's nothing out here but forest for the next ten miles. I think I'll be safe enough."

Jack's smile faded. "Seriously, Dev. You do not mean to harm her?"

"I haven't sunk that low, Jack. God willing, I never will. What did you think I'd planned?"

"That you planned to seduce her to spite Olney, then return her to him as damaged goods."

Devlin wished he could deny that such a thing had even occurred to him, but it had. How sweet the thought of having Olney presented with *his* leftovers. That was still a possibility, but his plan was a bit more subtle and would have the same results. In fact, the first ripples would be spreading on the London pond at this very moment.

"Then what are your intentions?"

He closed the carriage door, looped the rope around the handle and knotted it to the window frame. "To give Miss O'Rourke a lovely holiday in the country, and then to return her home, none the worse for wear."

"Don't cozen me, Dev. You do not kidnap a bride from under the groom's nose for no apparent purpose."

"Miss O'Rourke is incidental to that purpose."

"You know you're making powerful enemies, do you not? From the Hunter brothers to Rutherford and Olney, they will not rest until you are dangling at Newgate."

Devlin ignored the oft-repeated warning. He took the driver's cap, climbed into the seat and smiled down at Jack. "I will see you back in London, Jack. Mind you keep your nose clean until then."

He waited while Jack untied a horse from the rear of the hackney and climbed into the saddle. At that moment, a faint moan and a subtle shifting of weight inside the coach alerted him that Miss O'Rourke was regaining consciousness. There was trouble ahead, and he'd better get away while he could. He picked up the whip and cracked it over the horses' heads.

Chapter Six

Lilly's head pounded as she labored to regain her senses. What had happened? The last thing she recalled was…was… No, the pounding was horse's hooves. She opened her eyes and braced herself as the coach hit a bump.

Struggling to sit up, she gripped a hand strap attached to the inside wall. She couldn't seem to orient herself. She'd been standing in the vestry talking with Mr. Devlin, and then…then she could remember nothing. Had Andrew come to walk her down the aisle? Had she actually said her vows and then fainted? And was Olney taking her away to his wedding hideaway to consummate the marriage? Consummate! She felt suddenly nauseous and breathed deeply until it passed.

The coach had slowed and she edged across the leather seat to glance out the window. They were traveling on a narrow lane—no, more of an overgrown track. Verdant trees formed a canopy overhead, and branches slapped the sides of coach as they passed. Whatever had traveled on this road before them could not have been larger than a single rider.

Despite the heat of the afternoon and the closeness of the coach, Lilly shivered. Olney had bragged more than once that he was one of the best in the four-in-hand club, a group of men who had turned driving coaches into a pulse-pounding sport, and that he would drive them away from the church. But something was very wrong. She knocked on the roof and called out. "Olney? Olney, where are we?"

Though her voice was loud in the rural stillness, he did not answer. The silence made her uneasy. He must be concentrating on not getting them stuck in a rut. Surely they could not be much longer? The track seemed to be narrowing with every turn of the wheels.

She leaned out the window, straining to hear any familiar sounds—the muffled conversation of village women, the rattle of other carriages, the hail of approaching traffic. But all she heard was the scolding of birds in the trees, the faint sound of a brook running over stones and the soughing of a breeze ruffling the leaves.

The odor of rich fecund earth, sweet grasses, ferns and wildflowers carried to her, mingling with the scent of roses in the coach. She noted her bouquet and decorated bonnet lying on the floor, the flowers starting to droop in the heat. How long had she been unconscious?

Another shiver skittered up her spine as she lifted her bonnet and tugged it over her hair. Why could she not recall anything? Nothing…*nothing* rose from the depths of her mind and she arrived back at her last memory.

I think you should go, sir.

I think we both should.

No. No, surely not! He would not. There was no possible reason.

Unbelievably, the track narrowed even further. She moved away from the window just in time to avoid the lash of a supple branch bent back by their passage and rebounding into the window.

And then she saw it—the telltale rope twined through the window frames and out again to secure the door. Cold seeped all the way to her bones. She tried to open the door, and although the latch moved, the door would not budge. She was a prisoner!

Wavering between terror and fury, she beat her fists against the top of the passenger compartment. "Mr. Devlin! Blast you, sir! Stop at once!"

A low rumbling laugh was all that answered her demand. Oh, it was true, then! She'd been kidnapped by Mr. Devlin. Quite clearly, the memory of his cold, calculating eyes came back to her, and the tingle at her neck, as if she'd tweaked a nerve. And, judging if that was the last she recalled, then she'd never been married. And, by the absence of anyone pursuing them, no one would know what had become of her.

She fell back against the cushions and groaned. She was completely and utterly at the mercy of a man whose motives were murky at best. What, oh what, did he intend to do with her?

Devlin drew the carriage up in front of the tiny cottage. A small curl of smoke from the chimney told him that Durriken, the leader of the Roma band that camped nearby each summer, had brought the provisions he'd requested, had started a small fire on the hearth and had thrown the windows open to air the place out. Cheerful striped curtains fluttered in the soft breeze, as if waving a welcome. Two rooms downstairs and two up assured him that Lilly would never be far from his sight. If she tried to escape, she would not get far. He knew the woods for miles around. A man in Devlin's position always knew the lay of the land.

When he'd bought the parcel and cottage ten years ago, he'd known he would be needing it. In his business, he had occasion to escape the city now and then. No one, not even

Jack Higgins, knew he owned property out of town, let alone how to find him. Yes, although his plans all those years ago hadn't included Miss O'Rourke, he'd known he'd have use for a remote hideaway one day.

He dismounted the driver's box and took a deep breath. Miss O'Rourke was going to be a hellion, and there was no way for him to prepare for that. An awful stillness pervaded the clearing as he untied the rope from the door latch. He had no more than opened the door and stepped back when his hostage burst forth, fire in her eyes and ice in her voice.

"How *dare* you! I should have known the moment I saw you in the vestry that you were up to no good!"

He braced himself for worse to come, and he was not disappointed.

"What sort of scoundrel are you, sir, that you would abduct a girl on her wedding day? What do you hope to accomplish? Why, if you think there will be ransom, think again! My family is poor and the duke and duchess are not fond of me. They will look at this as a reason to withdraw from the marriage contract."

"Poor, eh?" He couldn't resist reaching out to touch her necklace as he'd done in the vestry. He'd rarely seen better. "We should all be so poor."

She gasped and the color drained from her face. Her hand flew to her throat. "Oh, dear Lord! These are the Rutherford Sapphires, on loan from the duchess. I was to give them back directly following the ceremony."

Devlin laughed. Oh, this was rich. Olney and Rutherford, both struck down in a single blow! Olney's bride and Rutherford's jewels! He could not have planned it better.

"You laugh? Oh, how could you? What have I ever done to you, sir?"

"Nothing, I confess it. I bear you no malice, Miss O'Rourke."

"Then why have you done this horrid thing? Do you not realize what people will be saying? What they will be thinking?"

He nodded. The thought had troubled his conscience but he couldn't allow that to change his plan. A chance like this might never come again. And no matter what people thought of Miss O'Rourke afterward, no matter the gossip, it would still be better for her than marriage to Olney.

Her lovely eyes widened. "You think this is amusing? You play games with my life and think it entertaining?"

No, never entertaining. Tragic for them both. Too bad for her that she had been in the wrong place at the wrong time. And the object of the wrong man's affection.

Ah, but the jewels. That was an unexpected complication for Miss O'Rourke. Now Rutherford doubtless believed her to be a cunning thief, seducing his son with the sole purpose of bilking him of the family fortune. He regretted that she was now in deeper trouble than he'd planned. Surely she would be able to extricate herself from that misunderstanding when she returned to London with the jewels and explained? Because, without their return, Miss O'Rourke was surely going to gaol.

He certainly didn't need them, didn't even want them, because there would never be enough money or jewels to pay the particular debt they owed him. He reached out to touch them again but Miss O'Rourke shrank back as if angry or disgusted. But not fearful, thank God. He did not like the thought that she might fear him.

"Why would you do this to a friend, Mr. Devlin? What has Olney done to you?"

"I believe I said that I knew him. And I do. But I never said Olney was my friend. In fact, I do not think he would even remember me. Too far beneath him for notice, you see."

She frowned. "When I asked him if he knew a Mr. Devlin, he said he did not. He said you must be a friend of his father's."

"I may as well set the record straight on that, Miss O'Rourke. I am no friend of either Olney or Rutherford. The family is well-known to me, but they would not recognize me. Do not look for a sympathetic connection. There is none."

"But you were at their ball. I met you in the gardens."

"I was an intruder. An uninvited guest, if you will."

"Who are you, then?"

Oh, no. He was not about to say the words and reveal a truth that would curl her luscious lips in contempt. He merely smiled again, hoping she would let the matter drop.

She paled. "Is Mr. Devlin even your name?"

"Part of it. Devlin is my first name."

She looked around the small clearing as if searching for someplace to hide or run, then back at the cottage. She swallowed hard and then turned to him again. "Are you…are you going to ravish me?"

To his shame, his body responded instantly to that question. He was long past his impetuous youth when his libido had ruled his decisions, but Miss O'Rourke, in all her stunning innocence, tempted him as none of his other women had done. He wouldn't touch her, but every instinct, every impulse, was to do just that. His lack of an answer was answer enough.

"Everyone will know, Mr., ah, Devlin. Someone will know who you are, see the direction your coach took. They will be here soon. I would escape while there is still a chance, were I you."

"Nice try, Miss O'Rourke, but no one saw us leave."

"But…but others have seen us together, and—"

"No one has seen us together. I have been very careful of that. Your maid may have seen my back, but she will not be able to identify me by that. And even if you mentioned my name to anyone, they will not be able to find me."

She looked astonished at his words. "How long have you been planning this, sir?"

"Almost from the moment I first saw you," he admitted. And it was true. He'd been taken with her even before Olney proposed, though the kidnapping scheme hadn't occurred to him until then. "I've had weeks to plan it, m'dear. Alas for you, it is the perfect abduction."

She looked down at the bouquet she still clutched in one hand, then back at him, and suddenly launched herself at his chest, using the flowers as a weapon. She did not stop pummeling him until the flowers were denuded and only the stems remained. He made no move to protect himself from her fury. He deserved it, after all. And more.

Moments later, her anger spent, she stepped back and said, "I hope they catch you and condemn you for the villain you are. You cannot get away with this, Mr. Devlin. Once you are caught, you will hang. I hope you do."

He was surprised by how much that stung. "You wouldn't be the first to make that wish, nor are you likely to be the last. And God knows I've done plenty to warrant such a fate. But it won't be easy to find witnesses against me, and it won't be today. So, were I you, Miss O'Rourke, I would resign myself to my fate. It is not so dire as you might imagine, you know."

"What is it you have in mind for me?"

"Why, for you to enjoy a few days of bucolic bliss, and then return to the bosom of your family." Her eyes narrowed and he knew she didn't believe a single word he said. "Now, may I suggest that you go inside? Your room is the second at the top of the stairs. There should be fresh water and towels if you'd like to freshen up."

"What are you going to do?"

"Unhitch the horses and take them to pasture. I shall be back presently." He glanced up, trying to gauge the position of the sun by the slant of rays through the trees. "When I return, we shall see what we can muster up for supper. Are you hungry, Miss O'Rourke?"

"Not in the least. In fact, I find I have lost my appetite entirely."

"More for me, then."

She blinked and he turned away before she could defy him again. Oh, this was going to be a long week, or his name was not Devlin Farrell.

On the edge of tears or fury—she couldn't decide which—Lilly stormed toward the thatched cottage. Would he take her home if she set it ablaze? She glanced over her shoulder at him. He was unhitching the horses from the carriage, having dismissed her entirely. The horrid man!

The veil trailing from her bonnet snagged on the thorns of a white rosebush next to the cottage door and she yanked savagely, ripping a long gash in the fragile fabric.

When she opened the sturdy door she stopped in surprise. She had expected rustic accommodation but found simple luxury instead. A sofa and overstuffed chair upholstered in French blue silk faced a cold hearth. Highly polished pine floors showed no trace of dust or dirt. An elegant oil lamp stood on a side table to illuminate the room at night. An array of gold-embossed, leather-bound volumes littered another side table to invite her attention and a small vase of wildflowers decorated the mantel. What a delicate touch for one so gruff as her captor. Charming.

No! She would not be charmed, no matter what Mr. Devlin had done to mollify her. If he thought he could lull her into complacency, he was sadly mistaken. Instead she would do all she could to make his life intolerable until he was forced to return her to London.

She turned in the other direction to find a wide archway leading to a kitchen. Another fireplace opposite the one in the sitting room held a small cooking fire, glowing with banked coals. A narrow stairway tucked alongside the pantry led to the second floor.

Her bedroom, Mr. Devlin had said, was the second room at the top of the stairs. She trudged ungracefully up the stairs, expecting the best now, but hoping for the worst. Then she would have something to complain about.

She blinked. An ornately carved bed with a warm ancient patina stood in the middle of the passageway. A deep mattress and lush jewel-toned coverings dressed it with style and sophistication. Heavens! Such a bed must once have belonged to a king.

But what was it doing in the middle of a corridor? No, not a corridor but an entire room—it was the entire width of the cottage, but not quite the depth. If this was the first room, then… She spied a door in the far wall and went to open it. A room, smaller than the first, was similarly furnished, though less grand and on a smaller scale. The bed was plain but plush and adorned in multicolored fabrics, almost garish in their splendor. Gypsylike in their patterns. The washstand bore an oval mirror, a china pitcher and bowl and several towels folded over a wooden bar. There was a desk by the door with a candlestick and tinderbox on the gleaming surface, ready for use. In all, it was a pleasant room, though not to her taste.

She turned back to the first room. If the smaller room was hers, then she would have to pass through Mr. Devlin's room to leave. Why, he would even know when she visited the privy! She looked down at the knob she still grasped. No lock. He would have access to her whenever he wished! He actually *did* intend to treat her like a prisoner!

Not on a snowy day in Hades! She whipped off her bonnet and threw it on the larger bed, her veil a pristine smear against the lavish bedding, before she hitched her white silk ruffles to midcalf and headed down the stairs.

She found Mr. Devlin with the horses at a water trough. He had shed his jacket and rolled his sleeves up to pump the water. She could not recall ever seeing a man in such a casual state. Well, except for the first night she'd seen Mr. Devlin in Rutherford's garden. She was momentarily confused by a visceral response that shot through her. Her chest tightened. Something unsettling about the way his muscles worked beneath the linen shirt and how he wiped his forehead on one sleeve. He was so…so *masculine*.

And then he noticed her across the trough. "Miss O'Rourke? Is something wrong?"

"Wrong?" she repeated. "Oh! Yes! That is…you do not expect me to occupy that…that room at the back?"

"That is precisely what I expect."

"I will not. Why, I would have no privacy at all."

"Regrettable, but necessary."

"Then…then I shall sleep on the sofa!"

"Alas, that is not possible, Miss O'Rourke."

"Why?"

"Because I cannot trust you not to sneak off and get yourself into some sort of trouble."

"I… You…" But argument was useless. She was a prisoner, after all. "How soon are you expecting the ransom?"

He smiled. "I thought you understood, Miss O'Rourke. There is to be no ransom."

"Then none of this makes sense."

"Please do not trouble yourself over it. It does not concern you."

Her head began to pound. How could it not concern her when she was the object of it? Unless it had to do with Olney. "Then it is my husband you dislike?"

He whirled on her with narrowed eyes and an angry expression. "He is *not* your husband, Miss O'Rourke. Believe me, that is a fact you will thank me for later."

She took a step backward, frightened by his fierce expression and icy coldness. "You dislike him. You've as much as admitted that when you said he is no friend of yours. And you are using me to punish him. But why? And how?"

"We have been over this, and I will say no more. I will leave you to your ablutions, Miss O'Rourke. You must let me know if I have forgotten to provide anything for your comfort."

She continued as if she had not heard his dismissal. "You are destroying my family in the process, sir. And me. What have I done to deserve your callousness and contempt?"

But he had turned away again, leading the horses across the clearing and into the forest. The pasture must be nearby. She glanced back to the overgrown lane they had traveled, then at the edge of the forest where Mr. Devlin had disappeared.

Alone. He'd left her alone. The fool! She hitched her skirts again and headed down the lane at a brisk pace. The faster she walked, the harder it would be for Mr. Devlin to catch up to her. She did not need to get all the way back to London, just to the first crossroad. There would be a sign to point the direction and she would find civilization soon after.

Within an hour, her spirits lifted. She could see a crossroad ahead. She was going to escape! Surely she had enough of a lead that the villain could not catch her now.

She smoothed her hair as she walked. She would not want to frighten the first person she encountered. Her hideous wedding gown would be frightening enough. Her white satin slippers were ruined, too. She'd stepped in a puddle in the wheel rut and soiled them beyond cleaning. Still, once she explained her predicament, she was confident that any stranger would assist her.

Breathless, she arrived at the intersection—a simple Y in

the lane. There was no direction sign, and no indication there had ever been one. Both lanes looked equally deserted. Would either lead her to a village? Or would she only go deeper into the forest?

Indecision muddled her thinking. All she knew for certain was which lane she'd come down. The canopy of branches and the growing twilight made it impossible to detect any signs of recent travel. An owl hooted, reminding Lilly that she had better make a decision soon. She did not want to be caught in the forest after dark. Either road would be better than standing still.

Making a hasty decision, she took the lane to her right and quickened her pace, saying a silent prayer that she would come to a village soon. Every sound, every whisper of the wind, threatened her now, and the approaching darkness urged her faster.

She had not walked another quarter of an hour before she had to stop. Something had changed, and she could feel the menace in the air. Her heartbeat raced and thumped wildly against her rib cage. The back of her neck prickled as a breeze lifted the fine hairs at her nape. She turned to look the way she'd come.

Directly behind her, as silent as a wraith, stood a dark man with an enormous black mustache. His obsidian eyes were piercing and angry. She screamed and stumbled backward as his meaty hands reached out to seize her.

Chapter Seven

A bloodcurdling scream shattered the stillness of dusk. Devlin wheeled his stallion toward the sound. He ducked beneath the low-hanging branch of an oak and galloped toward the sound. Blast the chit! If she had just followed instructions, she wouldn't be in trouble now.

But this was his fault, too. He'd been a fool to give her credit for good sense after their last conversation. Telling her the truth would not have mattered. In fact, she'd have fought him harder if she had known how callous he'd been, how single-minded in his purpose—a fact he now regretted.

She must have taken the west fork—another poor decision. That track only led deeper into the forest. As it was, he was amazed she had gotten so far.

Another scream, choked off in the middle, followed close on the first. Devlin said a quick prayer that she had not encountered a wild beast. Or worse. It had never been his intention that she come to physical harm. How would he ever explain his carelessness to her brother-in-law? Hell! How would he ever explain *any* of this to Andrew Hunter?

He saw Miss O'Rourke first, her wedding gown glowing

in the deepening shadows. She had her back turned to him and did not know he was there. A gypsy had seized her upper arm to prevent her from fleeing and was growling angry curses in the Romany dialect as she flailed against him.

He swung down from his stallion and walked forward. The gypsy's gaze flickered upward to meet his and his grip on Miss O'Rourke tightened—Devlin could see the indentation of his fingers on the soft flesh of her upper arm. He controlled the quick stab of anger that shot through him, reminding himself that he was not entitled to such an unguarded response. She was not *his,* after all.

"Need help?" he asked.

Miss O'Rourke spun as far as the gypsy's grip would allow and the two answered in unison. "Yes!"

"Release her, Durriken," he said in Romany, and the gypsy obeyed with another spate of curses.

"Do you see what your hellcat has done?" he asked, still in the gypsy dialect. He held out his left arm to display red welts where fingernails had raked four jagged lines from elbow to wrist.

Miss O'Rourke flew against him, fastening her arms around him, almost like an eager lover. "Make him go away! He was… I think he was going to ravish me!"

Durriken snorted and shook his head in denial. "Violca would slit my throat if I touched this one."

Devlin suppressed a smile and slipped his arms around Miss O'Rourke, partly to comfort her, and partly to keep her immobile if she should somehow decipher what they were saying. He had no doubt his sudden appeal had to do with what she perceived to be a greater threat.

"What is he saying?" she asked.

"That you are a great prize and that he does not want to give you up." He lied without the slightest twinge of con-

science. He'd have sworn the moon was made of cheese if it
would gain her cooperation.

"Oh, but…"

"I told him that you are my woman." He held her tight as
she raised her arms to push him away. "That is the only thing
that is keeping him from claiming you, Miss O'Rourke. To
him, you are fair game—alone, in the middle of his woods,
without a protector."

"But—"

"Your choice, Miss O'Rourke. The gypsy? Or me?"

Her blue-green eyes widened in disbelief as she glanced
at Durriken and then back at him, clearly weighing the lesser
of two evils. "I… You, Mr. Devlin. You, at least, have not man-
handled me as this man has done."

Oh, no. He'd only rendered her unconscious and carried
her away from her family and fiancé on her wedding day. It
would be a tactical error to remind her of that, however. "If
you are certain."

Her hesitation was enough to tell him that she wasn't
certain at all, but her final nod gratified him, nonetheless.

He turned back to Durriken. "Thank you, old friend, for re-
capturing my prize. I will bring you a reward tomorrow, eh?"

"Welcome to her, Rye, though she is worth a fine ransom.
And may you have joy of her." He rubbed his left arm and
shook his head. "And may you not turn your back on her."
With that warning, Durriken turned and took long strides
into the woods.

"What did he say?" Miss O'Rourke asked. "Did he ask
for me back?"

Devlin grinned. "To the contrary, m'dear. He wished me
good luck with you. He thinks I will need it. Will I?"

She looked down at her slippers and a delicate pink infused
her cheeks.

"Never mind. I would not believe a promise given now. You have too much at stake and are liable to say anything."

He turned and went to take the reins of his horse and swing up into the saddle, then rode to her and held out his hand. She took it and he lifted her to sit across the saddle in front of him and reached around her to grip the reins.

He returned the way she had come, not willing to let her learn the shortcuts he had used or betray other lanes she might use to escape. It would be better for them both if she could simply accept her temporary captivity. Would she have the good sense to reach that conclusion?

And would he have the strength to ignore the way her hip nested against his groin? The way she rested one palm across his thigh to brace herself? Or the heat that shot through him when she did?

They were nearly home when she turned her head to look up at him. "I cannot understand, sir, why you say that no one will look for me. They will not imagine that I simply fled the church without clothes or coin."

She was so deuced lovely, so soft and clean, that he had a sudden pang of regret. If only things could have been different between them—but no. He was, and always would be, beneath her notice. And now it was necessary for him to deliberately frighten her so that she would be more cooperative. "Without clothes or coin, perhaps, but as a brilliant stroke of luck would have it, my dear, you had all you needed around your lovely neck. Having dealt in it, I am a fair judge of stolen jewelry, and I wager, broken into individual stones, that necklace could set you up for life in a quiet village. Perhaps in France?"

Miss O'Rourke's eyes grew round. "Who would think… Surely not! They know me better."

"Your mother and sisters, perhaps. But not Rutherford or

Olney. They will be seeing themselves as duped. But come, you will be returning the necklace—and yourself—whole and intact. No need to worry."

High color filled her cheeks at his unsubtle reference to her virginity. "Still, they will know I am not to blame."

He heaved a resigned sigh and tightened his arm around her, relishing the feel of her warmth and softness against him. "I am afraid not, Miss O'Rourke. Not until you return to tell them so. Do you recall the envelope I had with me in the vestry?"

She nodded.

"'Twas a letter signed with your name. You expressed a deep regret that you could not bring yourself to go through with the marriage. Nor could you face the consequences of a public denial. You further stated that you would write once you were safely settled elsewhere."

"They will know it is not my handwriting."

"Alas for you, my forger is quite adept."

"How—"

"You dropped a list, m'dear, and I retrieved it. That was all he needed to contrive a convincing document. Your own mother will not know the difference."

Her lips pressed together in anger and two sharp lines formed between her brows. "If you have gone to such trouble and have been so thorough to throw any pursuers off the track, do you actually intend to return me? Or are you just telling me that to keep me complacent? Do you mean to keep me here forever?"

He laughed and shook his head. "Lord save me, no! Why would I want you forever? You are far too much trouble. I am as anxious to *have* you gone as you are to *be* gone."

"Can you not simply answer a forthright question? Tell me why you have taken me, Mr. Devlin."

He contemplated her question for a few minutes as they rode in silence. To make a fool of Olney? To repay an ill deed?

To exact his rough justice? Or to save Lillian O'Rourke from herself? Each of those reasons were true to various degrees, and now they were becoming jumbled in *his* mind.

"You will know soon enough, Miss O'Rourke," he stalled. In fact, she'd know when he did.

She stiffened against his arm and her chin lifted just enough to indicate carefully controlled anger. He grinned, encouraged to think she could, indeed, control her indignation. Oh, but the feel of her against him was insanely distracting and he could not rid himself of his lustful thoughts.

The remainder of their ride passed in silence. The twilight had deepened to a purplish dusk by the time they arrived at the cottage. A single lamp burned in the lower window, and a faint curl of smoke filtered up through the treetops. *Home,* he thought, and was alarmed by the notion. He could not afford such countrified ideals.

He dismounted and held his arms up for Miss O'Rourke. After a brief hesitation, she braced her hands on his shoulders and allowed him to lift her down. She wobbled and he steadied her with a firm hand on her waist. She did not look up at him and he was left to study the top of her head and the remains of her elaborate hairstyle, long silken strands escaping the white ribbons that had been tucked beneath her bonnet at the church.

The scent of her skin wafted up to him and brought his blood up yet again. He wanted to tilt her face to his and plunge the depths of her delicate mouth, and then plunge himself into… He could not think of the last time he'd had so many salacious thoughts in a single day.

He suspected that she sensed the direction of his thoughts because she shivered and pushed against his chest to break his hold on her waist. "I…I must have caught a chill," she said as she made a dash for the cottage.

He shook his head at his own folly. He could ill afford to

indulge such thoughts of the untouchable Miss O'Rourke. He took a deep, bracing breath and led his horse toward the trough.

Fie! She'd been so certain she could find her way to a village that she hadn't allowed for failure. Now she had undoubtedly ruined any chance of escape since it was most unlikely that he would leave her unguarded again. In fact, she would count herself lucky if he didn't tie her to a chair for the remainder of her captivity.

Oh, but if he just knew it, he only needed to come as close to her as he had during their return to the cottage. That was enough to keep her immobile and senseless. Pray all the gods in heaven that he did not suspect that awful truth. She slammed the cottage door behind her, wondering how much of a respite his task of unsaddling the horse would give her. Surely enough to collect her wits.

The aroma of a rich beef stew simmering over the fire wafted from the kitchen and her stomach growled. She could not recall the last time she had eaten. This morning, she'd been too nervous, thinking of her wedding night and the Rutherfords' expectations, and she'd forgotten about food entirely in the confusion afterward. But where had it come from? Had Mr. Devlin put it on to simmer before coming after her?

Lilly collapsed on a wooden chair at the table and buried her face in her hands. Her stays were crushing her ribs and she wished she hadn't let Nancy pull them so tight. She straightened to ease the pinch. She was exhausted, famished and worried sick. What could her mother and sisters be thinking at this moment? Were they worried about her? Did they believe she had abandoned them? Absconded with the Rutherford jewels? Were the authorities in pursuit?

She did not care what Mr. Devlin said. Her loved ones knew her better than to think so ill of her. Even Olney would know she had not willingly abandoned him. The duke and duchess might be a different matter.

She adjusted the flounces at her neckline and sniffed dejectedly. It was not in her nature to give up. She would just have to bide her time and wait for an opportunity to flee. After all, the man had to sleep sometime. Meanwhile, if at all possible, she could try to be civil. The axiom was true—that you could catch more flies with honey than with vinegar. If she could just lure him into relaxing his guard…

Good heavens! What was wrong with her? She actually *could* have escaped the blackguard in the forest. All she'd had to do was choose the gypsy over him, and yet she'd chosen him. Not just chosen him, but had been relieved to see he had come after her, even though he was no better than the gypsy. They both terrified her, though in different ways, and her fate in both cases was likely to be the same, so why hadn't she chosen the gypsy? That, at least, would have foiled his secret plan—whatever that was. He seemed to have some sort of strange power over her. Almost as if destiny were intervening.

She jumped when the door opened and a glowering Mr. Devlin strode through. His shirtsleeves were rolled up and his hands and hair were damp. He must have washed himself at the pump. He hung his jacket on a peg and turned to her. "I am famished. Have you taken an opportunity to freshen yourself, Miss O'Rourke?"

She felt heat rising in her cheeks. Did he intend to follow her to the privy? As if reading her mind, he shrugged and went to a cupboard to remove two bowls and a loaf of crusty bread.

"I shall give you five minutes, Miss O'Rourke, before I come after you," he said over his shoulder. "Do not disappoint me or I shall, indeed, escort you in the future."

Lilly scrambled to her feet and hurried for the door lest he change his mind. Before she returned to the kitchen, she, too, stopped at the pump. Lacking a towel, she dried her face and hands on her petticoat, then smoothed her gown over the damp folds.

Mr. Devlin glanced in her direction when she entered the kitchen again. "Ah, you look refreshed, Miss O'Rourke." He had placed the simmering pot on a wooden mat on the table and was ladling stew into the bowls. A bouquet of wildflowers was centered on the table and Lilly glanced back through the archway at the sitting-room mantle. The flowers were gone. Mr. Devlin had brought them from the mantle to grace the table. What a delicate touch for one so rough and stern.

She sat at the chair he indicated with a sweep of his hand and waited for him to be seated, too. Would he say grace?

No. He cut thick slices from the loaf with a wicked-looking knife. She'd never seen one like it in her mother's kitchen, and she guessed it had other, more unsavory uses for Mr. Devlin. She'd best not think of that now or she'd lose her appetite entirely.

"When did you have time to make stew?" she asked as she lifted her spoon.

"I didn't." He smiled. "I have friends hereabouts, Miss O'Rourke. They readied the cottage and brought supper. I am not much of a cook, I fear, and I did not think you would be amenable to cooking. *If* you can cook, that is."

"Do you think I am so spoiled—"

"Cosseted, Miss O'Rourke, not spoiled. You have the look of one who has been provided for, rather than one who had done the providing."

"Pampering was not allowed in my family, sir. We were not much indulged."

His smile turned to an outright grin. "I stand corrected. Then shall I expect you to cook tomorrow?"

Oh! She had stepped right into his trap. She swallowed a spoonful of the stew and sighed. It was heavenly—rich and salty, with hearty chunks of meat and vegetables. "Oh, I think not, Mr. Devlin. I could not possibly do better than this."

He laughed and filled her cup from a wine bottle. "I should have seen that coming."

She hid her own smile. It would never do to have him thinking he was winning her over.

"And while we are at it, you may as well call me Devlin. I've already confessed that is my given name."

"Too familiar," she said between bites. "What is your last name?"

His smile faded and he turned his attention to spreading thick, creamy butter on his bread. "It would mean nothing to you, Miss O'Rourke, and you will know it soon enough."

"Why the mystery, sir? Do you hope you will not be caught if I do not know your name?"

"I am prepared to bear the consequences of my actions."

"How will you make reparations to my mother? She has already lost one daughter, sir. She must be beside herself with worry at this very moment." The truth was that her mother was likely unconscious from laudanum by now. It was Gina and Bella who would be worried sick.

"I am sorry for that, but it could not be helped."

"What if she should have apoplexy? She could be dying—"

"Enough!" he snapped, all pretense of good humor gone. "I do not wish to discuss this again."

Her appetite failed and she pushed away from the table, glancing out the window as she stood. Inky darkness had swallowed their little clearing, permeating the air with danger. There was nowhere to go but her room. She lifted her cup and downed the wine in a quick gulp before she shot him a defiant glare on her way to the stairs.

"I would like a needle and thread. I have some repairs to make," she announced without turning.

"You will find both in the drawer of the desk in your room." She did not expect him to follow her, but she was a little disappointed when he merely watched her go without further comment.

Lillian O'Rourke was certainly the most infuriating female Devlin had ever encountered. He'd done everything within his power to make her comfortable and to reassure her, yet she defied him at every turn, rendering it impossible for him to make her stay pleasant.

Alas, there was no getting around the fact that she was, after all, his prisoner. He had stripped her of her choices, forced her into a situation she never would have chosen for herself and kept his motive murky, at best.

Did she fear him? Fear what he would do to her? That he would rape or despoil her in any way? Did she think he would kill her when she had served her purpose? Was there any reason he should not simply tell her what he meant to accomplish and why?

His stomach twisted at that thought. No, there was not a single reason to keep his motives secret, save one. Pride. He did not want to see the disgust on her face or the derision in her eyes when she knew the truth about him. Anything but that. Good God, anything but that.

He'd thought he was immune to such attitudes. He'd thought he'd made peace with the unfortunate circumstances of his birth and upbringing. But Lillian O'Rourke had smiled, and he was a timid but hopeful lad about to get his yearning for something finer dashed again.

When he'd embarked on this venture, he hadn't antici-pated the effect Olney's fiancée would have on him—the reawakening of his youthful desires. Bitter experience had taught him that he was what he was, and that would never change. Lusting after what he could never have would only bring him pain.

Ah, but it was too late to turn back now. Miss O'Rourke was above stairs, his plan was under way, and it was far too late to turn back. His only chance of coming out of this encounter unscathed was to harden his heart. He mustn't think of her as Miss Lillian O'Rourke, or as the sister of his friend's wife. No. She'd have to remain Olney's fiancée in his mind. The mere taste of those words on his tongue angered him. He would not soften if he held that thought in his mind. He would not have regrets over what he'd done to her future.

He would not care in the least what became of her.

Chapter Eight

Lilly secured the latch above the knob of her door before she groped for the candle and tinderbox she'd seen on the dresser earlier. When the room was bathed in soft light, she rolled her eyes again. Closed in now, she felt more than ever as if she were locked inside a gypsy caravan. The colors and patterns were foreign to everything she knew.

As she turned, she caught sight of her reflection in the washstand mirror. Her hair had come down and the ribbons were drooping dejectedly while her hideous wedding gown reminded her of what she *ought* to be doing tonight. She shivered, not altogether disappointed that she was not in Olney's bed.

Suddenly repulsed by the gown, she unfastened the hooks at her bodice and reached over her shoulder to loosen the laces in back. By tugging the sides, she was able to wrench it over her head. Exhausted, she collapsed on the bed to remove her slippers and stare at the offending garment, now lying in a grotesque white silk heap on the floor.

The emotions she'd been denying all day welled up in the form of hot silent tears. Frustration, anger and fear mingled in an angry brew. She snatched the gown off the floor and began ripping the absurd flounces from the neckline and the rows of ruffles from the skirt. The delicate stitches gave without tearing the fabric and soon she was surrounded by gathered strips of ruffles, flounces and bows. All that remained were the short puffed sleeves and a deep ruffle at the hem. She'd had to leave that or reveal her ankles.

A close inspection showed that there were only a few small gaps in the seams where the ruffles had been tacked. She would make the repairs in the morning when the light was better.

She collected herself and stood again, removed her petti-coat and was determined to remove the white embroidered corset over her knee-length chemise. But no matter how she contorted, she could not reach the strings. When Nancy had laced her up this morning, she'd pulled the strings extra tight, making a joke of how this would make Olney's job a bit more interesting. She had, evidently, tucked the laces beneath the stays. Good heavens! She could not spend the next week bound "extra tight." She'd expire from the lack of one good deep breath. She backed up to the bedpost and rubbed her back against it to see if something might give. Alas, nothing did.

The single candle on the desk flickered as she opened the drawer to find the needle and thread and, hopefully, a pair of scissors. She'd cut the wretched thing off if necessary. But she only found a delicate pair of embroidery scissors, too fragile to cut through multiple layers of fabric.

Drat! She could not *live* in the contraption! She kicked the desk chair and cursed when it toppled to the floor, then hopped on one foot, certain she'd broken a toe. "Fie, fie, fie!" she muttered, angry with her own folly.

A sudden thumping at her door shifted her attention from her throbbing toe. Her display of temper had drawn Mr. Devlin.

"Miss O'Rourke? What has happened? Are you well?"

"Go away!" she shouted.

"Open the door, Miss O'Rourke, or I'll break it down."

"You wouldn't dare!"

The door splintered around the latch and banged against the wall before rebounding, but Mr. Devlin was already inside. She'd never seen him look fiercer, nor more determined. His gaze went from her to the remnants of her gown on the floor, the overturned chair and back to her. "What the hell is going on in here?"

She crossed her arms over her chest, trying to preserve her modesty. "Have you no manners at all?"

"Very few. Do not toy with me, Miss O'Rourke. I am not in a mood for it. This is not one of your country weekends with society. I am your captor, and you answer to me."

Oh, how she wanted to defy him! But she backed away from him and dropped her gaze, nonplussed by this new ferocity. "I...I stumbled over the chair."

Silence met this admission. She tried again. "I cannot remove my corset."

"Turn around," he ordered.

She finally looked up again. "Why?"

"So that I can attend your corset strings."

Her two involuntary steps backward were followed by his two deliberate steps forward. "No. You cannot do that."

"Why? I have undone more than a few corsets ere now, Miss O'Rourke."

She gasped. She could only imagine under what circumstances this man would have unlaced corsets. But not hers! She'd never been so exposed in front of a man before, and she could allow him to go no further. "Please go away. I shall stop complaining."

"Don't be ridiculous." He reached out and spun her around so that her back was to him. "You cannot remain in a corset for days on end. I regret that I did not think of this before. Perhaps I should have employed a lady's maid."

His fingers slipped beneath the back of her corset and located the laces. A quick tug had them released but not undone. "Someone has knotted the strings."

Nancy! Had she thought knots would heighten Olney's excitement? "M-my maid," she said.

"Hmm. Well, Olney would have had a deuce of a time with these."

"And you will not?"

"I believe my experience to be greater than his. I doubt many of Olney's liaisons are…shall we say, voluntary. Likely done with corsets on."

She did not want to think of what Mr. Devlin was implying. She had much more important things on her mind at the moment. Like the heat of Mr. Devlin's fingers through her chemise as he worked at the knots of her laces. And the admission that he had performed this intimate task frequently.

Once again, she caught her reflection in the dressing-table mirror, her arms still crossed over her chest. In the shadows behind her, she could see Mr. Devlin, his dark head lowered as he attended his task, his fingers leaving little fire trails in their wake. His concentration was so complete that he did not realize she was observing him.

"There," he said, his breath tickling the back of her neck. "The knots are loose, but you are laced so tight that you won't be able to unwind them."

"I have unlaced myself before."

He looked up and met her reflection in the mirror. A slow smiled curved his lips and his former fierceness turned to something more…heated. "You will be a long time at it, Miss O'Rourke. Allow me to undo you."

He deemed her silence to be consent. He moved a bit

closer, and she could feel his heat surround her. The faint movement of his breath stirred the hair on the back of her neck, tickling in the most delicious way. She shivered.

"Afraid, Miss O'Rourke?" he whispered.

"N-no."

"Liar." He bent closer to her ear. "Are you sorry I am not Olney?"

And then she realized that the things she should have been doing with her new husband she was doing with Mr. Devlin! A mere twenty-four hours ago, she never would have imagined such a possibility. But was she sorry? She met his gaze in the mirror.

"You are a study in confusion, Miss O'Rourke. Quite telling. You were not looking forward to this familiarity with him, were you?"

"I…"

"Be honest. Did you ever allow him more than that little kiss in his garden the night of his proposal?"

"That is none of your business, sir."

"I think it is. After all, I am claiming Olney's wedding night, am I not?"

She gasped. Did he mean—

"Relax, Miss O'Rourke. Breathe, if you can. I meant that I am standing here, not Olney. I will return you to him unsullied. I would like to know one thing, though." His sure and knowing fingers worked the laces of her corset, loosening a little at a time, his tugs working in rhythm with his words. "Did you…ever…give him…a…proper…kiss?"

She would not answer such a personal question, though her heart thudded and she wet her lips nervously.

He chuckled and gave one last tug before her corset fell away in his hand. "I thought not."

Now clad only in her thin silk chemise, she was entirely

vulnerable. Frozen, she watched in the mirror as he tossed her corset onto the bed. He came around to stand in front of her— him now, not his reflection. He tilted her chin up to his face.

"Let me show you how 'tis done. Not like the insipid kiss you gave Olney, or the little buss we shared in the park."

He slipped his arms around her, his hands on her back pressing her against him until she was compelled to drop her arms. Oh, this was wicked. Completely sinful. But she looked up into his blue-gray eyes, so pale they mirrored her own, and she didn't care. His lips met hers, as tentative as they'd been in the park, but not so briefly. He nibbled her lower lip with lazy patience, kindling deep warmth in her belly, and he did not relent until she parted them to make his task easier.

The first explorative sweep of his tongue left her half shocked, wholly wanton and forever lost. She moaned. He made a sound like a muffled growl and tightened his arms as he deepened his kiss. She was lost to the feeling, swept into the sheer sensuality of his mouth. The heat, the passion, the deep intimacy of his mouth made her tremble long after he released her and stepped back.

His eyes had darkened and he looked as bemused as she felt. He retreated another step, a haunted look on his face. "Close your door, Miss O'Rourke, and secure it as best you can until morning."

Devlin stood in the cottage doorway, waiting for the sunlight to crest the trees. He'd given up trying to sleep. Lying there in that monstrous bed, the cool silk sheets and velvet counterpane soothing his heated skin, had done nothing to banish the sight of Miss Lillian O'Rourke exposed to his view, the sound of her helpless moan, nor the smell, taste and touch of her. Just knowing she was mere feet away, available and vulnerable, wreaked havoc with his libido. Something unexpected had happened when he'd kissed her. Something so surprising and impossible that he'd been stunned. Something that had sent all his firm resolve to keep her distant whistling down the wind.

He didn't know when, nor how, but the chit had actually gotten under his skin. It was so sudden, so absurd that he'd told himself it was the blasted corset, the necessity of seeing her half-clad, of touching her intimately and feeling her warmth, of the kiss that had even surprised him. He told himself that if he had her, lay with her, he could purge her from his mind.

Then he'd tried to tell himself that his nearly overwhelming desire for her was because of Olney—to cheat him of that last victory. To have what Olney never could—his bride's maidenhead. To take from Olney a fraction of what had been taken from him.

If it could only be that damned simple. But what remained of Devlin's conscience and honor forbade it. He'd never possess the thing he now wanted most because he could not bear to defile it. He'd had her in the palm of his hand. From the way she'd responded to his kiss, he knew that she'd been his for the taking. In her innocence, she could not know his appetite, nor the consequences of her appeal to someone as unscrupulous as he. Only the last shred of decency his mother had managed to instill in him had saved Miss O'Rourke last night. Pray it would be enough to save her today, and the days to come.

He turned back to the kitchen and found Miss O'Rourke descending the stairs. She'd remade her wedding dress into a simple white gown. Freed of the flounces and ruffles, the light fabric molded to her curves as she moved. The neckline was more revealing without the absurd gathers. Even her rich golden hair was simpler, not tied up in ribbons to fit beneath her bonnet, nor falling down in charming disarray, but bound by a single white ribbon at her nape. And she was barefooted! Why that fact should charm him, he could not think. But it did. She looked innocent and pure. Like a fairy princess or woodland sprite come to enchant him.

She paused for a fraction of a second when she saw him, then continued to the foot of the stairs. Would she berate him for last night? Curse him for the bastard he was? Demand that nothing of the sort happen again?

"Do I smell ham?"

He swallowed and nodded.

"Are there eggs?"

Sublime indifference? Or simply ignoring the ghost of last night? Either suited him well enough. He shrugged. "No chickens," he said. "No eggs."

"No pigs," she countered. "Yet you have ham."

He laughed. "There is porridge in the kettle and tea in the pot."

She nodded and went to help herself. "What are you going to do with me today, Mr. Devlin?"

"We are going fishing."

"*We* are?"

"We have no meat for supper. And since I cannot leave you alone, you will have to accompany me wherever I go."

"Wherever?" She raised an eyebrow and he sighed, pleased to see that her sauciness had returned.

He came to rest his shoulder against the archway into the kitchen so that he could watch her. "I am pleased to find you more tractable this morning, Miss O'Rourke."

"Oh?" She poured herself a cup of tea and sat at the table. "Well, I would not become too comfortable, were I you."

He went to refill his own cup and sat across the table from her. "Are you hatching some plan to foil me?"

"Not particularly. You have assured me that you will return me in a day or two, and I have decided to believe you."

"That is very sensible of you, Miss O'Rourke. It will make both our lives easier."

"Though—" she paused to give him the faintest of smiles "—should an opportunity to escape present itself, I shall likely take it."

He gave her a slight bow. "I would expect no less. But I think we should reach agreement on several matters."

"Which matters, sir?"

"You will not question me again regarding my actions or my motives. That is a troublesome subject and one I find tedious."

"And you, Mr. Devlin, will not go out of your way to annoy me. Nor is a repeat of last night to occur."

"What? That little episode in your bedroom? Not likely, since I gather you are not wearing your corset today."

Her color heightened and she looked down into her porridge bowl. "I was not speaking of my corset. You took liberties."

"You did not stop me."

"Next time, I shall. And in a most unpleasant way for you, Mr. Devlin."

He chortled. "I take your meaning, miss."

"And you may as well call me Miss Lillian. My sister Gina is older and therefore rightfully Miss O'Rourke."

"Miss Lillian," he acknowledged. "And you may call me Mr. Devlin."

"I thought that was your given name, not your surname."

"Trying to trick me into revealing more than I intended, Miss Lillian? Perhaps we should make that one of our rules."

She looked up through her lashes and another of those captivating smiles lifted the corners of her mouth. "Agreed."

He exhaled in relief. "Do you fish, Miss Lillian?"

"I used to go with my father, but that was many years ago."

"I shall fetch my fly rod and creel. Can you see what there is to muster for a lunch?"

* * *

Lilly cleaned up the remainder of breakfast and found a basket. She filled it with the leftover loaf of bread, a wedge of cheese, a few apples from the larder and a bottle of wine, the only beverage she could find in a container. She added a corkscrew and folded a light blanket from her bed over the top.

Her slippers were still soggy from the cleaning she'd given them this morning, so she decided to go barefooted. A flash of memory from lighthearted days passed through her mind—of her and her sisters running across the meadows near their home, looking for berries and wildflowers. The thought put her in a happy frame of mind.

Mr. Devlin led the way across the meadow to the edge of the forest and into the cool quiet of the trees. She heard the trickle of water before they came upon it—a swift-moving stream with a pebbled bed perfect for wading if one did not go too far. He stopped and took the basket from her.

"Shall I fix you a rod and reel, Miss Lillian, or would you prefer to lounge?" he asked as he shook out the blanket and spread it on a grassy bank dotted with wildflowers.

"I would hate to show you up, sir. Heaven only knows how you might choose to punish me."

He frowned, then caught her smile and laughed. "I might punish you for teasing, chit."

"Ah. Then I must conclude that you are not a good sport."

"Not in the least," he said, stooping to remove a hook festooned with brightly colored bristles from a small box. "I do not like to lose, whatever I'm doing."

"No one likes to lose, sir. It is how you handle the loss that reveals your character."

"Ah, well that would be ugly indeed. As you have already seen, my character leaves much to be desired."

She sat down on the blanket and drew her knees up to hug

them to her chest. In truth, she was in doubt about his true character. She wanted to hate him. To be afraid of him and disgusted by what he'd done. Instead, she found herself trusting him despite every reason he'd given her not to. Her rational mind warred with her instincts, and neither won. If only she knew his motives…

He turned to her and offered the rod. "But if you'd like to cast your line, I promise not to punish you with my bad temper should your fish be larger than mine."

"Thank you, but I believe I shall sit here and watch you while I take your measure as an angler. Then, after we lunch, I shall try my hand."

"As you wish." He tugged his jacket off and rolled his shirtsleeves up. With a wink over his shoulder, he headed for the river bank.

Lilly rested her chin on her knees as she watched him. The longer she knew him, the greater the enigma. She had always thought him good-looking, and the possessor of a rough sort of charm, but there was something more.

His bearing spoke of pride and a sense of purpose. His voice was assured, as if he was used to being obeyed. And though he'd forced her into a situation she would never have chosen, he'd gone out of his way to make her comfortable.

Still, he'd made comments that led her to believe he'd been raised on the streets of Whitechapel. She'd encountered men like that—they lurked on the streets of Mayfair, waiting to pick a pocket or cut a purse string. They feigned injuries and sat on corners with tin cups, begging a tuppence. At best, they swept chimneys or delivered coal. How had he risen above that? Could she trust him to be a gentleman? Did she want him to be?

More heat than the day could account for swept through her when the memory of last night surfaced. From the moment he'd kicked down her door until he'd warned her to secure it as best she could, he'd had her at a complete disadvantage. Yesterday morning she'd been shocked to see a man who was not a member of her family in shirtsleeves. By the time the day was done, she'd been nearly nude in front of that man, heated by his touch, bemused by his kiss.

She kept telling herself that it should have been Olney. *He* should have been the one to introduce her to a man's touch. To the stunning intimacy of his kiss, his tongue. But he hadn't. And a treacherous part of her was glad. She did not think Olney was capable of eliciting such a response. At least, not from her.

She tried not to think that Mr. Devlin held her future in his hands. She'd seen enough to know that he was completely focused on his scheme, whatever it was. Her future was secondary to that, and she knew he'd sacrifice her if necessary. But she'd also come to believe he bore her no particular animosity. He'd been telling her the truth when he'd said he'd return her soon, and untouched.

She released her knees and reclined on her side, watching as he hooked a trout and reeled it in, skillfully playing the line to avoid losing the fish. A warm breeze ruffled his dark hair and something inside her tingled. He really was a handsome man—more so than Olney, who was like a pale copy of Mr. Devlin. His arms flexed as he unhooked the trout and dropped it in his creel. He cast again and then began to reel in his line. His white shirt was open at the throat and tucked into snug buff-colored breeches, revealing more of a man than she'd ever seen or noticed before. The tanned flesh at the V of his shirt, the strong muscles revealed beneath the fine linen fabric, his lean hips, and the slight curve of his…good heavens!

He turned to look at her as she scrambled to her feet, desperate to banish her wayward thoughts. "Hungry, Miss Lillian?"

Oh, yes. She was hungry for another of those kisses. "I will wait for you, Mr. Devlin."

He glanced up at the position of the sun and she realized she must have lost track of time while she was watching him. "I'm ready now."

Odd how his day improved when he'd turned to see her there, her bare feet peeking beneath her hem and her cheeks flushed from the warmth of the sun. She nearly took his breath away, and that was not an easy feat. Somewhere in the back of his mind, a little censor warned him not to get used to this.

He put his rod down by his creel and went to sit on the blanket beside Miss Lillian. She handed him the wedge of cheese and he removed his knife from the sheath at his waist and cut several slices, then turned his attention to the bread.

He ate in silence, watching her distraction, unsure of what he could say or how he could engage her interest. They were beyond polite pleasantries about the weather or politics. He didn't give a farthing for the news of society, nor did he have the social skills for inconsequential banter. They had nothing in common, but the pull he felt toward her was undeniable, so he'd try anyway, the silence more awkward than stumbling conversation.

"Do you think the weather will last the week, Miss Lillian?"

"Unlikely," she answered, as if by rote. "'Tis August, after all. The nights are already carrying a chill."

"Ah. And here I thought the chill was from a different source than the nights."

She blinked those wide eyes. "Have I offended you again?"

He cursed himself for challenging her. "I am sorry. You didn't deserve that."

He reached for the wine bottle. She had remembered to pack a corkscrew, but she'd forgotten cups. Well, they'd have to improvise. He removed the cork and offered the bottle to her. She shook her head and he took a swig from the bottle before wiping it and setting the bottle down between them.

"That is not the only thing I don't deserve, sir."

"And that would be…?"

"I do not deserve to have been kidnapped. This was no fault of mine, sir. My only crime was in consenting to be Olney's wife."

"Then perhaps you should show more care as to whom you say yes to."

"I felt it was my responsibility."

"To whom?"

She frowned and pressed a spot between her eyes as if to hold back an impending headache. "I have tried so desperately to do the right thing for my family, despite my own personal wishes. I went to all the right places, said and did all the right things, and I consented to a marriage that would restore my family's good name and ease the way for a good marriage for my sister. How, when my intentions were so good, could things have gone so dreadfully wrong?"

"Good intentions?" He nearly laughed. Miss Lillian certainly excelled at self-deception, he'd give her that. "My dear, do you not know what the road to Hell is paved with?" He shook his head. "And, were I you, I would examine my 'good intentions.' You stood to profit both socially and economically by your marriage. How was that a sacrifice? It was, in fact, quite a large step up for the O'Rourkes. I hardly see you as a martyr."

Those wide eyes now narrowed in anger, showing the first spark of fire from her. She drank deeply from the bottle before she answered. "And what could a man like you possibly know of what a woman like me might want or need? How dare you presume to see me as a…a…."

A man like him? Someone so far beneath her that he could not possibly understand the finer emotions? He answered her charge with as much vitriol as she had delivered it. "As a social-climbing opportunist?"

She gasped. "You think I am an opportunist?"

"Can you look me in the eyes and tell me that marriage to Olney was a love match? Or that it would create a hardship for you, but one you would endure for the sake of your family?"

"No, but he was kind, in his way, and fond of me. I thought we could be congenial if only he could find it in him to defy his father and mother on occasion."

"Olney is a milksop? Why does that not astonish me?"

"Only where his parents are concerned. I think he is merely a good son."

"What would you have had him defy?"

"Just…just, oh, I don't know."

He watched her confusion as she drank again and suspected that Olney had somehow failed her. The fool. To have such a woman as Lillian O'Rourke and let her down was a mistake worse than any Devlin ever hoped to make.

"I am practical, Mr. Devlin. People think I am soft and silly. They think I am incapable. But I am far more practical than my mother or sisters. I see what should be done, and I do it."

And how could he fault her for that? Wasn't that what he'd done when he'd kidnapped her? "And *that* is why you consented to marry Olney?"

"Yes."

"That sounds so bloodless. I thought women were ruled by emotion, not cold reason."

She shrugged. "Perhaps I am not like other women."

"Now you have caught my interest. If marrying Olney was not your personal wish, what was?"

Consternation showed on her face and she put the bottle

down in favor of an apple. "I…I had not thought about it. I mean, it is every girl's wish to make a good marriage, I assure you. But what is the definition of a 'good marriage'?"

She had cocked her head to one side in a query and held the bright apple in front of her as if it were an offering. She was the primal Eve, tempting him even without knowing it, and he was about to give her an answer that would make her blush. A little more wine, and he might learn more interesting things. And then he heard a shrill whistle in the distance.

"Stay here, Miss Lillian. Do not make a sound." He stood and retrieved his jacket and knife, wiped the blade on his trouser leg, then slipped it in his waistband instead of the sheath.

"But—"

"Believe me, you do not want to chance an escape at the moment. Do you want another repeat of last night? Until we know who has come, you'd do best to keep out of sight."

She nodded, and he knew she would cooperate. She was practical, after all.

He made his way toward the sound. A message from Mick Haddon? Who else would know how to find him? Durriken must have come to the cottage to deliver it and found them gone. And it must be important if he had come at all.

When he emerged from the clearing, he saw the gypsy coming across the meadow toward him and knew he'd been right. Something was afoot. Something that could not wait for his return to London. Mick was not one to raise a false alarm. And if he'd gone through Durriken instead of coming himself…

Without a word, Durriken removed a folded paper sealed with a drop of red wax from inside his shirt and handed it to Devlin.

He broke the seal and read.

Dev,
I cannot tell you what has provoked it, but we have just

had a visit from James and Andrew Hunter. They were displeased that they could not talk to you at once. Their business is very important, they said. Urgent, and the very highest priority. They wanted to know how to find you and when you might be available. I told them I did not know, but that I would give you their message the very moment you returned. They were suspicious, but accepted my explanation.

My friend, I would hasten your return before they come looking for you. Whatever they want, they are determined and said they would be back. Are they not the men you said had high connections and the resources to uncover the darkest secrets?

I trust this message will find you in good health and with your plans in place.

Mick

Hell and be damned! Had the Hunters found out? Or did they merely suspect? He folded the parchment and slipped it inside his own shirt.

"Problems?" Durriken asked.

"When are there not?"

The gypsy thumped his chest and nodded his agreement. "*Life* is a problem, my friend. Does this have to do with the woman?"

Devlin sighed. "Aye. And this woman is more trouble than most. Too much, I think."

"You want me to take her off your hands?"

"I will return her to her kin, but not for another day or two, I think."

"Then wherein is the problem?"

"I must go to town tonight, but I cannot take her and I cannot leave her alone."

"Bring her to us. Violca will keep an eye on her."

Durriken's wife was a notorious meddler. She had one finger in everyone else's pot, and one eye to everyone's business. Miss Lillian would not be able to sneeze without Violca taking notice.

"But," Devlin cautioned, "then she would be able to identify you."

"Identify? You kidnapped the maid?"

"It is not an ordinary kidnapping. I am not going to ask ransom. I will return her after the passage of a few days."

"Her manner of dress. She was a bride?"

"Aye. But the vows were not said."

"Is she still a maid?"

Devlin contrived to look insulted, but it was a waste. Durriken could read men as easily as he could read the weather.

"A maid, but not for long, I think," the gypsy concluded.

"I will return her untouched."

"Then why have you bothered?"

"To spite her betrothed, and to save her from him."

"How can you save her if you return her?" Durriken's laugh boomed over the meadow. "Ah, the lies we tell ourselves to excuse our desires, eh? You want her. That is easy to see. Take her. Then she will have to marry you."

"Not that simple, my friend. She would not have me under any circumstances. She hates me."

"Hate? Love? Different sides of the same coin, Rye. She chose you when asked for a choice, eh? She will choose you again."

"You are dreaming, Durriken."

The gypsy clapped him on the shoulder. "When a gypsy dreams, it is sure to come true. Now, bring her to us. We will keep her safe until you return. And do not worry she will betray us to the king's men. She will not be able to find us. It is yourself you should worry for."

Chapter Nine

Lilly picked up the remains of their meal and folded their blanket, ready to bolt if she had the opportunity. Vagabonds, gypsies, ruffians, highwaymen? She had come to dread Mr. Devlin less than the unknown. But she would escape if given a reasonable chance.

She thought she heard a faint laugh and she frowned. How friendly would Mr. Devlin be with strangers? After all, he had a secret to keep. Her. She crept forward, careful to keep silent. A moment later, Mr. Devlin came striding along the path, as bold as you please. She tried to hide her relief.

He stopped when he saw her. "Coming to see if I needed rescue?" he asked.

"Ah, no. But I wanted to know what had become of you. I mean…if you had been murdered…or…something."

"Then you could find your way back to London?"

"Well…"

He grinned and her stomach did a little flip-flop. "Quite right, Miss Lillian. A girl must have an eye to her safety and reputation, mustn't she?"

"That is already ruined," she reminded him.

"And, alas for you, I am quite well. But go ahead, if you'd like. I'll just fetch my rod and creel and catch up to you."

She waited where she was instead, using the moment to collect herself. She hadn't realized how worried she was. If something had actually happened to Mr. Devlin, she'd have been free. And why did that thought not cheer her?

By the time he returned, she was curious. "Who was it?"

"Just a neighbor. We've been invited for dinner."

"Dinner? I thought you did not have neighbors. Who are they? *Where* are they?"

"A bit too excited, Miss Lillian. Are you even now plotting to climb out your window tonight and beg sanctuary from them?"

She laughed. "I have already noted that the drop to the ground is rather far."

"Ah, well, as it happens, I have accepted the invitation."

They emerged on the meadow and he glanced at the position of the sun. "In fact, I think we should go there straightaway."

"I should freshen up first and at least fetch my slippers. They should be dry by now."

"Our neighbors will not mind bare feet, I assure you."

"Your fish—"

"My contribution to the pot."

"Pot? But why—"

"Patience, Miss Lillian. All will become clear presently." He lowered his head and she could have sworn he muttered, "Unfortunately."

What was he up to now? He set a pace that made conversation difficult and she concentrated on her steps, lest she tread on a sharp rock or something less savory.

The faint sound of music grew louder as they approached a shaded glade. A flute, tambourine and fiddle kept a merry measure and Lilly knew this could not be good.

A young man dressed in a white shirt, loose breeches and a colorful sash at his waist came forward, smiling, his hand extended to Mr. Devlin. They spoke a few words in the language he had used to address the gypsy yesterday. Gypsy! Good heavens! They'd walked right into their camp.

But perhaps this was not to her disadvantage. Maybe she could persuade the man to return her to London for a price. She stepped forward and interjected herself. "Hello. I am Miss Lillian O'Rourke, late of London," she said in her best society voice. "Mr. Devlin here has kidnapped me for some nefarious purpose. Will you help me? I can promise a generous reward."

The young man blinked and then laughed heartily, slapping Mr. Devlin on the back. "Good choice, Rye. Are there any more in London like her?" he said in perfect English.

She blinked, then whirled on Dev. "Rye? What is this? You *know* these people?"

Unabashed, he nodded. "Aye."

"You lied."

"I most certainly did not. I said they are neighbors, and they are. They camp here every summer."

"Gypsies!" She stood back, her hands on her hips as her gaze swept the full length of him. "I should have known. Rye, is it? *That* is your real name?"

"It is my gypsy name," he admitted.

"And that man last night? Did you know him?"

The man in question stepped out of the crowd that had gathered at the edge of the woods. "Durriken," he said with no small measure of pride.

"Oh!" She flushed and spun on Mr. Devlin. "You horrid man! You lied to me. You tricked me."

"How? You did not ask if I knew him. And I gave you a choice which of us to go with."

"But you let me think—"

At that moment a young woman with luxuriant dark hair wound her way through the crowd and flung herself against Mr. Devlin, holding tight with her arms around his neck. "Rye! Oh, Rye! You have come to see me at last!"

He pried her arms away apologetically. "Hello, Drina." Then he continued in a spate of Romany words she could not understand. The gypsy girl turned to Lilly and hissed the word *"Gorgie,"* before turning and running back the way she'd come.

"Miss Lillian, may I present Brishen Petulengro." He paused while the young man grinned and bowed. "And Durriken Grey."

The older man, the one she'd been terrified of last evening, came forward and bowed. "Miss Lillian. I regret to be the cause of your distress." His accent was faint and she wondered if it came from his native Romany language or his origin in another country.

She sighed, giving in to the inevitable. "Shall I assume, then, that you will not help me get back to London?"

"Alas, no. My brother, Rye, does not want it so. But come. My wife, Violca, is curious to meet you. We do not welcome many *gajo* here."

She glanced at Mr. Devlin with a raised eyebrow.

"Non-gypsies," he interpreted.

Durriken took her by the arm and led her into the glade and she looked over her shoulder at Mr. Devlin. "Your brother? Mr. Devlin is gypsy, too?"

"He does not boast of Romany blood. He is a brother of the heart, yes? Our kinship is in spirit."

Rascals and thieves, she thought. Mr. Devlin had alluded to that in the past. It should not surprise her that he would have questionable connections.

Brightly colored caravans lined the glade in a semicircle on the banks of the same stream they had picnicked by. Most campfires were banked, but a few were cooking fires, fitted with black iron pots and spits for meat.

Men and women alike called greetings to Mr. Devlin in their odd dialect. He was, it seemed, a favorite in this camp. And then it occurred to her that this was where their stew had come from, and the flowers in the vase. And perhaps it had been Drina or Violca who had decorated her bedroom. Oh! How familiar was Drina with Mr. Devlin? The simple thought of them kissing as he'd kissed her last night infuriated her. Oh, not because she was jealous, but because it was proof of his duplicity. To think she had been on the verge of trusting him!

Mr. Devlin handed his creel to a short, heavyset woman. "Here you are, Violca, my love," he said, kissing her on the top of her head. "Do your magic on them."

She laughed. "Durriken had better keep an eye on us, eh? I just might run off with you this time." She gave him a familiar pat on his bottom and then turned to Lilly with a wink. "You come with me, eh, Miss O'Rourke? I will show you how to cook trout as Rye prefers."

How did Violca know her name? And why should she have any interest in how *Rye* liked his fish? "But I do not care in the least how Mr. Devlin…Rye…prefers—"

"Come, Miss O'Rourke. Leave the men to their boasting and bellowing. We have woman things to talk about, eh? More important things than they know." She took Lilly's arm and led her toward the most garish of the caravans.

Devlin watched Miss Lillian disappear into Durriken's caravan with mixed emotions. He needed to talk to his friend, but he wasn't certain leaving her with Violca was a good idea.

Gypsy women were apt to speak quite frankly, and he suspected his captive would be quite shocked.

"Not to worry, my friend," Durriken said as he clapped him on the shoulder and winked at Brishen. "Come, we will drink and you will finally tell me what you are about. Your directions to prepare for your arrival yesterday did not mention a captive. The camp is buzzing with curiosity. I could tell that Drina fears you've taken a bride."

Devlin cast an apologetic glance in Brishen's direction as they walked toward the back of a small wagon where a cask of ale waited. The young man had loved Drina since childhood, but Drina seemed blind to him. As for Devlin—well, he did not return her feelings. He would always think of her as a young girl, playing with rag dolls and following him with huge dark eyes.

"I think Miss Lillian would sooner wed the devil than me."

Durriken laughed. "So I see, but I think there is more than she is saying, yes? More than meets the eye."

"Perhaps she'd like me dead. I could hardly blame her."

Brishen shook his head. "Not dead, I think. Perhaps she would like to see you suffer, but not dead."

"I could not blame her if she did since I took her from the church on her wedding day and brought her here. I have not told her why nor when I will return her."

Brishen laughed. "Was this before or after the wedding, Rye? Is Miss O'Rourke now Mrs. Someone Else?"

"She is yet unmarried. But the worst of it is that I kicked her door in last night."

Durriken laughed so hard that Devlin thought he'd split the seams of his shirt. "And did that profit you?"

"Not in the least."

Brishen frowned. "Why? If you desire the girl, take her. Is that not why you stole her?"

"Not exactly."

Durriken took a pewter tankard from a shelf beside the cask, held it beneath the spigot and handed it to Devlin. "Then why did you steal her? Ransom? Is she rich?"

"She says not."

Brishen gave a thoughtful look as he tipped his tankard. "If not for love or money, then why?"

"Revenge," Durriken answered. "What else is there?"

They raised their tankards in agreement.

"Revenge, then. For what?" Brishen asked.

"A wrong done many years ago."

"Her father?"

"Her would-be husband. And *his* father."

"Ah, excellent! Will you make him poor to reclaim the woman?"

"Much better than that. I will make him a laughingstock."

Brishen shrugged and Durriken asked, "How is that better than gold, Rye? Will you send her back with a bellyful of your seed?"

Devlin paused. The thought had occurred to him, and every fiber of his physical being yearned for that, but then he would have stooped to their level. And they would have won again. Reluctantly, he shook his head. "The man and his father are arrogant and self-important. The bitterest blow is to their pride."

"Ah, but what a blow to his pride to have his bride bear *your* babe!"

"He would denounce her first. I considered waiting until after the vows were said and then taking the prize he had anticipated, but I have no quarrel with Miss O'Rourke. I am content that he will be regarded a cuckold. His friends will laugh at him behind his back. Conversation will stop when he enters a room. Rumors will spread that Miss O'Rourke found him wanting in some regard."

"A pale revenge," Durriken judged. "I think you should take the woman. *Know* her before your enemy."

He drank deeply. It would take very little to convince him to do what he wanted.

"Is this what the message was about, Rye? Has the enemy found you?"

"This is another matter that requires my attention. You said I could leave Miss Lillian with you. If the offer still stands, I will take you up on it."

"Aye. We will watch her. She can share Drina's bed." He laughed again. "No doubt they have much in common. They will chatter like little birds long into the night."

Devlin doubted Drina and Miss Lillian would have a single thing in common, but he knew he could trust the gypsy girl to do as he wished. Even if she didn't like it.

"A few cautions," he ventured. "Miss Lillian is not to know your location. Nor is she to be told what my purpose or my intentions are. She'd be sure to revolt."

"We will have to tell her something, Rye."

He waved one hand in dismissal. "Tell her anything. Just be certain she is not abused, and that she will be here when I return."

"Which will be…"

"Tomorrow, if all goes well. If not," he said with a shrug, "someone else will be coming for her."

Durriken filled his tankard again. "Will you tell her you are leaving?"

He turned to watch her emerge from Durriken's caravan. She was wrapped in a green paisley shawl with deep silk fringe and looked as exotic and captivating as any gypsy. When she turned, her glance caught his and she paused. Violca followed her gaze and said something that made Miss Lillian laugh. Even across the glade, he could see her color come up. She gave him the faintest of smiles and turned back to Violca with a comment of her own. He'd have given a week of his life to know what they were saying.

"When will you go?" Brishen asked.

He remained silent. He knew he should go now, this very minute, but the thought of staying was seductive. His mind conjured possibilities. Miss Lillian by firelight? Miss Lillian dancing in the moonlight?

Miss Lillian in her wedding gown, ready to walk down the aisle to Olney's side.

"Now," he said, finishing his ale. "I will go now."

Chapter Ten

That night, Devlin sat at his desk at The Crown and Bear after midnight, watching the door, a glass of whiskey near at hand. Waiting was not one of his few virtues, and he chaffed at the inactivity, his stomach churning at the possibilities. Since receiving Mick's letter earlier, he'd been wondering if the Hunter brothers had somehow discovered that he was behind Lillian O'Rourke's disappearance.

Well, if they had, there was nothing to be done about it now. He knew how to face the consequences—he'd done it often enough. A man in his position did not expect any latitude in his dealings. He'd scraped and scrambled his whole life. Why should this be any different?

He heard the soft footfall of boots in the corridor and sat forward in his chair, schooling his features to relaxed unconcern as he opened a ledger, hoping to appear as if he had nothing else on his mind.

He called entry to a soft knock and made a show of closing the ledger as he looked up. Ah, it was Jamie *and* Andrew Hunter. Whatever was afoot, it could not be good for him if it was going to take both of them.

He waved at a chair in front of the desk and another against the far wall, then took two more glasses from the liquor cupboard behind him. "Mick said you came by last night. What can I do for you?" he asked when they were seated.

"Can't you guess?" Jamie asked him.

He poured straight whiskey for both of them and raised his glass to them. "Is this a riddle?"

Andrew drank and gave him a piercing stare. "Where were you, Dev? You're rarely gone from here during business hours."

"Visiting my maiden aunt."

"And how is she?" Jamie asked in a tone of voice that clearly said he didn't believe Devlin.

"Well, thank you."

Andrew sighed. "Enough of the pleasantries, eh? Why so hostile, Dev?"

"Am I hostile? Guess it's just habit. When a Hunter comes calling, they usually want something. Rarely something simple."

Jamie nodded. "You're right. We want something, and we need you. I brought Andrew this time. Thought he might be able to convince you."

"Then this is about…"

Andrew nodded. "The Blood Wyvern Brotherhood. We need to pull them in now, Dev. We can't wait another day, let alone another week."

"And this is my business?"

"You helped us last month."

"I helped myself. You just happened to benefit."

"Good God! I've never known a man who went to such lengths to be disliked. Put your stubbornness aside for a moment and think of someone else."

He sat back and breathed deeply. They weren't here about Miss Lillian. That much was a relief. He could afford to hear them out. "Why the urgency?"

"Because they are on the move. We've been watching those we could identify, hoping they would lead us to the rest, but we believe they are making plans to escape. Getting their affairs in order, transferring money abroad, selling assets. If they get away—"

"What? England is rid of them? How is that a problem?"

Andrew frowned and Devlin had never seen him look angrier. "It's a problem because they will get away with having murdered innocent women, my sister-in-law among them. Of torturing and slaughtering them like sheep. They'll be free to continue their practices abroad. Is that what you want?"

Jamie nodded. "They've acquired a taste for it, Dev. They won't quit now. You know the sort of man we're dealing with. A few of them might have been curious or thrill-seekers, but the rest were common killers."

"And, if those few get away, we will never know who the rest of them were. Those remaining will continue their depravity, but they'll be more clever about it," Andrew added.

Devlin was thoughtful. What they were saying was true. The curs were clever enough not to use women who would be missed again. They would prey on the vulnerable—prostitutes, girls fresh into town from the villages, shop girls who lived alone.

As if sensing his indecision, Jamie leaned forward. "You have resources that we don't, Dev. You can ask questions and go places no one else can."

He stood and began to pace. He was reminded that there was always the possibility that he could uncover Rutherford's involvement, and wouldn't that be a plum? Even Olney's. Yes, that would be icing on the cake of his revenge.

"If I do this, Jamie, will the government stand behind us? Will they take action this time, or let the blackguards get away again?"

"They are prepared for the scandal. They know now that

the aristocracy is behind this, and they are willing to proceed. No more cover-ups. No more favors called in."

"Can you guarantee that?"

Andrew tossed down the contents of his glass. "Dash is dead. Throckmorton has been brought in but won't, or is afraid to, talk. But Henley is still in hiding. He'd be the mastermind of the Brotherhood now. Dash trained him. Booth and Elwood will be following in close step. But the others…who they are and where they are hiding, that is what we need to know."

Devlin had a quick flash of memory. *Henley. Poised above Miss Lillian's sister, ready to rape her in clear view of a chanting crowd of England's nobility.* His stomach burned with anger. Helpless. She'd been as helpless as his own mother….

"Are you certain there is no other way? Are those the only names you could come up with?"

Andrew cocked an eyebrow. "I might have caught a glimpse of the Duke of Rutherford. His whelp could have been there. Aside from them, I could not recognize anyone beneath their robes."

But that was enough. That was all the Hunter brothers needed to say to win his cooperation. "I'll help," he said with every appearance of reluctance. "But I need another day."

"What for?" Jamie asked.

"To clean up a few matters." And once he'd done that, he wondered if the Hunters would even want his help.

Jamie nodded. "We can wait that long. Drew has a few personal matters to tend to, as well."

Ah, Miss Lillian, no doubt. "I've heard rumors," Devlin ventured.

"I doubt they do justice to the situation," Andrew grumbled. "I love my wife dearly, but her family has been a bit of a trial."

"Bit?" Jamie laughed this time. "They've run him a merry race. The last, not so merry."

Devlin knew he should stop them. Anything they told him now would be remembered tomorrow. "Too bad," he said, hoping that would end the conversation.

"'Too bad' would be an improvement," Andrew said. "I am certain everything you've heard is true. Bella's sister has jilted Lord Olney in a most public and humiliating way. Not that I am disappointed about that. Olney is not a man I'd choose as a brother-in-law. But to make matters worse, she has disappeared with the Rutherford jewels. The duke has sworn a warrant for her immediate arrest."

Devlin squelched a pang of guilt. There'd be some damage to undo, but he knew Andrew was up to the challenge.

"I could deal with all that if only she would come home to us," he continued. "Her mother has taken to her bed. Her sisters are beside themselves. And I...I haven't mentioned it to the family, but I find myself fearing that, somehow, the Brotherhood has got their hands on her. They killed Cora, and kidnapped Gina and Bella. And now Lilly is missing. Are they taking revenge on me for stopping their scheme?"

"That is the reason for your urgency."

"In part. The O'Rourkes have had more than their share of misery. But wherever Lilly has got herself to, I only pray that she is safe."

Jamie stood. "Perhaps we should ask Dev for his help finding Lilly."

"Done," Devlin said as he opened the door for them. "I shall bring her home safe and sound the day after tomorrow."

Both men laughed politely. He hoped they'd still be laughing tomorrow, but he doubted that. It was far more likely that he and Andrew Hunter would be facing one another across a dueling field.

* * *

After they had bathed in the cool stream, Lilly wiggled her toes in the water as she sat beside Drina, combing her hair over her shoulder. She could feel Violca's dark eyes boring into her back, reminding her that she was not on holiday but was, in fact, a prisoner. If only she could convince someone to help her.

She glanced at Drina. Last night, before they had made peace, Drina told her that Rye had sold her to them and that she was to be Drina's slave. Violca had tweaked her ear for that impertinence.

She couldn't help but wonder what the girl's relationship was with the man she called Rye. She broached the subject they had carefully avoided until now. "Drina, are you and Mr. Devlin…betrothed?"

The girl's dark eyes flashed with anger. "Rye does not see me as I am. To him, I am a child, as I was when my people first camped on his land."

"When was that?"

"Perhaps five years ago. I was but ten, then."

So Drina was scarcely fifteen years? She appeared to be more than that—at least as old as Lilly's own twenty-one.

"But I see in his eyes that he loves you. I must give him up or rend my clothes. I like my clothes."

Lilly laughed. The girl really was a charmer. If Mr. Devlin was not interested in her, it was his loss, even if she was too young for him. And she had certainly misjudged the relationship between her and Mr. Devlin.

"I think I will call you Florica," Drina said. "That will be your gypsy name, eh? You must not tell it to any but the Roma. If the *gajo* know your name, they will have power over you."

"Florica," she repeated. "I like that."

"I like your underdress. It is as soft as a butterfly wing. I gave you a name. Will you give me your—"

"Chemise," she supplied. "But if I do that, what will I sleep in? All I have is what I have on my back."

"Sleep as nature made you, Florica. Rye will give you more. He is most generous."

"So I have heard."

She had been treated with respect by the gypsy band, and that was due, she had no doubt, to the fact that they believed she was Mr. Devlin's woman. They were loyal to him, and no amount of bribery had been able to buy her freedom. But Lilly hadn't given up. Surely she'd find someone to help her, or some way to escape before Mr. Devlin returned.

Brishen, though, was different. He had smiled sadly and shook his head. "If only I could, miss, I would. But Rye would have my head and call down curses upon me."

Later, he had come to visit Drina's caravan, and Lilly suspected he was in love with her. She glanced sideways at the girl and decided to pay the girl back for her teasing with some of her own.

"You can have Rye. I like the man you call Brishen. So tall and handsome. I think he would know how to treat a woman, yes?"

Drina shrugged and busied herself with weaving a crown of blue and yellow wildflowers.

"And his mouth. Have you noticed how soft his lips appear? How full and plump they are? His kiss would be sweet and soft, would it not?"

She shrugged again. "I would not know. He never speaks to me."

"Never?"

"He thinks I am a child, too. But I am not. I am a woman, full and true."

"Perhaps he is afraid to talk to you. Some men become tongue-tied when they are in love."

Drina laughed. "Love? Brishen? You dream. You would not make a good gypsy. We can tell what people are thinking and we can see the future."

Lilly smiled. She was perceptive enough to see that Drina was aching from Brishen's lack of attention, and that she was probably using Mr. Devlin to make him jealous. She glanced over her shoulder to see the man in question coming toward them. "If you could tell the future, you would know that Brishen is coming to see you now."

Drina jumped to her feet and turned. "Florica! You must have Roma blood."

She shrugged innocently. "Perhaps I do."

Brishen looked confused. "You are Roma, miss?"

"Florica," Drina corrected. "Florica is her gypsy name."

He smiled at her and Lilly's heart almost broke at the sweetness of it. She'd give anything if someone would look at her that way.

Brishen shuffled his feet and looked down. "Durriken would like to know how you are, Florica."

"And I would like to know when Mr. Devlin will be back for me."

"He did not say. Perhaps today. Perhaps tomorrow. But he will be back for you, Florica. He swore it."

Warmth seeped through her when she realized how comforting that thought was. When he'd left without a word, she'd felt abandoned. Oh, what was wrong with her? She liked him and hated him by turns. She wanted him back and she wanted to escape. She wanted another of those extraordinary kisses he had given her, and she dreaded his touch because of what it would do to her. Everything about Mr. Devlin created confusion in her.

She stood and wrapped her arms around herself, suddenly chilly in the late afternoon sun. "Is that all, Brishen?"

"There is to be a celebration tonight. Grandmother Jofranka has entered her year of eighty. There will be dancing." The yearning he felt was clear for Lilly to see when he glanced at Drina. Was he working his way up to asking Drina to dance with him? Did gypsies do that?

Perhaps if they had privacy… "I will go tell Durriken how I am. Brishen, would you stay with Drina and keep her company until I get back?"

"Yes!" he said, a bit too eagerly to be missed by Drina.

The girl flushed and looked uncharacteristically shy. Lilly smiled as she walked away. Some things were the same, whether in a gypsy camp or in a grand ballroom.

She came to a Y in the path and stopped. The path on the left would take her back to the caravans. The path to her right led to freedom. She knew the gypsies went to town to sell their wares and buy supplies. She could follow that path to the nearest town, and from there, to London.

He had only managed to catch a few hours of sleep after his meeting with the Hunter brothers but it was dark by the time Devlin arrived at the gypsy camp. He had gone to the cottage first, to leave his horse and clean up before fetching Miss Lillian. The summer night was warm, and he'd left his jacket behind, favoring rolled-up sleeves and an open vest. No doubt Miss Lillian's delicate sensibilities had been calloused by the gypsy disregard of social niceties by now. He wagered shirtsleeves would no longer shock or dismay her.

He heard the music and laughter before he entered the glade and wondered if his hostage would be sulking in Durriken's caravan. He had quickly learned that she could be quite off-putting when angered or out of sorts. And charming and funny when relaxed and trusting. But always amusing. Always surprising.

The campfires illuminated the clearing and cast ever-changing shadows against the caravans. There was dancing, laughter, drinking and revelry. A celebration. A woman with dark, silver-threaded hair sat in a chair in the middle, her shoe tapping as she clapped in time with the music. Ah, Grandmother Jofranka's birthday.

Durriken and a few other men were dancing in a circle, trying to best one another with intricate steps while an equal number of women were dancing in their own circle, twirling and dipping in a lovely pattern.

Devlin scanned the crowd, looking for Miss Lillian. She should be easily recognizable by her white gown, but he could not find her. He saw Violca, standing by her caravan, and went to talk to her.

"You are back too soon," she greeted him. "Florica has been telling us stories of you."

"Florica?"

"Your Miss O'Rourke. Drina has given her a gypsy name."

"She has not caused you trouble?"

"Trouble? Yes. She draws too much attention. But even Drina likes her. They have traded clothes."

"Where is she?"

Violca laughed. "You do not know her?"

He glanced around the clearing. Though it was dark, he could see clearly but for the shadows at the edge of the forest. "Is she lurking somewhere?"

She nudged him and pointed toward the revelry around Grandmother Jofranka. The unmarried gypsy girls were dancing around her chair, chanting good wishes. Three times right, then three times left before repeating their steps. And then he saw her.

Dressed in brilliant blue with the red paisley shawl tied around her waist and hips, was Miss Lillian. Gone was the pristine bride of two days ago, and in her place was a vivid, stunning woman, animated with laughter. The shawl was snug against her form and revealed her waist and hips. Entire legions would have gone straight to hell for their thoughts if they'd been watching "Florica." God knows, he would have. And from the looks on the gypsy's faces, they, too, would be doomed.

The tops of her pale shoulders were revealed by the wide neckline, as well as the tempting shadow between her breasts, barely covered by the lace edging of the gown. And if he was any judge, Florica wore no undergarments—no confining corset, no modest chemise and no drawers.

He'd have to box Drina's ears for this.

But first he'd watch Florica. He took a tankard from Violca and drank deeply of the *mul*—gypsy wine—thirsty from his long ride. Florica twirled and her skirts flared above her calves. He drank again. Thank God she was going home tomorrow. He wouldn't vouch for her purity if he was around her much longer.

The dance was over and the girls stopped, laughing and panting. Drina whispered something in Florica's ear. Her hair had been brushed back but left to drop in a smooth fall of gold down her back. Wildflowers crowned her head and she looked like some sort of woodland nymph. To him, she'd never been more beautiful.

Brishen approached the group with another man named Chik—a strapping young fellow with a ruddy complexion. He did not like the way Chik was sizing her up. He started forward, but Violca stopped him with a hand on his arm.

"Go easy, Rye. Not with a heavy hand. Florica is gentle and not used to men who take what they want. *Dukker* her."

Charm her? Devlin didn't know if he had that in him. He'd never played anyone's admirer before. That was best left to the aristocrats. He was more comfortable with prostitutes and charwomen. He and Miss Lillian were not lovers. They were adversaries, and he'd do well to remember that.

He finished his tankard and handed it to Violca. "I am taking her back tomorrow morning, and that will be an end to it."

Violca's laughter rang in his ears as he went toward the center of the clearing. First, he bowed to Grandmother Jofranka and gave her a kiss on her weathered forehead, and then he turned to the group around Florica.

"Miss Lillian, I see you have not suffered in my absence."

She gave him a wary look, as if she were trying to decide if he was angry. He smiled to soften his words. Violca would be proud.

She returned his smile. "I have made the best of the situation. I did not know when to expect you back. Drina told me you sold me to her people. That I would have to be her slave."

He bit his cheek to keep from laughing as he turned to the girl. "Did you say that, Drina?"

She grinned. "Yes, but Florica did not believe me. She thinks you are a good man. A gentle man."

"Pish-posh!" his captive said. "I said nothing of the sort. Drina is making things up."

"Then what *did* you say?"

She tightened the knot fastening the shawl around her hips. "I said…I said that you were a perfect gentleman."

He laughed at her outrageous lie. "Have you been drinking?"

Drina affected wide-eyed innocence. "Not very much, Rye. She said she was not accustomed to strong drink, so I did not give her much *mul*."

"Only a few mugs." Miss Lillian nodded.

Drina was a minx. She knew the gypsy wine was potent and that a *gorgie* would have little resistance to it. He gave her a severe look. "If I have to carry her back to the cottage and all the way up the stairs, Drina, I will be very unhappy."

"Ah, and that is why living gypsy is better than living *gajo*. There are no stairs in caravans. All that up and down, up and down. It is a waste of time."

Miss Lillian regarded him with amusement. "Oh, I rather think Mr. Devlin is fond of the up and down, up and down, and I doubt he considers it a waste of time."

Devlin nearly choked on his *mul*. Had the prim little bride-to-be really made a bawdy jest? "Oh, no, you don't, Miss Lillian. You are not going to charm me so easily."

"Charm you? Why, I cannot imagine how such a thing could be done. Tell me, Mr. Devlin, what *would* it take?"

Not much more than she was doing at this exact moment, he thought. Her smiles, her teasing and puckish wit were captivating enough. He wondered if it was too much to hope that it signaled a softening rather than the *mul*. He ignored her question because he didn't know how to answer it without betraying his own feelings. "How have you occupied yourself in my absence, Miss Lillian?"

"After I recovered from the shock of finding you gone without a farewell and the news that I was now a slave? Hmm. Well, I tried to persuade Durriken to set me free. After that, I asked Violca's help to return me to London. Failing that, I importuned Brishen, and he was most regretful that he could not assist me. Drina, however, offered to guide me to a thoroughfare if I would give her my chemise." She glanced down at the low scoop of her blouse. "I hope she likes it."

"But you are here. Did Drina lie to you?"

"Unashamedly."

Devlin turned to the gypsy girl. "Drina, give Miss Lillian back her clothing."

"She has got the better of me, Rye. She has taken my best dress. And Violca gave her red shawl to Florica."

"For shame, Miss Lillian. You must give the girl back her clothes. And take your own."

"No!" Drina's eyes widened. "It was a fair trade."

He grinned and looked at Miss Lillian. "Do you want them?"

"I thought Drina might have better luck with the wedding silk than I."

"I have never had silk before," Drina pleaded. "Please?"

"You will not mind returning to London in gypsy finery?"

"Better than a ruined wedding gown."

He shrugged. "If it is your wish."

Drina clapped her hands in delight and seized Miss Lillian's hands to spin her in a circle. Devlin held his breath, certain her dress would slip down one shoulder. The red shawl slipped instead, snugging the curve of her buttocks. Oh, and what a sweet curve that was. With a bottom like that, it was a shame women's current fashions often showed their busts to advantage, but left the rest of them shrouded.

She stopped suddenly and he looked up from the curve of her hips to meet her gaze. Though color rose in her cheeks, she did not flinch or look away. Was that a challenge? An invitation? A question?

Nausea twisted his stomach and resentment crowded out reason when he remembered that he'd be taking her back to Olney. Curse the fates that had made him base-born and Olney the heir. "Drina, tell Durriken I have taken Miss Lillian home."

Chapter Eleven

Lilly trudged along in the moonlight at Mr. Devlin's side, wondering where the amusing man had gone. When he'd first returned to the camp, he'd been more at ease than she'd seen him since London. But now he was moody and morose again. Had things not gone well for him while he was gone?

"I…I told you there would be no ransom," she ventured, a little breathless from the pace he set.

"Ransom? What are you talking about?"

"Is that not why you were gone? Arranging my ransom?"

"I told you I had not taken you for ransom, Miss Lillian, and that has not changed."

"Then where did you go?"

"To London, for my own reasons. 'Twas business, and nothing to do with you."

That should have reassured her, but it only rankled. Was she so unimportant to him, then, that he could just abandon her at a gypsy camp and return when the mood struck him? Oh, she should have escaped. She should have taken that path. But the thought of dealing with Olney was daunting. And what would she say to her family?

Laughing and teasing with Drina and the others today had seduced her into thinking she could make another life that had nothing to do with society and responsibilities. Drina had taught her some Romany words and said she was no doubt a gypsy herself, taken by the *gajo* and raised as one of them. Silly words, she knew, but she had almost been ready to abandon everything familiar for…for the gypsies? Or for Mr. Devlin?

That thought was sobering. She couldn't be falling in love with her kidnapper, could she? Why, kidnappers were horrid men who mistreated their captives and ofttimes slit their throats rather than return them unharmed. They were greedy, unscrupulous beasts. Unwashed and uneducated.

But Mr. Devlin was none of those things. He was as gentle as she'd allowed him to be. And funny, patient and considerate. And handsome. Devastatingly handsome. And his kiss was the most distracting thing she'd ever experienced—so intimate and yet so innocent. Innocent? No. Not with the feelings that kiss had awakened.

She looked up at him in the moonlight, wondering what he was thinking. He must have sensed her attention on him because he turned to her with a quizzical look.

"What is it, Miss Lillian?"

"I am wondering when you intend to take me back."

He looked introspective again. "Are you anxious to see Olney again and explain that this wasn't your fault?"

How could she ever explain to him that she was not certain she even wanted to go back or face the problems that lay ahead? "Olney is the least of my concerns, Mr. Devlin. I doubt he would ever consider marrying me now."

"Are you sorry for that?"

Was she? Good heavens! Was *that* her reluctance to go home again? Oh, if she were to be honest, she would have to admit that a part of her was relieved. Actually relieved! She had never wanted to marry Olney for himself. Only for the ease and comfort it would bring her mother and Eugenia. "No," she admitted. "I am dreading it. I must tell him that I think it was not meant to be."

"Fatalistic," he mused. "I had not expected such pragmatism from you, Miss Lillian."

"Spilt milk," she said, and Mr. Devlin nodded.

A cloud drifted across the moon, darkening the night and the forest along with it. Lilly shivered in the sudden shift from filtered moonlight to utter gloom. She stumbled, stubbed her toe and hopped about on one foot. "Ouch!"

Mr. Devlin steadied her. "What is it? Were you bitten?"

"No. Just…just… I think it was a rock."

He lifted her like a child and carried her to a fallen log, where he sat her down and cupped her foot to rest on his knee and bent his head to examine it.

The patchy clouds shifted again, casting a shimmer of moonlight on his dark hair, revealing the waves and rich color. She had to clasp her hands together to keep from touching him and slipping her fingers through the cool strands. His scent— soap, leather and something tangy—rose to her and made her head spin. Or was that the *mul?* Whatever it was made her slightly dizzy, and she caught herself with a hand on his shoulder. He looked up at her and smiled.

"'Tis nothing much." His fingers kneaded her foot, restoring the circulation and tickling her. "You'll be right as rain tomorrow."

She giggled and then covered her mouth, not wanting him to think her childish. "Mr. Devlin, you have a deft touch. My foot feels better already."

His smile widened into a grin. "Deft touch? I am gratified that you think so, Miss Lillian."

She returned his smile. "Durriken said you had the lightest

touch he's ever seen until you grew and your hands became too large."

"I shall have to have a word with Durriken."

"I gather you have known each other a very long time."

"We met when we were young. His people had come to town to pick a few pockets and tell fortunes. It was he who taught me my light touch when picking pockets. When my hands grew too large, I had to find other talents."

She laughed. "Dare I ask what other talents?"

"No." He released her foot and stood. "You have a lamentable lack of calluses, Miss Lillian. Can you walk, or shall I carry you the rest of the way?"

She took his offered hand and stood. "Walk," she said.

He offered his arm as if they were strolling in Hyde Park and she took it. He was a surprising man. A complicated man. They walked in silence for a time, and she tried to reconcile what she'd learned about him from the gypsies and what she knew of him from her own experience. Who was Mr. Devlin, really? A criminal, indisputably. A gentleman, possibly. And certainly unlike any man she'd ever known before. His manners, when he chose to use them, were impeccable. His education might not be extensive, but it was adequate when paired with his excellent mind. His experience with women was evident in the way he'd charmed her, undone her corset and had half the gypsy maids following him with their heated eyes.

The Romany people loved him—that much was certain. She'd been told half a dozen stories by the men, and that many again by the women, of how he'd saved them from the local authorities on many occasions, how he'd made his land a sanctuary for them and how he'd saved Durriken's life when the townspeople accused him of stealing their livestock. How he'd rescued Drina from rape at the hands of drunks returning home after a night at the public house. And how he'd brought the local physician to cure Grandmother Jofranka of the grippe when she'd been in so much pain that she'd begged to die. To a man, Brishen had told her, they would die for him if he asked it.

But what she really liked about the man was that she did not have to behave around him. She did not have to watch her manners or her words. In fact, he seemed to enjoy her rebellions and defiance. He tolerated her eccentricities rather than trying to change them—unlike Olney, who'd alluded to the possibility of finding a tutor for her in the "social protocol" necessary for the wives of the upper aristocracy. Oh, and the duchess! Every occasion was an opportunity to correct and instruct her future daughter-in-law. Well, at least that was in the past. Despite the impending disgrace to her family, she sighed deeply with a small measure of satisfaction.

The cottage, an outline in the darkness, was visible across the clearing when they came to a small stream. Mr. Devlin barely hesitated before he swept her up in his arms and jumped the distance. He did not put her down, but took long strides toward the cottage.

"I can walk, Mr. Devlin."

"I know you can, Miss Lillian. But you do not weigh much and this is quicker and will result in less damage to your bare feet."

She chuckled. "Yes, but at what cost to you, sir? Why, all those stairs…"

"No cost at all. As you were so quick to point out, I am rather fond of the up and down."

"It isn't necessary.…"

"I do not mind wasting my time in the least."

She laughed, despite her chagrin. "If you were a gentleman, sir, you would not throw a lady's words back at her."

"Ah, then lucky for me that I am no gentleman."

"I might be forced to debate that." She slipped her arm around his neck to help support her weight, and looked up into his unfathomable eyes. "Who is the real Mr. Devlin?"

"Do not ask unless you want the truth, Miss Lillian. I am done with lying to you. Tomorrow you will know exactly who and what I am."

"Tomorrow might not come. I want to know now," she whispered, not at all certain that was the truth but knowing she did not want these feelings to end.

"You like to tempt fate, do you not?"

"Yes," she admitted.

"We shall test that theory, I think."

They had arrived at the cottage door and he dipped to twist the knob and kick the door open. So slowly that it made her heart pound and her breath catch in her throat, he released her until her toes touched the floor. His arm still around her waist, he pressed her close and Lilly could feel the hard length of him through her cotton gown. His hands slipped down to her hips and unfastened the knot of her shawl.

"You are coming undone, Miss Lillian." He held the red paisley wrap up in one hand to show her.

Oh, yes. She certainly was. And there didn't seem to be a single thing she could do about it except look into those deeply stirring eyes and shiver.

He draped the shawl over her shoulders. "Are you cold?"

To the contrary, she was burning in a way that had nothing to do with the hot summer night. She shook her head, unable to form intelligible words. She lifted her arms to rest her palms against his chest, feeling the trip-hammer beat of his heart.

He groaned. "You cannot know what you are doing to me."

If it was anything like what he was doing to her, she could hazard a guess. "Kiss me," she managed. "Kiss me like you did before."

He lowered his lips to hers and spoke a warning against them. "This was not my plan. You cannot play with me this way. I'm not a gentleman. You'll get burned."

"I could have escaped at Durriken's camp, but I stayed. I'm tempting fate, Mr. Devlin," she reminded him. And she knew it was the truth, knew that, whatever his intention had been, Mr. Devlin had rescued her from a disastrous marriage. Olney was not half the man that Mr. Devlin was. And she was glad—deliriously happy—that he had never claimed his marital due. *That* right belonged to Mr. Devlin. If he wanted it.

With an unintelligible curse, he lifted her again and headed for the stairs.

In the end, he had needed very little encouragement to do what he wanted to do, Devlin thought wryly. Between the urgings of Durriken, Brishen and Lilly herself, he'd cast his few scruples to the wind in favor of his base desires.

She felt as light as a feather when he lifted her and turned toward the stairs. She slipped her arm around his neck and fondled the curls at his nape as she leaned her cheek against his shoulder. The feeling was so tantalizing that he almost stopped to savor it better. But by now he was feeling so urgent that he couldn't have stopped if all the legions of Hell had been waiting at the top of the stairs.

Thank God they weren't. He was beyond caring about anything but the way Lilly felt, the way she smelled, the little sigh that was half gasp, half yearning. He stood with her at the foot of his bed, wondering if he should undress her now or as they made long, lingering love. But if what Lilly had said was true, all that was remaining of her clothing was Drina's blue gown. Everything else had been traded to the gypsy girl.

He put her on her feet and held her at arm's length as she

swayed toward him. "Last chance, Lilly O'Rourke. Flee now, or take the consequences."

She smiled, her eyes soft and certain in the dim moonlight filtering through the sheer curtain. "Very sporting of you, Mr. Devlin, to give me a last chance."

She didn't even know his name. He didn't want her to make love to a stranger. "My name is Devlin Farrell."

She paused and gave him a strange look, as if she'd heard his name before. Then she shrugged. "Devlin. Rye. Does it matter?"

"Not the name, Lilly, but the man behind it. You don't know me. Who I am. What I am."

"I know enough."

Dear God, the girl was reckless! His kindred soul. And she was ready to give herself to a stranger. If he were a gentleman, he wouldn't let her. Ah, but that ship had sailed long ago.

He pushed the sleeves off her shoulders and down her arms. His mouth went dry as the soft fabric slipped, little by little, revealing an inch of her, then two. She made no move to stop it, but held his eyes with her own, waiting, perhaps, for some word, some response from him. But he was frozen, finding more power in her innocent simplicity than he ever had from the practiced seductions of courtesans and prostitutes.

Lilly was a world of firsts for him. His first woman of quality. His first coupling with someone he had feelings for. The first woman he could really believe wanted *him,* not just his coins. His first…virgin.

The thought was sobering. What he did to her tonight would be with her forever. Would color her attitude toward love and making love.

She caught the sleeves of her gown just before her breasts were completely exposed, a deep color staining her cheeks. Even shrouded in darkness, he could see every nuance of her, every shade and movement. He leaned forward and nuzzled her ear, whispering, though there was no need.

"You are beautiful, Lilly. More beautiful than any other woman I've ever known. Let me see all of you."

She sighed and he could feel her tension through his hands on her shoulders. "Let go," he told her. "Give me the reins."

She nodded, and he was humbled that she trusted him. God knew, he had given her every reason not to.

Inch by inch, she was revealed to him, and he felt like a lad again, seeing a woman for the first time. She was a goddess—fresh, innocent and yet ripe. Her breasts were stunning—pert, pink-tipped and firm, neither too large nor too small. A tiny mole above one aureole reminded him of a star above the moon. He bent to kiss it, and Lilly made a mewling sound. She swayed again and he steadied her.

"A bit more," he said, urging the gown over the curve of her hips.

Ah, heaven. It was as she'd said—nothing beneath. No corset this time, no drawers, no garters or stockings. Just Lilly. Glorious, barefoot Lilly. The sweet curve of her buttocks, the swell of her hips and the dark V of her mons. He wanted to kneel before her and pay homage with his mouth and tongue.

Alas, she shivered. Why she should be cold when everything inside him was burning was beyond him, but he could not bear to think of her being uncomfortable. He lifted her again and laid her upon his bed.

"Please," she said.

Her plea was soft and shy, and he knew she would be feeling exposed and vulnerable. He pulled the green silk coverlet over her and stepped back to unfasten his shirt and trousers.

Lilly watched him disrobe with a mixture of curiosity and trepidation. Every part of her was still humming from his touch, from the brief stirring kiss, and the cool coverlet he had drawn over her. She did not want to turn back now, but her separation from him had cleared her mind. If he did not hurry, she would surely change her mind.

Heel to toe, he wedged his boots off, then tugged his shirt over his head. She could not help but stare at his chest. Lightly matted with dark hair, defined by strong muscles and a tapering waist, she found the sight deeply stirring to her senses. She yearned to touch his skin, trace the ridges of his muscles and test the texture of the dark hair.

She swallowed hard when he unbuttoned his trousers and pushed them down. Now clad only in his drawers and stockings, he was beyond her imaginings. Long, lean legs revealed themselves and, when his drawers followed his stockings to the floor, she was suddenly hot. Burning. Whether from modesty or anticipation, she could not begin to guess. Everything now was unknown to her.

She was not naive. She'd seen animals—had witnessed the neighbor's hunting dog mating with a female in the pack. She'd actually found it a bit off-putting and could not imagine how that would correspond to humans. She still couldn't.

He caught her gaze and smiled as he came down beside her. "Take a breath, Lilly, and believe that I will not hurt you unnecessarily." Then he lifted her chin and met her lips.

This kiss had all the sweet passion of the night he'd removed her corset, but with something more. A softness that spoke of patience and concern. That promised heaven and, perhaps, a touch of hell.

His hands moved down over her hips, defining her curves and warming her skin. The tension drained from her and she found herself falling into a velvet abyss where only Devlin's touch remained, only his mouth and tongue. Every time she caught her breath in surprise or wonder, he groaned.

She did not protest when he pushed her back against the pillows and hovered over her, paying exquisite attention to her lips. Nor did she attempt to stop him when he moved lower to cherish the little mole he had kissed before, and then dip lower still to nibble and draw the firm tip of one sensitive breast into his mouth. Oh, that made her knees feel weak and her breathing heavy.

No, she did not ask him to stop, but instead twisted her fingers through his hair, holding him closer as she moaned his name over and over again to tell him what she had no words for. He seemed to understand and gave her what she wanted, always taking her further and further into the dark space where only they existed. And again, she did not protest when he slipped his hand down farther to find that part of her that was aching for his touch.

"I want…I want…" she moaned.

"What?" he asked. "What do you want, Lilly? Ask it, and 'tis yours."

"I want you…you…"

"There is no rush, Lilly my love. We have all night to make you a woman. My woman."

And then he began stroking that secret place in a steady, even rhythm and she nearly cried out when an unexpected heat washed over her. She rose to his hand and he sighed.

"Perfect. You are perfect, Lilly. You were made for me."

She wanted to make him feel the way she felt, but she didn't know how. She pushed him onto his back and poised herself over him. "What should I do? Tell me."

He tugged her hair to pull her mouth down to his and gave her another of those deep kisses before he spoke. "You need do nothing," he said. "You intoxicate me with your smile. Just smile for me, Lilly, and I'll count myself a fortunate man."

She did and moved one leg across him, as if to straddle him.

Her leg brushed his erection and she was startled by the size and strength of it—like steel sheathed in velvet. He groaned. "Easy, Lilly. A man cannot take too much of that."

She retreated, afraid she might have hurt him, but he followed her, covering her with his body but bearing his weight on his forearms.

Again, he kissed his way down her body, stopping to give attention to the places that cried out for him. But this time, he moved lower, trailing his tongue to where his fingers had been. She caught his hair and tugged, shocked to her very core that such things were done. He only laughed, the vibration sending little shock waves of pleasure coursing through her.

Within seconds, she was incapable of shock. Incapable of even moving. Her world narrowed to that one tiny spot where intense pleasure rocked her very being.

Moments later, or hours, he cradled her and wiped her tears away with his thumbs. "Rest, Lilly. We will finish this later," he whispered in her ear as she felt the earth dropping away.

Devlin leaned against the doorjamb, watching a pink dawn stain the sky above the trees. *Hell! Bloody goddamn hell!* This hadn't played into his plan at all. Never in his wildest imaginings had he thought Lilly would desire him. Or that he could fall in love. That they would make love.

In the end, he hadn't been able to go through with it. He dared not. The memory of her would sear into his soul. He'd never be free of her if he lay with her. Worst of all, he would prove himself no better than Olney and Rutherford if he simply took what he wanted without thought of the consequences. No, like the coward he was, he'd left Lilly as she lay sleeping.

She wouldn't suffer pain or degradation at his hands. His touch, his love, would defile her. But she had ruined him, too—making it impossible for him to settle for any other woman. How could he content himself with anyone else now that he'd known Lilly? And how would he live with Lilly's contempt when she found out what he'd done?

Now he was left to clean up his mess. To, somehow, redeem Lilly's reputation and standing in society—the very things he'd stripped her of mere days ago when he'd carried her from the church. Oh, he'd had his revenge, but at what cost? How had he thought Lilly's good name less important than his selfish desires? He should have waited, should have found a different way to bring them down.

But today, he would take Lilly home to her family. He would face Andrew Hunter, knowing he'd lost a friend, if not his very life. Because if Andrew called him out, he would face him across the field, but he would not lift a hand against him. He'd forfeit his life if that would restore Lilly's honor.

Chapter Twelve

Lilly came downstairs to find Devlin standing in the doorway, his back to her. Heat scorched her cheeks when she thought of the things he'd done to her last night. And the things they hadn't done. Was she somehow deficient? Lacking in some essential way? Not up to his standards?

Oh, but how could that be? He'd been so kind. So gentle. He'd brought her such delight, and had praised her for her response. And he'd left her while she slept.

He hadn't even wanted to wake with her.

She straightened her gown and tied the shawl around her waist in a savage knot. Well, she had too much pride to beg his attention. If he did not want to give it, she would not ask it.

"Have you had breakfast, Mr. Devlin?"

He turned, and she was pleased to see shadows beneath his eyes. "Yes. I've made a breakfast of hard-cooked eggs, cheese and bread for you. It is in a basket in the coach."

"Coach? Are we going somewhere?"

"I am taking you home, Lilly."

Good heavens! She'd been so awful that he couldn't wait to get rid of her! "Now? But I thought…"

He nodded and straightened. "I'd planned on keeping you longer, but circumstances… Well, London is the place for you now."

"And your reason for kidnapping me?"

"Accomplished."

Where, moments before, she'd been burning with embarrassment, she was now frozen to the bone. *Accomplished.* He'd kidnapped her to seduce her before Olney had the chance. And now that he'd done what he'd set out to do, he was finished with her. But she'd make him say it. Admit his perfidy. "Then last night was just the completion of your plan?"

"No. Lilly, please. That is not what I meant. Last night took me by surprise. I hadn't planned—"

"You kidnapped me to exact some sort of revenge on Olney, and seducing me was not in your plan? Oh, I should have known better! I should have realized your kindness was merely cozening up to me so you could…*oh!*"

She turned her back to him so she wouldn't have to look him in the face. Oh, he looked regretful enough, but that hadn't stopped him from getting his revenge. "What did he do to you?" she asked. "What was so awful that it made you so cruel? I've done nothing to you, and yet you've ruined me. I hate you, Mr. Devlin."

"Lilly, I…"

But he did not finish. She heard his boot scrape the threshold as he walked into the rising sun without another word. She was so confounded that she couldn't think what to do. She looked around the little cottage that had actually grown dear to her in the past two days, but poisoned now by its owner's treachery. The pain of his calculated betrayal washed over her, saturating her every pore until she could think of nothing but escaping from him and the scene of her disgrace. There was nothing but shame for her here.

She followed him outside, determined to hide her tears until she was inside the coach. But if it was the last thing she did, she'd find a way to exact her own justice against Mr. Devlin.

Devlin couldn't imagine what Lilly must be thinking. He'd wanted to hold her, tell her how he felt about her, but perhaps it was better this way. She'd have no regrets to see the last of him. She'd been silent for the duration of the ride, no doubt cataloging his crimes and preparing her denunciation. And she'd never know how much it was costing him to return her when he knew that, given a chance, she would go to Olney's bed now. If Olney was man enough to defy the old man. Doubtful.

He maneuvered his coach through London traffic thinking that, as much as he dreaded it, he hoped Andrew Hunter would be home. He was anxious to settle matters—for better or worse. And anxious to return Lilly to her loved ones, where she'd be safe from…him.

He rounded the corner onto a quiet street opposite a square with lush verdant growth. Trees, hedges and summer flowers gave the impression of gentility and refinement. Just the sort of place a man like him would never be invited. He drew up outside the address Jack Higgins had given him.

He secured the reins and dismounted the driver's seat. He had barely opened the coach door when the front door flew open and a disheveled woman screamed as a host of people poured out onto the street.

"Lilly! Lilly, is that you?"

Lilly did not accept his assistance in getting down, stepping onto the street just in time to brace herself for the onslaught. "Yes, Mama."

"Oh!" The woman hesitated long enough to take in Lilly's appearance, then reeled and threw the back of one hand against her forehead in a gesture of deep shock. "Gypsies! The damned gypsies had you! Bella! Fetch Mr. Hunter!"

The woman Devlin recognized as Andrew's wife turned back from the door and disappeared inside. A lovely woman followed Lilly's mother, her face ashen. This would be the other sister Lilly had mentioned—Miss Eugenia. He'd seen her once before on the altar the night he and the Hunters had raided the Brotherhood's last ritual. Not under the best circumstances.

"Oh, Lilly! Are you all right? Say they did not hurt you."

"Hush, Gina. Let Lilly talk. Tell us, sweet girl, did you come to harm?"

But Mrs. O'Rourke was hugging Lilly so tight that she could barely speak. She managed to disengage herself long enough to turn to him and give him a freezing glare before saying, "I am well enough, Mama."

Andrew appeared in the doorway, his wife by his side.

"Gypsies!" Mrs. O'Rourke screeched at him. "Gypsies had our girl, Mr. Hunter! What are you going to do about it?"

Andrew grinned at Devlin, no doubt thinking he had kept his promise rather than simply returned his hostage. To make matters worse, Jamie Hunter appeared behind him, a look of astonishment on his face.

"I said what are you going to do about it, Mr. Hunter? Should you not be sending the king's men after them? Why, they will get away if you do not act fast."

Devlin stepped forward, hoping to forestall any such rash action. "Here, now. They—"

"And who are *you?*" Lilly's mother asked.

"I—"

"He is a friend of the gypsies, Mama, and they did not harm me at all."

"But where have you been? Why did you disappear? Olney and Rutherford are infuriated! They—"

"Not on the street, please, Mrs. O'Rourke," Andrew interrupted, motioning them all inside.

Devlin followed, feeling like a condemned man. When they were all in a spacious foyer, Andrew asked, "Do you need medical attention, Miss Lilly?"

She shook her head and her sisters both sighed in deep relief.

"Go calm your mother. I will send for you later."

In a flurry of skirts and handkerchiefs, the women disappeared down a long corridor, supposedly to glean whatever information they could from Lilly. Andrew motioned Devlin to follow him and Jamie in the opposite direction.

Once inside a quiet library, Andrew closed the door and went to a sideboard to pour them all a glass of sherry. "Damn me if I didn't doubt you, Dev. I thought you were joking when you said you'd bring her back today. Did one of your contacts catch wind of the scheme and tip you off?"

"It wasn't a gypsy scheme," he said, accepting a glass.

"They helped you, then. Tell us where to find them and we shall see that they are amply rewarded. I cannot begin to tell you what a relief this is."

Jamie sank into a chair and sighed. "Now we can begin to untangle the mess. Another day, and there might have been chaos. Rutherford has not taken this well at all."

"He was worried about Miss Lillian?" That surprised Devlin. He hadn't thought Rutherford would be much affected by the kidnapping other than the distress it caused his heir.

"Not worried, worse the luck. Did I mention yesterday that there's a warrant out for Miss Lilly's arrest."

Worse and worse.

"Rutherford wouldn't wait. Within hours he had called in the police and sent runners in every direction. Lilly was wearing the Rutherford jewels when she disappeared."

Devlin gulped his sherry and put the glass down. "That's

my fault, I fear. I hadn't planned on her having anything of importance. I am certain she has brought them back with her."

Andrew frowned. "You hadn't planned? What are you saying, Dev? What do you know about all this?"

"It was my scheme."

Andrew put his glass down. "I don't understand. It was your scheme to kidnap Lilly? But why?"

"I wanted to spite Olney and Rutherford."

"*You* did this? *You* arranged the kidnapping?"

"I carried her from the church," he admitted.

Devlin saw Andrew's fist coming, but he didn't flinch. He took the blow square on the jaw and, even though he was ready, he tumbled backward from the force of it. Andrew advanced again, but Jamie held him back.

"Easy, Drew. We'd better hear him out if we're to get to the bottom of this."

Devlin rubbed his jaw and got to his feet, almost savoring the pain. He wanted it. He deserved it. And maybe it could wash away some degree of guilt.

Jamie poured him another sherry and handed it to him with a scowl. "Good God, Dev. What the hell got into you? Kidnap Bella's sister?"

"I didn't know who she was until it was too late," he said. "There was a moment, brief though it was, when I could have turned back, but I was committed to my course."

"Hogwash!" Andrew shook the hand he'd hit Devlin with and then finished his own sherry. "You always have a choice, Farrell."

Devlin winced for the first time. Andrew was using his last name instead of his first—a sure sign the friendship was over. "Everything was in place. I did not want to turn back."

"But what did Lilly ever do to you? Were you smitten? And when did you meet her? It is not as if…" Jamie let the thought trail off.

Not as if you ever would have introduced one of your womenfolk to the likes of me? Though Devlin knew that to be true, it still stung. He took a deep breath, still guarded about how much he would tell them. "I met her in Olney's garden the night he proposed."

"Have you been seeing her secretly?"

He shook his head. "It wasn't that. I encountered her once or twice in public and we exchanged a few cordial words, but that is all. Do not blame Lilly for any of this."

"What is this about wanting to spite Olney and Rutherford? And how did Lilly become a part of that?" Jamie asked.

"She had the misfortune to be in the wrong place at the wrong time. And the object of the wrong man's attention."

"I cannot disagree with at least part of that," Andrew admitted. "I tried to persuade her to change her course, but she was convinced it was the best thing for her mother and sister."

"I wondered why you would permit such a match."

"Had she been my sister or daughter, it wouldn't have happened. But Martha O'Rourke was determined. She was ambitious for Lilly and wanted to be the mother of a duchess. Lilly might have changed her mind if not for that." Andrew sighed and shook his head. "Damn you, Farrell. You cannot know what a hornet's nest this has become."

"You'd better tell me the worst." If there was a chance of extricating Lilly from this quagmire, he would.

"Why the hell should we tell you anything? I cannot make up my mind whether to call you out or call in the Home Office and have you arrested."

Pragmatically, Jamie held up one hand. "A moment, Drew. If he's locked up or dead on a dueling field, how will he help us round up the Brotherhood?"

"Do whatever you want," Devlin told them. "But first I want to help you bring in those demented sons-of—"

Andrew poured another sherry and sat behind the mahogany desk to regard Devlin with a scowl that portended pain. "I think I can delay dealing with you for the sake of stopping the Brotherhood, but do not test me."

"Why would I? You want the Brotherhood, and I want Olney and Rutherford. You alluded to the possibility that they were involved, did you not?"

"Tell me, first, why you want to 'spite' them."

"That's my business. They wronged me in the past, and that's all you need to know."

"Can you assure me that your vendetta will not jeopardize our operation?"

"Yes. If they are involved, they will deserve what they get. If not," he said with a shrug, "I will find another way."

"Good!" Jamie rubbed his hands together. "Now we need a plan. How to proceed. Both with Lilly's pickle and the Brotherhood."

"Lilly, first. I want to assure you both that she is as virginal as she was the day I took her from the vestry. Whatever she suffered at my hands, she did not suffer that."

"The gypsy rags?"

"I left her with a friend when you summoned me to town. I could not take the risk that she'd wander away and come to harm."

"Her greatest danger, at the moment, is from Rutherford and Olney. They had gone to a great deal of trouble to keep this as quiet as possible, but when Lilly is arrested, all hell will break loose."

"The jewels complicated things." Devlin took a seat across the desk from Andrew. "I thought Olney would be made a laughingstock. And that Rutherford would look foolish, as well. But will they not forgive and forget when she returns the sapphires?"

"I do not think so. I offered to pay for them just to keep this quiet, but they refused. Lilly's letter—"

"Lilly didn't write the note. I hired a forger to do it."

Jamie groaned and Andrew just stared at him. Devlin knew he was devising several decidedly ugly means of death for him.

Jamie paced in front of the windows. "Surely, when Lilly tells them it wasn't her, they will forgive. Given time, the buzz will die down and we can all go on. Why, if Lilly actually marries Olney—"

"No!" Devlin and Andrew said at once.

"Yes, I suppose that would be too high a price." He continued his pacing. "But what will satisfy their bruised pride?"

"It is more than pride, I think. It's principle. Her disappearance made them look foolish—Olney standing at the altar, the duke and duchess by his side." A small grin curved the corners of Jamie's mouth upward. "It was rather…droll. I knew Drew had been hoping to change her mind, and I thought he might have succeeded. Alas…"

Andrew tented his fingers thoughtfully. "Alas, we are dealing with the consequences. And now add Lilly's wishes to the mix. We must resolve to give her a choice in this. After all, she is the damaged party, and the one that stands to lose the most if Rutherford continues with his charges. Jamie, ask Edwards to bring Miss Lilly to us, please."

Lilly was almost relieved when the summons came. She could barely make sense of what was being said. Her mother would not stop talking and Bella and Gina kept trying to ask her questions. Nancy, efficient maid that she was, brought tea and cakes and kept fluffing the settee pillow behind Lilly.

The only thing she could decipher was that her mother was certain, now that she was back, the marriage could continue as planned. Poor Mama. Did she not understand that Olney would not want her now?

Gina kept casting her sympathetic glances, as if she wanted to talk to her alone, and Lilly knew what to expect. She would ask if Mr. Dev—Farrell had taken advantage of her. And how could she answer that? She could say that he had given her indescribable delight, but that he had not breached her. How would Gina or Bella respond to that? How did *she?* Oh, what a muddle.

She knocked softly at the library door and entered at her brother-in-law's call. Her knees weakened when she saw all three of them watching her—Andrew, James and Mr. Farrell. She took a deep breath when she turned to close the door to keep Mama from eavesdropping.

"Come, sit," James said, holding a chair for her.

Lilly did as she was bid and folded her hands in her lap.

Andrew noted her trembling hands and poured her a small glass of wine. "This will calm you, Miss Lilly, and make this interview easier."

She glanced sideways at Mr. Farrell, perceiving a dark discoloration along his left jaw, then looked back at Andrew. It seemed they had already been discussing the matter. Despite the new bruise, however, he did not look in the least contrite.

"Miss Lilly, we have been discussing your absence," Andrew told her. "Mr. Farrell has told us some rather disturbing things."

What, exactly, had he told them? Had he blamed her? She glanced at him again, then back at Andrew. "Yes?"

"I would like to hear anything you might have to say on the matter."

"Mr. Farrell came to the church, found me in the vestry, and took me away." She touched her neck where he'd applied pressure to render her unconscious but said nothing. "He took me to a cottage in the woods, where he kept me until this morning. Oh, except for the gypsies."

James nodded. "And what are your wishes, Miss Lilly? What would you like to do now?"

"I… Well, I haven't thought. I would like Mr. Farrell's assurance that this will never happen again. And I would like to speak with Olney, to explain matters. Mr. Farrell tells me he left a forged note telling Olney that I had changed my mind about marriage. I would like him to know that is not the case."

Andrew frowned as if he disapproved. "It might not change anything, Miss Lilly."

"I realize that, sir. I just think it is the courteous thing to do. He must have looked foolish in front of his friends. Whether that was my fault or not, I believe he is owed an apology."

James cleared his throat. "There is a warrant for your arrest, Miss Lilly. The jewels, you see."

"Oh! Mama did not say a thing about this!"

"She does not know. I have kept it from the ladies to spare them further distress. Rutherford has not made it common knowledge yet."

"But perhaps he will drop the charges when you return them." Andrew leaned forward across the desk in his earnestness. "If you will fetch them for me, I will personally return them and request an end to the matter."

"I…I…oh, dear!" She'd forgotten them entirely after Mr. Farrell's coldness and her haste to leave this morning. "They are still on the dressing table in my room at the cottage."

Mr. Farrell groaned. "I shall leave when we are finished here. I can be back with them by morning. Will that be soon enough?"

"If we can keep Miss Lilly's arrival home quiet until then. That is the only way to forestall an arrest."

Lilly took a deep drink of her wine and waited while the liquor settled in her stomach. Arrested! Olney had wanted her arrested!

"And then, what? Do you still want to marry Olney?"

"No!" she exclaimed then tried to cover her horror. "I

mean, if he wants me arrested, he would not want to wed me." But it was no use. She saw Mr. Farrell's secret smile. He knew she could not go to Olney now. He'd seen to that with his sly seduction.

Andrew drew a paper from his desk drawer and dipped a quill in his inkwell. "I will ask Olney to call here tomorrow at four o'clock, but I will not say why. We should have the jewels back by then."

"I could go to him," Lilly suggested.

"I'd rather you meet him where you will have protection, Miss Lilly. Olney is known to have a temper."

"He would not…that is, I only want to make amends. I just want to forget all this unpleasantness and go back to the way things were before."

To a man, they looked at her in disbelief. Heavens. It was even worse than she'd thought.

Andrew went to the window as if to check for the impending arrival of the authorities. "I doubt that will be possible. In fact, I think we may be fortunate to escape prosecution."

She blinked back tears. She and her family were ruined in society, and it was Mr. Farrell's entire fault. Everything, *everything,* he had said and done since the moment they'd met in the gardens at Rutherford House had been lies and deliberately calculated to embarrass and humiliate Olney. He didn't care about her; he'd merely used her. She'd been his pawn.

And she'd get even with him if it was the last thing she did.

Chapter Thirteen

It was nearly teatime the next day when Gina steadied Lilly's shoulder as she hooked the back of her gown. "Stop fidgeting!"

"Sorry." She made a face at Gina's reflection in the mirror. "I want to look my best."

"I gather Olney is quite angry. Mama sent a note to the duchess while you were gone and was rebuffed rather abruptly."

Lilly had been so tired last night that she'd gone to bed early and avoided the family. Now she wondered how much she should tell Gina. Oh, but they were sisters and had always shared their thoughts and feelings. "Gina, you mustn't say a word to Mama, but Andrew says that there is a warrant for my arrest. The Duke of Rutherford had it done when the jewels were not returned."

"Jewels? What jewels?"

"Oh, I forgot you didn't know. Well, just before I was to walk down the aisle, the duchess came to the vestry and insisted that I wear the Rutherford Sapphires. Then, when Mr. Farrell took me away, I forgot about them entirely."

"But you will give them back." Gina's pretty face furrowed with concern.

"I forgot them at the cottage and Mr. Farrell has gone to get them. I hope he arrives before Olney."

"What do you intend to say to Olney?"

"I shall tell him that I did not desert him of my own volition, then beg his understanding and ask if he will agree to say that he and I had mutual misgivings."

"But he was standing in the nave, waiting for you. Who would believe that?"

"No one, perhaps, but they would not call us liars to our faces. Whether they believed it or not, they would be forced to accept the explanation."

"This whole thing has turned into such a muddle. I wish you had never accepted Olney's proposal."

"If I could go back… But never mind. We shall untangle this mess today, and then go on as before."

Gina rolled her eyes. "Well, not quite as before. A few invitations have been withdrawn since you, ah, have been gone. I think the duchess is wielding her power. Mama is beside herself and no one knows what to do."

Neither did she, Lilly thought. She did not want to have Mr. Farrell charged with kidnapping because that would lead to speculation as to her chastity. Nor did she want the truth to come out. If only she could think of some logical lie that would spare Gina and Mama embarrassment and shunning. As for Mr. Farrell, well, she would take care of that herself.

Gina flopped onto Lilly's bed and sighed. "What will you do if Olney will not agree to your plan?"

"I could say that Olney and I argued before the nuptials and that I thought he did not want to go through with it. Or that, oh drat! I cannot think of anything that would not reflect poorly on you and Mama."

"Lilly, are you truly…well?"

"Truly…oh! If my own sister does not believe it, how will I ever expect society to believe it?"

"I only ask because I see a sadness in you. As if you are not quite happy to be home."

Gina was right, but how could she explain that she'd rather be in the woods with "Mr. Devlin" and the gypsies? And that, for some inexplicable reason, she did not want to have Mr. Farrell locked away. "I am happy to be home, Gina. It is just that there are so many things to think of and so many problems to solve. I am praying that, once the jewels have been returned, and once Olney and I reach an agreement on what story to tell society, the dust will settle and we will be able to get on with our lives."

"I hope you will not be cross with me, Lilly, but I am glad something happened to interrupt the wedding. I did not like Olney or his family. Such great prigs! The O'Rourkes never would have been good enough for their son."

She smoothed her willow-green gown over her hips and tugged the embroidered neckline a bit lower to entice Olney's attention. If he found her appealing, he might agree to her plan. Nancy had swept her hair up at the crown and left a fall of curls in back. Olney loved to fondle her curls as they talked. At first she had found it endearing, but now it annoyed her.

Gina sat up on the bed. "Stop fussing. Olney will think you are stunning. Now tell me the truth of what happened while you were gone. I give you my oath that I will not breathe a word to Bella or Mama."

"Nothing important, Gina. I did not wake until we were nearly at the cottage. It was along a deserted track, and the coach could barely get through. I think only horses and foot traffic had used it in years. The cottage was quite remote. We had a stew for supper, then I went to my room."

"Is that all? Did he not tell you why he had stolen you?"

"He still has not told me the particulars. Just that he wanted to spite Olney and his father."

"And you were allowed to sleep unmolested?"

Lilly thought of the knowing way he had undone her corset, the sure and steady way he had seduced her, and his coldness the next morning, but she nodded her head. "Quite unmolested. Really, my time away was quite unremarkable. Even the gypsies were kind. Drina, a young girl, wanted my wedding dress, so we traded clothes. I hated that monstrosity anyway. And that is all there is to tell."

"You make it sound like a holiday."

Her door burst open and Nancy stood there, her eyes as wide as saucers. "Oh, Miss Lilly! The Marquis of Olney is in the library with Mr. Hunter. Mr. Hunter whispered for me to bring you to them!"

"Drat! I had hoped Mr. Farrell would be back by now. Gina, will you watch for him? If he comes, send him in immediately."

The look of shock on Olney's face was enough to tell her that her brother-in-law had not informed him that she was back. She gave him a tentative smile as she closed the library door.

"Hello, Edward."

"Miss Lillian! But…where…how…"

"Yes," she agreed. "It is all so confusing, is it not?"

He took several steps toward her before he stopped himself. His eyes hardened and his lips formed a thin line. "I hardly think this is appropriate. I should have been informed of her presence."

"Would you have refused to see her?" Andrew asked.

"I would have been prepared for her appearance."

"Well, she is here now. She arrived back yesterday afternoon. Given that your father has sworn a complaint against her, we thought it prudent to keep her presence a secret until she had an opportunity to talk to you."

"I see." Olney's stiffened posture relaxed a bit. "You have something to say to me, chit?"

Lilly gave him her best look of profound regret. "So much to say, Edward. Will you sit down and hear me out?"

He didn't answer but went to sit in one of the overstuffed chairs. She took a seat opposite him, and Andrew sat at his desk, clearly unwilling to leave her alone with her former fiancé.

"First," Lilly began, "I want to tell you how deeply I regret any discomfort or embarrassment you have suffered as a result of my disappearance from the church."

Olney snorted in disbelief. "If that were true, you would not have gone."

"That is just it, you see. I did not go. Not willingly, at least. I was taken."

"Who?"

She could feel Andrew's eyes boring into her. He fully expected Lilly to tell. Perhaps she should, but then Mr. Farrell would be beyond *her* reach.

"I do not know. It was a man, hired by someone else, no doubt, who put me in a carriage and sent me away. I was taken to a secret place and held there until yesterday."

"A likely story."

"It is true, nonetheless. If I had wanted to cry off, I would not have come to the church. I would have sent for you and told you in person in this very library."

"You've made me a laughingstock, Lillian. Not even my friends can keep a straight face when I walk into a room. I hear their whispers and snickering. It is beyond enduring."

"Neither of us asked for this, Edward. And both of us have suffered for it."

His eyes widened. "Suffered? Were you raped?"

"No!" she exclaimed, shocked by his indelicacy. "But I

know what people must think of me. They will be calling me a jilt. And that will be the kindest thing they say."

Olney looked down, as if trying to assimilate this news, and Lilly used the moment to look at Andrew. He gave her a reassuring smile and went back to his papers.

"Lillian, perhaps there is some way… We must speak privately."

"Mr. Hunter knows everything, Edward. We can trust his discretion."

"Alone," he said, more firmly this time.

She turned and gave Andrew a nod. He picked up his papers and crossed to the door. "I shall be just down the hall," he said.

When the library door closed after him, Olney leaned forward and took her hands in his. "Perhaps all is not lost, Lillian. Perhaps there may still be a way to be together."

She tried not to show her dismay. "How?"

"The jewels. Give them to me, and I will take them to my father. I have never seen him so angry. He says it is the first time in his life that he has been duped. But once I tell him your story and he has the jewels in his hands, I could possibly persuade him to drop the charges against you."

This was just what she had hoped for. "Thank heavens. You know I never would have taken them, do you not?"

"I didn't know what to think, Lillian. It was the most exciting day of my life, and then suddenly, I was made a buffoon. Let me tell you, Mother was worst of all. The things she called you and your family! But never mind that. Just give me the jewels."

Stall. She had to stall him just a bit longer and pray for Mr. Farrell's return. "I shall get them when you are ready to leave. But tell me first how you think we may still be together."

"Once the charges are dropped and the gossip wanes, we

could rent a flat, or I have a small cottage just outside town. I'd keep you like a princess, Lillian. You'd want for nothing."

Back to that. Back to making her his mistress. He couldn't marry her now without looking a cuckold. But making her his mistress would be a triumph. He would have at his disposal and discretion what he'd been willing to marry, and then be free to marry someone his parents deemed more suitable. And once again, he'd thought nothing of what such an arrangement would do to *her* family.

"We were to marry," she reminded him.

"But you see that is not possible now, do you not?"

No, she did not. But she remained silent, knowing if she opened her mouth it would be to vilify him.

Encouraged, Olney dropped to one knee in front of her. "Bring me the jewels, Lillian, and we can begin anew."

"I…I do not have them."

"But you said you did."

"I do. But not here."

"I need them. My father will not withdraw charges until they are in his hands, and until he has had every last stone confirmed as genuine."

"Mr. Hunter offered to pay for them. Surely your father could buy more with the money."

"Gads!" Olney stood and regarded her down his long aristocratic nose. "Hunter does not have enough. He would have to borrow from all his brothers and then be in debt the remainder of his life. The Rutherford Sapphires are irreplaceable."

"But—"

"They were gifts from kings and popes over the past four hundred years. The center stone in the necklace was a gift from Queen Elizabeth to my ancestor for faithful service. How can you replace that, Lillian?"

She stood, defeated. "I cannot."

"But I can think of ways you can make the loss sting less." He seized her around the waist and pulled her against him. "Give us a little kiss, puss. Then down on your knees to kiss another part of me, eh?"

Instead, Lilly brought her slipper down on his foot as hard as she could. "You are an animal, Olney! A pig! Get out!"

Devlin was startled when he raised his hand to knock at Hunter's door and it burst open. The Marquis of Olney brushed past him without a single flicker of recognition. He gathered things had not gone well at Lilly's interview.

As he stood there staring after Olney, Hunter pulled him inside. "Good God, man. Do you want him to see you?"

"He did not even recognize me." Devlin laughed. "All the better for me, I think."

"Did you get them?"

"The jewels? No."

Hunter took a direct course for the library, Devlin close behind. Lilly was pacing, her hands clasped into fists. She heard Hunter slam the door behind them and turned.

"There you are! What has taken you so long? Why could you not have been a moment earlier?"

Devlin was startled by how distraught she was. He'd never seen her so angry. "I came as quickly as I could."

She looked down at his dusty breeches and boots. "I see that. But you said you would be back by teatime today. Olney has already been here."

He nodded. "He passed me on the way out. What did you say to him to make him so angry?"

"Me?" She was magnificent in her anger. "What did I say? Why, that I would give him the jewels. When I could not hand them over immediately, he had other ideas as to how I could pay him back."

His amusement faded to fury and he turned to the door.

"Come back here!" Hunter shouted as he sat at his desk. "You'd only make things worse."

"Oh!" Lilly threw her hands up and went to stand before Hunter's desk. "You cannot know the vile things he said to me! Suggested to me! And what am I supposed to do now?"

She was wrong. Devlin could hazard a good guess as to what a man like Olney would ask of her. And Olney would pay for that, too. As to what she should do next, he wondered that himself.

Hunter motioned her to sit, then turned to Devlin. "Sit down, Farrell. We need to get some things settled, and quickly. Tell me why you have not brought the jewels."

"They were not there. I looked on the dressing table, in the sewing box, under the blankets—everywhere. I tore the cottage apart, trying to think where you might have hidden them. Where did you stash them?"

"I did not stash them anywhere. I swear it. I left them on the dressing table. In front of the mirror. Durriken! Or Violca? They seem to come and go as they please. Perhaps they…"

Devlin shook his head. "I went to their camp. Durriken swore to me that he had not been there. And Violca had not come to clean because the beds were still…the beds were unmade. Nothing else was missing, Miss Lillian. Only the jewels."

She narrowed her eyes at him, those brilliant eyes. "And you, sir? Did you think this might be another splendid way to spite Olney and Rutherford?"

"You think *I* have them?"

"You told me you were a thief."

"Once. Long ago. I haven't stolen anything in years."

"Spots and leopards, Mr. Farrell."

"Stop it!" Hunter snapped. "We haven't time for this. Do you have any theory as to what happened to the jewels, Mr. Farrell?"

"Only that perhaps the temptation proved too great for your sister-in-law. They would make a nice little nest egg to start life anew, would they not?"

She gasped in outrage. "How dare—"

"Bloody hell!" Hunter shouted. "How in blazes did the two of you spend three days without killing one another?"

"Sorry," he muttered.

"Does anyone have any idea how to proceed?"

"The cottage is quite remote," he explained. "It isn't as if there are many people wandering by. Even the nearest village has forgotten its existence. There is a possibility that someone could have happened upon it and searched the house. But why wouldn't they take anything else?"

"Because nothing else held the same value," Lilly said. "The furnishings were fine enough, but not portable. Only the jewels would fit in a pocket and hide away easily."

"And the stones, broken down from the settings, would fetch a king's ransom. I've thought of that. As soon as I get back to my office, I will be sending out men to make inquiries of all the local fences. If anything of that quality turns up, I will be informed."

A worried frown knit lines between Lilly's eyes. "Oh, but that will be too late. Once they are separated from their settings, how shall we prove they are Rutherford's? Or how can we return them as they were loaned?"

Hunter had nothing to say to that, and Devlin could not give them any reassurances. That was the classic problem with stolen gems. Only the center stone would be identifiable by its size and color. The rest…well, the rest were likely to be swallowed up by jewelers and made into other pieces.

He drew a deep breath and told a comfortable lie. "We will find them, Miss Lillian. They have to be somewhere. And someone will know about them. Meantime, I'd recommend paying Rutherford for them. I'll leave you with an open voucher for the cost."

"Olney told me in no uncertain terms that he would not accept payment." Lilly looked down at her lap. "The jewels are a part of his heritage."

Hunter nodded. "I offered, and was summarily dismissed."

Damn! It was just like the arrogant duke and his son to make this more difficult than it needed to be. "Then we shall just have to come up with the jewels, no matter the cost."

Hunter gave him a wary look, and he knew the man was thinking that Devlin would do all sorts of mayhem to achieve his jail. Well, he wasn't far wrong. Short of murder, there wasn't anything he wouldn't do for Lilly.

"Now that Olney knows Lilly has returned, he will be running to his father, and the king's men will not be far behind."

Devlin raked his fingers through his hair and muttered a curse under his breath. "You cannot mean to hand her over? D'you know what Newgate is like? She'd be raped by the guards and her things stolen by the other inmates before you could even bribe the guards."

Lilly paled and Devlin immediately regretted his unguarded words. They were true, but he should not have said them in Lilly's presence.

Hunter winced. "Damn! Were there time enough, I could make arrangements to send her away. I cannot think where to hide her that the authorities would not look."

Devlin ran through a number of possibilities in his mind. The women he knew well enough to ask such a favor—hiding a fugitive from the law—were bawds, barmaids and serving girls. Not suitable companionship for gently reared Lillian O'Rourke.

"My sister, Sarah, and her husband would shelter you, but it would not be safe for you there," Hunter told her. "She is rather notorious for helping women in need."

Devlin took a deep breath. "I'll take her. There'd be no reason the authorities would think to look for her at my apartments."

Dead silence met his offer. Hunter only gave him a blank look, as if he had not heard him right. Lilly's eyes widened and her mouth opened in surprise. Hell, *he* was surprised.

"Bella would have my head on a platter," Hunter finally sputtered.

"Then do not tell her. In fact, we shall never tell anyone. Do you not see that Miss Lillian's safety is paramount? Her virtue will be safe enough. We can make up some plausible story later to explain where she has been. Who would ever look for her with me?"

He watched a thousand emotions pass over Lilly's face, but thank God none of them were fear.

"You'd kill each other."

"I doubt we would see each other much. You know the hours I keep, Hunter. I have a spare room, and Knowles will be a proper chaperone."

"Your valet? What would he know about—"

"Knowles was a valet to a duke before he came to me. He knows what is proper, and how young ladies should deport themselves."

Hunter turned to her. "Lilly?"

"The…the gypsies?"

"They are decamping by the end of the week. I believe Durriken said they were going to France for the winter. Is that what you want, Miss Lillian?"

"France, Newgate or Mr. Farrell? Heavens, what a choice."

He nodded. "Have your maid pack you a few things. Hurry. We haven't long."

Chapter Fourteen

Lilly had never been to Whitechapel before. The sights, sounds and smells were almost more than she could take in. Mr. Farrell was not inclined to linger or indulge her curiosity. Darkness had fallen by the time he helped her down from the coach, and she was assaulted by the noise emanating from an establishment named The Crown and Bear. She could scarcely believe it when he ushered her inside to a long corridor with a staircase at the end.

"A gin house? You live in a gin house, Mr. Farrell?"

"I do indeed, Miss Lillian. In fact, I own it."

"Does Mr. Hunter know this is where you are bringing me?"

"He has been here before. If he had not thought it suitable, I doubt you would be here."

And this would be the reason they would think she'd be safe here. Neither Rutherford nor Olney would think to look so low. And how could a gin-house owner have run afoul of Olney and Rutherford? Or have made enemies of them? For that matter, how had he made acquaintances with the Hunter brothers? When he'd told her he had grown up here, she hadn't suspected he still lived here. He did not speak with the broad uncultured accent as the others, nor did he dress or deport himself as such.

He dropped her valise, unlocked the door at the top of the landing and held it open for her. "I would appreciate it if you would not go into my study. You may have the run of the rest of the place."

"Sir?"

Lilly jumped and turned to see the quintessential valet. He was tall, straight, thin and had a long face with an equally long nose. One eyebrow had shot up in surprise or disapproval, she couldn't tell which.

"Miss Lillian, this is Knowles, my valet. He is in charge here, and if you need anything, you must let him know." Mr. Farrell turned to his valet. "Knowles, this is Miss Lillian O'Rourke. She will be staying with us for a few days. Please make her comfortable."

"But, sir, I do not know how to…*maid.*"

"Miss Lillian is capable of doing for herself. She will take her meals at the usual time. If she requests something, please do whatever you must to provide it. Now, here is her valise. Please put it in my room. I shall take the small guest room."

The moment Knowles disappeared, Mr. Farrell turned to her again. "Now, I must leave you. I have business to take care of, not the least of which is your predicament—"

"Which you caused."

"—so I will not join you for supper tonight. Please remember a few things, eh? Do not come downstairs after dark. It is not a suitable establishment for young ladies. Do not go outside after dark, either, as the potential for disaster is even greater. Do not go running to your family. The authorities will be watching for just such a thing, and blundering in could put them all at risk. And, Miss Lillian, do not quiz Knowles about me or himself. Neither of us likes prying."

She was beginning to think there was little difference between Mr. Devlin's premises and Newgate Prison. "What am I allowed to do, Mr. Devlin?"

"Read…uh…" He looked confused, as if he hadn't the faintest idea what a woman might do with her time. "Whatever you wish, Knowles will bring it to you. A sewing box? Paints? Embroidery? Just tell him, and he will acquire it."

She sighed and said a silent prayer that the jewels were found quickly. "I shall make a list." Just for the pleasure of confounding Knowles.

She glanced around when the door closed behind Mr. Farrell. The apartments were elegantly appointed. If she hadn't just climbed the back stairs of a gin house, she wouldn't have believed such luxury possible in the middle of Whitechapel. Deep club chairs, a dark blue silk tapestry sofa, rich cherry and mahogany tables and paneling along with deep Persian rugs gave the appearance of a society drawing room. She could barely hear the noise from the taproom downstairs or the street outside, nor did any of the smells filter upward.

Knowles had not returned, so she walked down the central corridor, peeking in rooms as she went. She found the inviolable study, a small library, a dining room and another stairway, hidden behind an imposing door. The moment she opened the door, Knowles cleared his throat somewhere behind her. She spun around to find that he'd been following her.

"Heavens! You frightened me out of my skin!"

"Did you need something, Miss O'Rourke?"

"Yes, Knowles. I need to find my room."

He came forward and gently pushed the door closed again. "If you will follow me."

"What is upstairs, Knowles?"

"My quarters, miss, and the kitchen."

She trailed after him, wondering what he was hiding up there. Or was he simply a private man?

At the end of the corridor, he opened the door to her right. "Mr. Farrell's chambers, miss. I have put your valise in the dressing room."

"Thank you. And what is the room across from mine?"

"The guest room, miss."

The room that Mr. Farrell would be occupying. Well, it was better than the cottage, where she'd had to pass through his room to get to hers. She glanced at the latch and was relieved to see that there was a lock.

"Shall I bring your supper to you here, miss, or will you take it in the dining room?"

"I… Here, Knowles."

He bowed and departed, leaving Lilly in the corridor. She shrugged to herself and entered the room. As gypsylike as Mr. Farrell's room had been in the cottage, this one was fit for a king. The furniture was enormous and ornately carved of dark exotic woods, the bed hangings and draperies were of heavy lined amber silk and the unlit fireplace was massive. A small stool had been placed at one side of the bed to give her access. Heavens! It was the most luxurious thing she'd ever seen. She'd dreamed that, on her wedding night, Olney might—no. She hadn't wanted that then, and she did not want it now.

She crossed the room to another door and threw it open. Her small valise rested on the floor in the middle of the dressing room. Here, too, were the wash stand, a small chaise to rest upon and a number of clothespresses and a cheval mirror. By the look of things, Mr. Farrell might have a taste for elegant surroundings but he was not an extravagant man. His clothing was stylish, but simple. But she did not see any evening clothes. Of course. How many fetes and events would a gin-house owner be invited to? That thought annoyed her. His manners were certainly better than some of the ton.

She heard the outer door open and the rattle of dishes as Knowles placed a tray on a side table, then a click as the door closed again. He was certainly doing his best to avoid her. That suited her, as well. She'd just go to the small library, select a book and come back to spend the rest of the evening in her—Mr. Farrell's—room.

And she'd best keep in mind that neither Mr. Farrell nor Knowles were to be trusted. She and Mr. Farrell were allies only for as long as it took him to find the jewels. If this whole thing wasn't an elaborate ruse and he hadn't stolen them himself. After all, once a thief…

By the time Devlin unlocked his office door behind the taproom, Jack Higgins and Freddie Carter had arrived and were waiting for him. He ushered them in and waved at the chairs in front of his desk.

"What has happened?" Jack asked. "I thought you wouldn't be back to town for another two days."

Devlin poured them both a glass of raw whiskey. "Other business interrupted. I have an old problem and a new one. Both are urgent."

Freddie, a Bow Street Runner who took private commissions when time permitted, rubbed his hands together. "Excellent. Things have been quiet of late. And I could use the money. What do you have for us?"

"For you, Freddie, stolen jewelry." He pulled a sheet of paper from his drawer and dipped his pen in ink. He drew, to the best of his meager talent, the jewelry Lilly had been wearing when he'd abducted her and slid the sheet of paper across the desk to Freddie. "Here's a rendering of the three pieces—a necklace and two earrings. I am hoping they haven't been broken down yet. The center stone looked to be quite valuable."

Carter looked at it and emitted a low whistle. "I recognize these, Dev. They are the Rutherford Sapphires. But there's no mystery where they are. Olney's bride absconded with them. Rutherford filed a complaint, and the sketches have been distributed to every runner and watchman in London. And half the country, I'd wager."

"But she didn't."

Both men just stared at him.

"I have information that acquits her of any wrongdoing. She does not have them. The jewels were stolen from her."

"Are you certain that's not just her story? She might be hiding them—"

"I'd stake my life on it, Freddie. But Rutherford is not the sort of man to listen to reason. Miss O'Rourke will hang if they catch her. And he still won't have the jewels."

Freddie took a swallow of the whiskey and watched Devlin for a long minute before he spoke again. "I am afraid to ask how you know this, Dev. It's my duty to bring her in, you know."

"I know. And I also know you and Jack are the best investigators in England. But I suspect no one is looking for the jewels. They just assume the bride has taken them because that is what Rutherford says. And if no one is looking for them, they will not be found."

"Do you know where Miss O'Rourke is?"

Devlin sighed and sat back in his chair. "Yes, I do. And I know she doesn't have the jewels. And, before you ask, I have satisfied myself that she is innocent."

Jack stirred uneasily in his chair and Dev realized that he suspected the truth. "I'd believe him, Freddie. Dev knows his women."

Freddie laughed. "I suppose you're right. And you're

also right that no one is looking for the jewels, just for Miss O'Rourke."

"You cannot have any conflict in me paying you for doing your official duty, can you? Find the jewels, and if Miss O'Rourke has them, I'll eat them for supper."

"And your interest in this?"

"Justice."

Freddie gave him a disbelieving look, but was wise enough to accept his words at face value. He picked up the sketch, folded it, and put it in his jacket. "I'll start with fences, then query the less reputable jewelers. I'll check their stock to see if there are any pieces featuring suspicious stones. Sapphires and diamonds, I believe?"

Devlin nodded. "They went missing two days ago. It may be a bit soon for them to show up in London, but grease palms, Freddie." He pushed a stack of coins across the desk to him. "Tell them there's more where that came from if they should see the pieces, and even more if they acquire them for me."

Freddie pocketed the coins as he stood. "I will start immediately."

"And, Freddie? No need to tell your superiors about this, eh?"

"None," he agreed. "Unless something shows up."

"Agreed."

Devlin waited until the door closed before he turned to Jack. "What I'm about to ask you is dangerous, Jack. Several men were killed the last time we investigated. I will understand if you do not want to get involved."

"Do not tease, Dev. You know how I like danger. Gets the juices flowing, eh?"

"The Blood Wyvern Brotherhood."

Jack's eyes widened. "Holy—! Are these the same fellows we ran down a few months ago?"

"What's left of them. You remember that they scattered down

tunnels when the charleys came? Well, some of them are still missing, and there's evidence that they are up to their old tricks."

"Are girls missing?"

"That's the rumor. But the Brotherhood learned their lesson. They are choosing their victims from women who will not be missed, at least for a very long time. They've got a taste for blood now, Jack, and I doubt they'll stop, unless…"

"Unless someone stops them. But Andrew Hunter killed Lord Humphries, did he not? Self-defense, I heard. I thought the group would disband without their leader."

"That is what we hoped. Unfortunately, it may be possible that Humphries was not alone in leading the Brotherhood. We collected Throckmorton and a few of the others, but they are too frightened to give names. Henley and Booth are in hiding but Lord Elwood is living as if nothing has happened. He knows the authorities lack proof of his complicity."

"It galls me to think of Elwood and the others getting away with mutilation and murder. We need to find proof, damn it."

"If proof is to be found. I tell you, Jack, whoever is holding those men in thrall must be a very dangerous man. But we are fortunate. You and I are not bound by laws or a sense of fair play. That is why I chose you for this job instead of Freddie. We can go after this scum in any way we must." Devlin finished his whiskey and pushed the glass aside.

"Kill them?" Jack guessed. "Manufacture 'proof'?"

Devlin hesitated a long time. What would he be willing to do to stop the killing of innocent women? How far would he go to find justice for those who had no voice in society? Women like his mother? "If it comes to that," he said quietly.

James and Andrew Hunter came next. Devlin had known they would. James, because he needed Devlin. Andrew, because he was Lilly's protector. And Devlin suspected it would not be a pleasant interview. He had to be careful how much he told them. The Hunters had been bred like Freddie Carter—bound by laws and fair play.

When they were settled in their chairs, Devlin waited for one of them to speak. In the art of negotiation, he who speaks first has the weakest position. Or the most at stake.

"Is Lilly settled?" Andrew asked.

"I believe so. Knowles is seeing to her needs. If you'd like, you may go up and see her. Just don't let anyone follow."

"Too late for that. You hadn't been gone a quarter of an hour when there were charleys across the street from Drew's house. Olney and Rutherford did not waste a minute."

Andrew sneered. "That little weasel. I never liked him and this just confirms the matter. He swore he loved Lilly and then failed the first test of his love. By God, I'm glad she didn't marry him."

Devlin did not know what to say to that so he sat back and tented his fingers thoughtfully as he waited for them to continue.

"But the long and short of it is that we are being followed. I doubt visiting a gin house will raise suspicions, as the Home Office knows Drew and I are working with Wycliffe to clean up the mess we left at that ruined abbey."

Ah, yes. Lord Marcus Wycliffe, whose title at the Home Office was a mystery, as was the name of his division. Devlin rather thought it was "ticklish" cases—cases too sensitive or too horrific to make public. He'd had one or two experiences with the man and respected his professionalism. "Then your watchers will not find it odd that you are meeting with me?"

Andrew waved one hand in dismissal. "I'm sure they expect it. They know how much help you were last time."

Devlin sighed in relief and then caught them up on what he'd done to find the jewels. "I hope to have some results soon.

At the least, Freddie will have talked to the fences and jewelers by tomorrow night. If I have anything to report, I'll send word.

"As for the Brotherhood, I've sent Jack Higgins to put the word out to everyone in Whitechapel that we're looking for blades who are in hiding. Loath as I am to use them, Jack is going to offer a reward to the Gibbons brothers for information."

Jamie gasped. "Good God! They're the worst scum in London. Hell, I wouldn't be surprised if they were the ones who procured women for the rituals. Is there anything those two won't do?"

"Nothing," Devlin said cheerfully. "And that's why they are so valuable to us. Use scum to catch scum, eh?"

A new look of respect dawned on their faces. "And that's why you're the underlord of Whitechapel," Andrew said with a smile.

He was surprised that they'd heard that appellation. It was not something he was proud of. But if he could use it to his advantage, he would not hesitate.

"What about Lilly?"

The question was so abrupt that Devlin blinked. "What do you mean?"

"Her mother is…being difficult. She wants to know where Lilly is and wants reassurance that she is well."

"If my word will suffice, she is well enough."

Jamie laughed. "Dev, you should see Andrew's home. Ever since he married Bella, he's been invaded with petticoats and fainting spells and unreasonable demands. Take that to heart. If you marry a woman, too often her mother comes with her."

Andrew chuckled. "I have my eye on a nice cottage in St. Albans. I think Mrs. O'Rourke is ready for a place of her own somewhere distant enough to discourage daily visits."

"Send her back to Ireland," Jamie suggested.

Over Devlin's dead body. If Mrs. O'Rourke went back to Ireland, she would take Lilly with her.

"I am paying for my wicked days," Andrew said. "And this predicament with Lilly is an example. I am now her closest male relative. I am responsible for her. And I have turned her safety over to a…"

"Gin-house owner?" Devlin finished for him.

"At the very least. You are called the King of Whitechapel. It's said there's nothing you haven't done," Jamie said. "Including kidnap our sister-in-law."

"I've become a law-abiding citizen, gents. I haven't picked a pocket since I was five and ten years old. Haven't burgled a house since…well, quite a while. And I gave up highway robbery when the king's men began patrols. Not much left for me to do but invest and trade in gin."

"Just keep it to that and we won't have a problem."

"I have other things that occupy my time these days."

"Watching after Lilly and your quarrel with Rutherford, whatever that is," Andrew said. "But that is temporary. What we need is a permanent solution for Lilly. We cannot leave her here with you for more than a day or two. If we could just get her married. The protection of a husband, especially a prominent and wealthy man, would go a long way in persuading Rutherford to drop his charges."

Marriage. The thought shot through Devlin like a bolt of lightning. He had nothing but wealth to offer a woman like Lilly, not that Andrew Hunter would even consider an offer from him for a single second. But perhaps there was something else he could offer. Something that Rutherford would trade for Lilly's freedom. Not jewels or money, but a secret and a simple truth.

"Between mourning and her sudden engagement, Lilly has not been enough in society to attract a suitor like that," Andrew mused. "Not that anyone would offer for her after her supposed jilt of Olney."

Jamie nodded his agreement. "She will be considered a high risk now."

"I may have an idea," Devlin said. "It is a vague possibility, but one worth pursuing. Be patient another day."

Chapter Fifteen

The rooms were silent as Devlin locked the door behind him, his head filled with possibilities. He would have to trade his revenge for Lilly's freedom. Mere days ago, he wouldn't have considered such a possibility, but today it seemed like a very fair trade indeed.

In the library, a clock chimed four times. He'd still have time to catch a bit of sleep before putting his plan into action. He untied his cravat and left it loose around his neck while he undid his shirt. He'd need a fresh change of clothes in the morning and he didn't know how long Lilly would sleep. His bedroom was the only entrance to his dressing room.

He knocked softly at her door and waited for a response. Nothing. She and Knowles would have retired hours ago. He tested the door and was surprised to find it unlocked. How very innocent of Lilly. He would have to warn her again that he was not to be trusted.

The room was lit by a single candle, guttering in the breeze caused by the open door. Lilly lay on top of the bed, still dressed in her chemise and corset. An open book lay beside her, as if she had dropped it when sleep had overtaken her.

Ah yes, the cursed corset. Lilly had been unable to unlace herself again. He was sorry he hadn't thought of that. He went to her side and touched her arm, but she sighed and rolled onto her stomach.

"Lilly?" he whispered in her ear. "Shall I unlace you?"

She did not move and he debated only a moment before deciding to take matters into his own hands, so to speak. He ran his fingers down the tightly drawn strings, then traced a swirl of embroidery on the fabric. Beautiful workmanship. Not like those of the women he'd lain with. Plain corsets, if they'd had any at all, were their stock in trade. But the courtesans he'd dallied with were a different breed. Like Lilly, they'd had the best of everything and were more expert in the slow teasing of senses.

Devlin enjoyed unlacing corsets. He relished the slow and sensual unveiling of a woman's charms, of laying her bare to his eyes and touch. But with Lilly it was more than that. Unveiling, yes, but Lilly's innocence and awakening sensuality were revealed, as well. He remembered her as she'd been on his bed that last night at the cottage in the woods. Modest, slightly embarrassed, willingly placing herself in his hands, trusting him not to hurt her. And in the end, she'd abandoned herself to him, eagerly anticipating more. Lord, where had he found the strength to leave her?

He slipped the knot and began unlacing her little by little, folding the corset back as he went. Her chemise was made of white lawn so fine that it revealed the flesh tones beneath, the shadows of the curve of her buttocks, the darker tone of the little mole he'd discovered on her right hip and the one on her breast. He grew hard, aching with the need to have her, to take her fully and make her his forever.

"God, but you are beautiful," he told her. Words he could not say when she was awake. "I want you as I've never wanted another."

But tomorrow, if his plan succeeded, he'd lose her forever. He would give up the only thing he'd lived for, the only thing that had driven him since he'd been a child, to redeem Lilly's future. She'd be free to leave him. To go back home and find another man who would love and value her in a way that Devlin hadn't. No, he had destroyed her future for the sake of his past.

Tomorrow, he would face his past—the disgrace, the pain, the shame and the loss. He would surrender his objective and acquit his enemies. For Lilly's sake.

She uttered a little moan and he leaned close to her lips to hear what she was saying. "Devlin…."

The single word seared his heart. Was it a curse or a prayer?

Lilly found breakfast in various dishes on the sideboard in the dining room. Evidently Knowles had gone to a great deal of trouble. She helped herself to tea, eggs, ham and potatoes and sat at the long, empty table.

Would Mr. Farrell be making an appearance? That thought brought heat to her cheeks. When she'd woken to find herself unlaced, she'd been mortified. She knew she should feel violated, as well, but given that Mr. Farrell knew how she felt about sleeping in corsets, it seemed a kind thing for him to have done.

And perhaps it would explain that very odd dream she'd had, where Mr. Farrell was whispering in her ear, saying lovely things. And would it account for the memory of his touch, light and delicate for hands as large as his?

"Do you require anything else, miss?" Knowles stood in the doorway, his hands clasped behind his back.

"No, thank you, Knowles. This is delicious. Will Mr. Farrell be joining me?"

"It is nearly midday, miss. He has gone on about his business."

"But did he not work late last night?"

"Mr. Farrell does not require much sleep, miss."

"I see."

"He asked me to give you this message, miss." He came to her side, brought one hand out from behind him and placed a folded sheet in front of her on the table.

"Thank you," she said, wondering if he was just going to stand there until she had read it.

"Will there be anything else, Miss?"

"No, thank you."

Knowles bowed and left the room, closing the door behind him. What an odd man, Lilly thought. She had seldom encountered a more proper servant, and to find him above a gin house in Whitechapel was extraordinary.

Alone, she unfolded the note and read.

Miss Lillian,
Please remain indoors today. With the news that you have returned to London, every watchman and charley will be looking for you.
     I shall return in time for tea, and I hope to have good news for you.
Your servant, Devlin Farrell

His penmanship was excellent and a shiver went up her spine with that knowledge. How had a small pickpocket from Whitechapel learned to read and write? How had he learned manners that half the ton ignored? How was it that his manner of dress was as good as any in the aristocracy? And how did his speech remain clear and free of the local accent? Heavens! How did he have a proper valet and elegant apartments? Acquired wealth could account for some of that, but it would not change the character of the man. And, odd as it seemed to her, she'd come to the conclusion that Mr. Farrell was, at his core, of good character. Despite being brought up in the poorest, most dangerous part of London, he had risen above his humble origins.

Lilly was not above prying when her curiosity was aroused—a flaw in her own character, no doubt. But first she would need to get rid of Knowles. She went to the bell pull and summoned him.

Scarcely a moment later he appeared in the doorway again. "Miss?"

"Knowles, I will require a few items, but Mr. Farrell has written me to remain inside. If I gave you a list and money, would you fetch them for me?"

There was a long pause and she knew he wanted to refuse, but his employer had instructed him to do as she asked. "Yes, miss."

"Thank you. I shall have the list ready for you in a few minutes. May I use Mr. Farrell's desk?"

"Yes, miss. The one in the library, miss, not the one in his study."

"Of course, Knowles."

Lilly stood in the doorway of Devlin's study. In whole, it was unremarkable—a desk, a lamp, several cabinets and chairs, a tray with a decanter and glasses and a plush expensive rug. The cabinets, she suspected, would hold all she could possibly want to know about Mr. Farrell. Perhaps the information would give her an insight into dealing with the man. Perhaps it would destroy her illusions.

She sighed, closed the door with a faint click and turned back to the library. She would be a very poor guest, indeed, if she violated the one thing Mr. Farrell had asked of her. "The run of the place," he had said, but for his study.

A cup of tea might settle her nerves. She'd been fidgety

ever since reading Mr. Farrell's note promising good news. Oh, pray he had found the jewels! She would just put a kettle on before settling in her room with a book to wait.

The stairs to the upper floor were rather steep and Lilly congratulated Knowles for his stamina. Kitchens were almost always below stairs, but this was an interesting arrangement. One of Mr. Farrell's making, no doubt, to separate his quarters from the business below.

The stairway gave out to a large open attic kitchen with a cooking hearth on the outside wall. A long wooden worktable would have accommodated several servants and preparations for a large family and many guests. A pantry door on one side of the room was unlocked, likely since there were only Knowles and Mr. Farrell who would be foraging.

The kettle was still on the table and she placed it back on the hearth to heat, then went looking for spoons. The second drawer she opened held a wooden case and she opened it to find several lovely silver teaspoons. On closer inspection, she could see that they were engraved *K from R 1812,* and the others were engraved with subsequent years, ending with the year 1818. They were of the highest quality and would have been given Knowles by a previous employer. She lifted one and turned it over to see the design. It was a simple crest— one she knew on sight. Rutherford! What was Knowles doing with silver from the Duke of Rutherford?

"Did you find what you were looking for, miss?"

It was late in the afternoon when Devlin stood in the foyer at Rutherford House, his hat in his hand, waiting to see if he would be received. He'd been barely nine years old the last time he'd stood here, his hand in his mother's. He hadn't understood, then, why they'd come. He'd been too over-whelmed by the wealth and elegance to think of anything else.

A butler, as stiff as Knowles, returned to him and bowed. "His Grace will see you, sir."

He was led down a wide marble corridor to a room with tall double doors. The butler opened them and bowed. "Mr. Farrell, sir."

The instant he stepped into the room, the butler closed the door and was gone. Devlin stood there for a moment, taking his bearings. Rutherford was not alone. Olney lounged in a chair near the massive fireplace at one end of the room and Rutherford himself sat behind a desk, his attention occupied by some papers in front of him.

"Well, what is it, Farrell? Are you bringing my tailor's bill or some such?"

Odd, how being face-to-face with this man after so many years affected him. He, who was self-assured under the direst circumstances, was nervous. And he noted a twinge of distress to see the man's face was pallid and tired. It was true, then. The old man was failing. Regardless, he could not allow himself to care for someone who'd never cared for him. "I'm bringing you an offer," he said.

That got Rutherford's attention. He dropped his pen and looked up. Not a single flicker of recognition passed across his face. "Offer? What could you possibly have to offer me?"

"A chance to retain your good name."

"Eh? Is this some sort of scheme to extort money?"

Olney's interest perked up and he came to stand behind his father's chair. "I say, do I know you? You look a bit familiar. Oh! You're the chap I saw at Hunter's yesterday, are you not?"

"I am," Devlin admitted.

Rutherford cocked an eyebrow. "Do you know anything about this debacle?"

"I know everything about it."

"Do you know where the jewels are?"

"Everything but that."

"Then you can take your leave, sir, since that is the only thing I care to know."

"That would be a shame, your grace, since then all of London would know your secrets."

"Pish! All of London already knows my secrets. This is a scandal-mongering town, sir. They have it with their tea and they serve it up at supper. What could you possibly think you know to use against me?"

Olney interrupted. "Just a moment, Father. I want to hear what he knows about Miss Lillian."

"Go ahead, then." Rutherford sat back in his chair and tented his fingers—a gesture Devlin silently vowed to never use again. "Astonish me."

"I know that Miss O'Rourke did not abandon Olney on their wedding day. In fact, she was abducted from the vestry mere moments before the vows."

"That is what she told me yesterday, Father. I didn't know if I could believe her."

"Why should you believe this man now?" Rutherford asked his cub. "Hunter could have hired him to say these things just to persuade us to call off the hounds."

"I know," Devlin interrupted, "because I am the man who abducted her."

They stopped quibbling and looked at him in openmouthed shock.

"It was my plan, you see, not hers. I only meant to take her away for several days and then return her uninjured. I had no way of knowing she would be wearing the Rutherford Sapphires."

"She left a note—"

"My forger."

"Why?" Olney asked. "What did you mean to accomplish?" Devlin took a deep breath, his contempt for the pair growing by the moment. "Your family's discomfort. Your shame and embarrassment. I hoped you would be made a spectacle, and to have society talking about how you'd been made to look like fools."

"Too late," Rutherford said. "We have our story in place. Tomorrow we are going to put out the news that the king himself asked us to delay the wedding due to the queen's death. And when interest has waned, we are going to say that there was a contractual problem, that the O'Rourkes are insolvent. They will look the fools, not us."

Devlin managed to shrug and look indifferent. "That will be nothing compared to the scandal I will cause."

Rutherford turned red and slammed the top of his desk with his fist. "Damn it all, man! Why?"

"Because of what you did to my mother," he said, his voice lowering to a growl, voicing his anger aloud for the first time in twenty years. "And to me, *Father.*"

Rutherford's eyes widened. "By God, you're Catherine Farrell's whelp, are you not? I thought I recognized something in the eyes, something condemning."

Olney could not seem to find his voice. His eyes had bugged out and his mouth worked without sound.

"Do you remember the last time you saw her?" Devlin asked.

Rutherford frowned, as if trying to recall. "I…I reckon it was in winter of 1801."

"'Twas a week before Christmastide. She begged shelter and a crust of bread for her son. Me, Rutherford. But you and your son stood there, in the freezing rain, laughing at us."

Olney's mouth made an O and Devlin knew he was remembering the incident.

"You told us to leave London and never trouble you again." He faced Olney squarely. "She'd been your governess, Olney. She'd wiped your ass and fed you your dinner. She'd taught you your numbers and letters. But you laughed at her. You called her a hag and me a bastard."

"B-bastard," Olney repeated. "And that's what you are."

Devlin had expected that to sting more than it did. "Because your father raped my mother when she was his employee. When she got with child, he threw her onto the streets to make her way the best she could. Seems to me the real bastard is our father."

"Damnation!" Rutherford came to his feet. "Why now?"

"Because this wedding was the first thing either of you cared about. The one thing that would make you a public spectacle."

"You hate us so much?" Olney asked. "Why, we forgot you even existed."

"My mother was dead within three weeks of your turning her away. She had barely managed to support me and keep body and soul together until then, but when her hands failed and she could no longer sew for the rich, her frail body gave out. She died of starvation, Rutherford. So that I could eat. Do you know what it cost her to ask you for help? Do you know how it crushed her spirit when you threw her out? You sent us from the foyer to make us wait for you in the stables, for God's sake! Like trash."

"And trash you were!" Rutherford snarled. "Catherine was a haughty wench, thinking she was better than the others because she was born of a good family. She had to make her own way when her wastrel father lost it all on the turn of a card. I've no stomach for whiners and beggars. She turned out no better than her father."

It cost Devlin every last ounce of strength to keep from pulling Rutherford across the desk and beating him to a bloody pulp. He kept his fists doubled at his sides. *For Lilly,* he told himself. *For Lilly.*

"Whatever you thought of my mother or me, she deserved better than she got from you, your grace. But I did not come here for that. I came here to make you a proposition."

"What could you possibly offer that I'd be interested in?"

"The jewels," Olney guessed. "You have the jewels. You took them from Lilly, and you're holding them for ransom."

Devlin could only shake his head. "I do not have them at the moment, and neither does Miss O'Rourke. But I will find them and return them to you on one condition."

"And what is that, pup?"

"Withdraw the charge of theft against Miss O'Rourke."

Rutherford sneered. "What, do you think *that* ridiculous gesture will make you a gentleman?"

He could only look at his half brother and father, and think that, if they were gentlemen, he did not want to be one. He shook his head again. "You will get the jewels and my silence."

"Silence? About what?"

"That I am your bastard son. I will take that fact with me to my grave."

Olney chucked and Rutherford roared with laughter. "Good God, Farrell. Do you think I give a damn for that? Had I a tankard of ale for every whelp who has claimed me for a father, I'd be drowning in a vat."

"But I can prove it."

"The deuce, you say."

Devlin took a small golden locket from his watch pocket. He opened it to reveal the engraving inside and held it out for the man to see. *To Catherine for a son, Rutherford.*

His smile faded but his confidence did not waver. "I thought I could cozen her back to my bed, but she would not hear of it, the stubborn wench. Well, and what of it? My wife knows I have had other interests. The ton does not care when their own bastards, recognized and not, are going about in society. But you're a fool if you think I will recognize you, Farrell. I won't give you that much."

It was Devlin's turn to sneer. "Do you think I want that? You're mad. But I am not just any bastard son. If you do not recognize my name, perhaps your wastrel son can tell you."

"Farrell?" Olney said, tasting the name as if it were something foul. "Farrell? Why, the only Farrell I've heard of is some mucker in Whitechapel. Owns a gin house and has a reputation for…"

"For damned near anything," Devlin finished with a grim smile.

"That's you?" An expression of distaste flickered over Olney's face.

"In the flesh, brother."

Rutherford remained impassive. "What of it?"

"Do you want it known you gave birth to—"

"The King of Whitechapel! That's it. That is what I've heard," Olney interrupted. "Bloody bugger! Why, he is a crime boss!"

Rutherford's lip curled. "Do your worst, Farrell. Tell whoever you want. Post it in *The Times*. But you won't get a farthing from me, nor will I buy your silence for Miss O'Rourke's freedom. As for you, I will not shift the blame to you. Let your little hostage pay the price for your folly."

"Why have you suddenly come over with a conscience?" Olney asked. "Have you been poking my fiancée?"

Devlin gritted his teeth. This was not going well at all. Olney's crudity was going to earn him Devlin's fist in a minute. "Acquit Miss O'Rourke. I will take the blame and the punishment. 'Twas my scheme."

He'd been prepared for their contempt, but he hadn't been prepared for their indifference to gossip. He had, evidently, overestimated the duke's stock in a good name. Perhaps when one was a duke, one did not need a good name. It galled Devlin that Rutherford thought he was above ordinary mortals.

If he could not buy Lilly's freedom with his silence, he had no reason to stay. Without a word of goodbye, he turned and headed for the library door before he could do something he would regret.

"Oh, by the by, Farrell," Olney's voice followed him, "how did you like the delectable Miss Lillian? Quite talented between the sheets, is she not? Is that a brotherly thing, d'you think—sharing whores? Have you any others you'd like to share with me?"

Lilly hadn't…surely she hadn't. Blast and be damned! He was a simpleton to have thought someone like Lilly was "taken" enough with him to have surrendered to him so easily. Her practiced innocence had duped him. She was, in fact, as unscrupulous as he. She had used her body to secure her future.

He recalled the way she had played on Olney's desire for her to gain a proposal, and her words that night rang in his ears. *It is all I have dreamed of since I was a child, sir.*

The anger, the humiliation began to build in him and the library door banged when he slammed it to the sound of Rutherford's laughter. By God, he'd been played a fool by everyone involved in this charade.

Chapter Sixteen

Nausea churned in Devlin's belly as he rode home. He was ashamed of his relationship to the Rutherford title and to the Manlay family. He was angry with his own culpability in the plan to disgrace them and disgusted that neither of his plans had worked—the one to make fools of Rutherford and Olney and the one to acquit Lilly. But worst of all was that he was the fool for having been deceived by Lillian O'Rourke.

Well, he hadn't acquired wealth, the respect of Whitechapel and the fear of the ton by playing the fool. He still had one plan to bring them down—the one handed to him by James Hunter. Everything now hung on proving Rutherford and Olney had been involved with the Brotherhood. With that proof, nothing could save them from disgrace and a public trial. Oh, he was not naive enough to think they would actually be convicted, but the damage would be done. Yes, he would ruin them utterly.

And Miss Lillian O'Rourke?

He climbed the back stairs and threw his door open.

Well, Miss O'Rourke would answer for her duplicity. And for making him believe and trust again.

"Knowles!" he shouted.

Knowles's footsteps clattered on the attic stairs. "Sir?"

"Where is she?"

Knowles appeared in the corridor in front of him, and a second later, Miss O'Rourke was fast on his heels.

"She sent me out for folderols and was snooping in the kitchen when I returned, sir."

Snooping? It was true, then. She was part and parcel with Olney. She'd played him for a fool, too. And that ridiculous business of prosecuting her? That was simply a ploy to make him find their jewels. Or was little Miss Lillian playing her own game with both of them?

"I was not snooping. I was making a cup of tea," she gasped.

What an accomplished little liar she was. Why, he could almost believe her. "Retire, Knowles."

The valet's expression changed when he saw Devlin's face. He was used to his moods and did not question him. "Sir." He pivoted and headed back up the stairs, closing the door behind him. Devlin knew Knowles would not be visible again until morning.

Lilly took two steps toward him. "Mr. Farrell, did you know that Knowles has silver spoons with the Rutherford crest?"

"Of course I knew." He advanced on her. "I hired him for that reason. He was Rutherford's valet before he was dismissed when Rutherford blamed him for the latest pregnant maid that either Olney or Rutherford himself seduced."

She looked chagrined. "Oh! Then he is not a spy for the duke?"

The feigned concern only infuriated him further. "No, Miss O'Rourke. They have left that task for you."

Her eyes—those lying blue-green eyes—widened. "Me? But why would I spy for Rutherford?"

"Why would you consent to marry Olney, my dear? Why

would you sell yourself to the highest bidder? Did you think you could worm your way into their good graces again if you brought them information about me?"

She must have realized she was in trouble because she began backing away from him. It was a long corridor, and nowhere to escape at the end of it. "What has gotten into you?"

"You, Miss O'Rourke. Into my blood. Into my brain so that I cannot think of anything else. I wanted to save you." He laughed, the sound as harsh as metal scraping cobblestones to his ears. "More the fool, I. Little Miss Lillian knows how to save herself, it seems."

"Now, see here! That is uncalled for, Mr. Farrell." She had reached his bedroom door and stopped. "I do not think I want to talk to you until you are in a better temper."

"We have some matters to settle, Miss O'Rourke, and I do not recall giving you a choice."

She slammed the door in his face. Oh, the poor, deluded thing if she thought that would stop him. Hadn't he taught her better at the cottage? One boot to the panel and the door flew open. She was no more than halfway to the dressing room when he caught her around the waist and spun her around to face him.

"You told me you could have escaped the gypsy camp. Why didn't you?"

"I…I believed you would keep your word and return me."

"Is that it, Lilly? Or is it that you were collecting information for Rutherford? That you were biding your time until you could betray me to him? And was that why he was so indifferent to my proposal today? He'd been warned, hadn't he?"

"What proposal? I did not know where you went today. How could I betray you?"

Devlin was beyond reason. He tightened his arm around her, crushing her to his chest until she had to tilt her head back to look up at him. "But worst of all, sweet Lilly, was making me believe that you were innocent and vulnerable. For making me feel guilty for what I'd done to you and your reputation. Absurd! Ridiculous! Were you laughing at me behind my back? Tell me, did you and Olney share the joke at my expense before I returned from the cottage yesterday?"

She pushed hard against his chest and stepped away. "I would never make that mistake, Mr. Devlin. I have thought you many things, but never a fool."

"Tell me, chit, just what do you think I am?"

"You…you are behaving like a…a bastard!"

Bastard! There it was, in the open now. The word he hated most in the English language. But from Lilly's lips it cut even deeper. He advanced on her again. "Precisely! And there are names for women like you, too, Lilly. Harlot, for one."

Her eyes grew round in surprise. What did she think? That she could get away with her behavior? "How dare you!"

"How? Easily. The words come without difficulty once you know someone's true nature."

"Get out!" she demanded, pointing one slender finger at the splintered door.

"You are here at my sufferance, Lilly, and I could just as well put you out on the street. Or send you back to Hunter with the warning that you are a spy for the enemy. I've known accomplished liars before, but you are the best. Is this how you do it, Lilly?"

He backed her against the bed, slipped one hand around her waist and twined his other hand through her hair. Holding her and her head immobile, he lowered a punishing kiss to her lips. She struggled for a moment, then grew still as his kiss deepened.

"Is *this* how?" he managed to say against her lips.

She parted them, granting him access to the honeyed sweetness of her mouth. Her heat, her softness, the tentative way her tongue met his astounded and humbled him.

He lifted her onto the bed and followed, covering her with his own body. "Or this?" He nibbled her earlobe, his breath coming fast and hard now. God help him, he was lost.

Lilly could not fathom what she had done to make Devlin so angry, but she had been terrified until he'd begun kissing her. And then she could sense his need, his utter passion, in his touch. Oh, she was not out of trouble yet, but something had changed. Something in his kiss and in the way he sighed her name.

He consumed her, set her on fire until she was burning in the most amazing places. He parted from her long enough to unfasten her gown, tearing the fragile fabric in his haste. The fine lawn of her chemise was in shreds by the time he had dragged it upward to pull it over her head.

"No corset," he groaned. "Thank God."

She wanted to tell him that she hadn't been able to put it on alone, but his mouth was on hers again, quieting her protests and muddling her mind. Oh, not enough to not know she should stop him or end this impossible situation, but certainly enough that she simply didn't care. Didn't care about anything but the trail of fire he left with his fingertips, the heart-stopping demands of his kiss and the growing tension in her belly.

Somewhere in the tangle of limbs and clothing, Devlin had managed to disrobe. She thought she was now accustomed to the feel of him, of his skin against hers, of the ridge of hard muscles across his chest and the light matting of crisp dark hair there. But this was different than last time. More urgent, less gentle. He was no longer asking or entreating. He was demanding with his every movement, possession in the way he held her—as if he knew what she wanted before she did.

This time he would not stop.

He pinned her to the pillows and hovered over her, kissing his way down her body, lingering to kiss her neck below her ear and the hollow of her throat. When he reached her breasts, he took one in his mouth and teased it with his tongue until she was writhing and arching to him. The deeper his pressure, the greater her delight.

She tangled her fingers in his hair and held him close, slipping one leg over his hip. "Devlin, please…" she moaned.

"Please, what?" he asked against her flesh.

What? What was it she wanted? More of these feelings. More of his mouth on her. More of his caresses. "More! Please, more." She gasped as he nipped one tight areola.

He continued there as he drew one hand down between them to find that secret part of her and began a rhythmic stroking that sent her arching to him. She could not speak, could not catch her breath.

He praised her. "Yes, Lilly. That's what I want. I want to be there, deeper, harder."

"Yes!" She moaned.

"Again," he said, still stroking and drawing her closer to the brink of…what? Madness? For she would surely go mad if this continued much longer.

"You are so bloody ready for me," he muttered against her breast. "Do you want me, Lilly?"

"Yes…yes!"

"Now? There's more, y'know. More I want to do to you."

"Now," she confirmed, not certain what it was she was agreeing to, only that every part of her was tingling.

He rose above her, bringing her knees up to enclose his hips, then held her steady as he lowered his hips to hers. She felt the pressure between her legs, the hot, hard length of him pushing against her. She froze, not knowing what to do.

"Easy," he urged. "Steady. A moment and I'll have you there."

He thrust into her, causing a burning pain to erupt deep in her center. She stiffened and looked up into Devlin's passion-darkened eyes. He looked surprised and somehow regretful. "Damn it, Lilly. Why didn't you tell me?"

Tell him? What? That she'd been a virgin? But what had he expected? Tears welled and trickled from the corners of her eyes. Not for sadness or regret, but that Devlin had thought anything different.

He kissed the tears away and whispered, "Stay with me, love, and I'll take you there."

Instead of thrusting as he had before, he rocked against her until that lovely pressure began to build again, undeniable and demanding. Craving the mingling of ache and pleasure, she tilted up to him, and he growled, increasing his pace until a blinding heat burst upon her, drowning out all other thought and sound. Only Devlin. Only her. Together.

Lilly's cheek rested on Devlin's chest, her arm draped across him. He watched her sleep, stroking her hair and memorizing the curve of her cheek, the dark fan of her lashes against the glow of pink in her cheeks. She was stunning. Too fine for him.

He had pulled her against him when she'd stirred from her lethargy, greedy for the feel of her in the crook of his arm, determined to remember it when she was gone. And she would be gone. His possession was only for a moment—a brief moment in time when she needed him, and he needed her. Soon she'd go back to Hunter's house. Perhaps, even, back to Olney.

If Devlin let him live.

His devilish half brother had lied to him. Why? Was he jealous of Devlin? Did he want Devlin to think that he'd had what he now might never have? That thought amused him and he wondered if he should taunt Olney with the truth the next time he saw him. A gentleman wouldn't. Ah, but events had just proven that Devlin was no gentleman.

There was no escaping the fact that he'd bitten on Olney's bait, and as a result, Lilly was no longer untouched. He'd gone back on his good intentions. He'd broken his promise to Hunter. Hell, he'd betrayed himself. He'd played Olney's fool in the worst possible way because his brother had known how to tap Devlin's deepest pain. He'd never learned to trust. A lifetime of betrayals and hurt had seen to that.

Years of necessity and deprivation had driven him to do things he knew were wrong, things he wasn't proud of, but he'd always maintained a rough set of morals and a strong sense of what he *wouldn't* do for any reason. A sense of his own dignity. His mother's situation had impressed upon him the right of a woman's sovereignty over her own body, but he had violated Lillian O'Rourke in a most unconscionable manner. And in the process, he had made himself as arrogant and heartless as his father and half brother had been.

He had two choices to correct the matter. The first was to take Lilly home and confess to Hunter what he'd done. That would end badly on a field of honor. No matter who died that day, it would not restore to Lilly what he'd taken.

The second choice was equally undesirable—at least for Lilly. He could marry her. He could protect her from Olney and other men like him who would never appreciate her uniqueness—who would never value her despite the fact that she did not come to them pristine.

She sighed in her sleep and nuzzled against him again, setting his pulse to racing. The feel of her next to him was almost more than he could bear, joy and pain in equal measures. Joy that she was with him, if only for tonight. Pain that she would soon be gone and that he'd never find another woman who could take her place.

And that thought made it painfully clear what he must do.

Lilly wound her way through the crowds at the farmers' market, her wide straw bonnet pulled close about her face and her market basket slung over her arm. She knew Gina came here every Friday to shop for vegetable marrows and fruit with the cook, and she wanted to talk to her. She wanted news of Bella and Mama, and how they were holding up under the disgrace.

Knowles had found just the right bonnet and basket yesterday and she had thanked him this morning. He had given her the most eloquent, heartfelt apology for his accusation that she had ever received when he'd brought the things from her list. And he'd made no comment about the broken bedroom door other than to say that there'd be someone coming to fix it soon. Devlin must have given some sort of reason for the destruction. Perhaps he'd even told the truth. Knowles did not say. Only that Mr. Farrell had gone out on business and would join her later for tea.

Her cheeks grew warm just thinking about seeing him again. Heaven only knew what he must be thinking. Would he act as though nothing had happened? Would he lecture her about having a care to her reputation and virtue? Or would he simply pack her up and take her back to her kin?

This was the second time she'd awakened to find him gone. Was she so dreadful and disgusting that he could not face her in the morning? Did he feel sorry for her, and was that why he had seduced her? How humiliating.

As for Lilly, her mind kept wandering back to the feel of his flesh against hers. And the gentle way he had eased himself from her and gathered her against him after... well, after. He'd caressed her until her trembling had ceased, murmuring gypsy words she couldn't understand. Everything, in fact, had been magical—the heavy, languorous way she felt, the comfort of his arms, the deep murmur of his voice against the top of her head, the soft lushness of his mouth as he kissed her cheeks and nibbled her earlobe as he entreated her to sleep.

Her memories were so distracting that she bumped into a broad-faced woman. "Watch where yer goin'," the woman snapped.

"Sorry," she murmured and moved on.

This was the first time she'd been out without an escort or chaperone. If there was proper decorum for a woman alone, she wasn't aware of it.

She purchased several apples, two peaches and strawberries for a tart. She hoped Knowles's regret extended to letting her use his kitchen.

A breeze lifted her bonnet momentarily and she tied the blue ribbon a bit tighter.

"Lilly! What are you doing here?"

She whirled around to find Gina, a look of astonishment on her face. The wind must have lifted her bonnet just enough for Gina to recognize her. She closed the distance between them and took her sister's arm. Cook, she noticed, was several stalls away, inspecting a crate of peas.

"I came looking for you," she whispered. "How is Mama? And Bella? Have they been suffering for my disgrace?"

Gina squeezed her hand. "Oh, Lilly. We miss you. Everything has gone from bad to worse since you've been gone. Mama has fallen into a decline. She says that she does not care for anything anymore. Andrew says he will send her home, but Mama will not hear of it until you are found. You see, we have not told her where you are. She would have apoplexy. Lady Vandecamp called and said there is nothing more she can do for our family. We are simply beyond redemption, she says. Bella, although she is worried about you, just walks about with that silly besotted look on her face, as if none of this touches her. I tell you, she hasn't been the same since she married Andrew.

"And, worst of all, Lord Rutherford and Olney called last night. There was terrible shouting coming from the library and, when they left, Andrew told us that Rutherford has refused to withdraw the charges of theft against you, even though Mr. Farrell went to his house and explained everything yesterday. They said that until they have the jewels back, they will not relent. I do not believe I have ever seen Andrew angrier. He said that the danger to you is worse than before."

Lilly was speechless. She had not known that Devlin had gone to Rutherford House to plead on her behalf. Was he that anxious to be rid of her? The heat washed through her again and she put last night from her mind.

She, the most conventional of her sisters, was the cause of the greatest turmoil. She shook her head. "Tell them all I am sorry, Gina. Oh, if only I hadn't lost track of the jewels. I can still see them in my mind's eye, lying on the dressing table in the cottage. Why did I not remember to bring them?"

"If only that horrid man had not kidnapped you. You should be Olney's wife now, and a marchioness," Gina muttered.

Oh, but that was the one thing Lilly was not sorry for. She glanced over her shoulder and noticed that Cook was coming their way. "Do you still walk with Bella in the park every afternoon? Yes? I shall come to you there when I can," she whispered before she turned and hurried away.

There had to be something she could do—some way of putting the pieces of her family's life back together. Some way of releasing Devlin Farrell of his obligation to her. She could only guess what it had cost him to petition Rutherford and

Olney on her behalf. He must be even more desperate than she had imagined. And if that were so, she would have to find a way to release him.

Chapter Seventeen

Just as Lilly was about to leave the market, a commotion drew her attention. A baker who'd been selling loaves of bread dangled a young boy by one arm. She recognized the lad immediately—the roguish little Ned who had filched her pound note the day she'd met Devlin in Covent Garden. And he was in trouble again.

"Someone fetch the watch!" the baker was shouting.

Stealing bread? The poor thing must be starving. Before she could think better of it, she marched forward. "Here now, you let the boy go! Shame on you!"

"Me?" the baker said with wide-eyed disbelief.

"You!" she confirmed. "Now let my boy go. I sent him to buy us a bit of bread, and this is what we get for our trade."

"'E was stealin', 'e was. Took what don't belong to 'im."

She gave Ned a stern look. "Did I not tell you to pay the man, Neddie? Come now, where's your coin?"

Ned looked a bit wary, but he was a quick study. "I, uh, someone picked me pocket, 'e did."

"I'll box your ears when I get you home. Haven't I told you to watch out for ruffians and pickpockets?" She took a coin from her basket and held it out for the baker. "Here you are. Now, let go of my boy."

A bewildered look spread over the baker's coarse features. "I didn't mean no 'arm, missus. I thought 'e was going to run off wiv it."

Ned landed with an agile hop and straightened his shirt. "I was goin' to my mum to get another coin." He took the loaf of bread and plopped it in Lilly's basket.

"Good day to ye, then." The baker backed away.

Lilly took Ned by the arm and turned around—right into Devlin's chest.

"Well done, Miss Lilly," he said with a touch of humor. "There's a bit of the larcenist in you, I see."

She realized that the baker had seen Devlin behind them and that had been the real reason for his sudden change of heart. Her memories of last night mingled with her embarrassment and anger at his desertion. "I, um, I—"

"No excuses. Young Ned is a lucky lad to have you come to his rescue. Is that not so, Ned?"

"Aye. Anything you wants, Miss Lilly, an' I'll get it for you."

Devlin shook his head with a rueful grin as he ruffled the boy's hair. "Just do not ask where he gets it."

He turned them toward Whitechapel and set a brisk pace. "I have been looking for you."

Lilly blinked. "I told Knowles where—"

"For Ned," he explained.

"I didn't 'ear about it," the boy said.

"I'm looking for some sparkly."

Ned gave a low whistle. "I don't see much of that, sir."

"Just keep your eyes and ears open. Tell the other lads I am offering a bigger reward than they can earn from fences if they find them or have word of where I can find them."

"You can count on me, sir."

"And there's something else, Ned. Something you must keep quiet at all costs, do you understand?"

"Aye. Is it dangerous?"

"Men have been killed over it."

Lilly frowned. What was Devlin thinking?

"Again, keep your eyes and ears open. You mustn't interfere, and you mustn't take matters into your own hands. Just send to me if you have news."

"Of what, sir?"

"There are some gents in hiding. Rumor is, they are somewhere in Whitechapel. Likely in the rookeries or somewhere in Thieves Kitchen. I only want news if you hear something—where they are, what they are doing. That sort of thing."

"I can do that right enough."

"Stay away from them, Ned. Just bring the news to me."

"Aye. That all?" Ned waited for Devlin's nod, then doffed his cap in a courtly bow to Lilly. "Thank you, Miss Lilly. You're a right one, you are." He ran off down a narrow row of stalls.

Devlin offered his arm and they began walking again. "I thought I asked you to stay inside, Lilly."

She looked at him and blinked. "You said I should not go abroad after dark. I did not think you would object to me disguising myself and taking a walk during the day."

"Disguise yourself?" He gave a short, mirthless laugh. "Lilly, I knew you the moment I turned the corner. Even with your back to me at fifty feet away, you are unmistakable."

"To you? Or to the charleys?"

"Well reasoned. No one knows you the way I know you now. That is not the point. I do not like you taking the risk of going where you might be seen and recognized. I have a long reach, Lilly, but I doubt even I could overreach Rutherford to pull you out of Newgate."

Her spine stiffened and her hand on his arm tensed, and she knew he would sense her rebellion. "Then I must stay shut away until this matter is settled?"

"'Twill be just a few more days."

"What if the jewels are never found? What if a thief has taken them and has gone to Scotland? Or France?"

"I will track them down, Lilly. Have no doubt of that."

"So you say. But what if the worst happens and you cannot recover them?"

"Do not doubt me," he repeated, as if to a child. "If that should happen, I will find a way to call Rutherford off."

There was, evidently, little he would not do to be rid of her. "I have not been afraid through all of this, and yet now I have misgivings. I did not anticipate how angry Olney would be, or just how little he cared for me."

"Olney only knows what he wants, and when he thought someone else had taken it first, he…" He stopped and cleared his throat.

"In any case, it is true now. Someone else *has* had it." She looked down at her feet because she could not look at his face.

"I am sorry for that," he said.

She was certain he was. Now he was stuck with her until he could find a solution to her problem. "Surely there is something you can say besides that you are sorry."

"If there is, I do not know of it. I cannot undo what happened last night, and I am not certain I would if I could."

They arrived at The Crown and Bear, and she remained silent as they walked up the side stairs to his apartments, all the words she wanted to stay straining to burst forth. But not in public. Not where they could be overheard.

She untied the ribbon of her bonnet, dropped it on a side table and turned to face him. "You are sorry, but you would not change it? Oh, you are the most infuriating man!"

* * *

This was worse than Devlin had thought. She was angry, and she had a right to be. But he'd thought…Olney had said…and she did not protest too much once he kissed her. Had he mistaken her shock for willingness? Had he taken advantage of her innocence and seduced her? As much as that thought grieved him, he could not waver now. She would have to listen to reason.

"Damn it, Lilly, when I came home and found you gone, I thought, well, no matter what I thought, I was afraid for you. Olney has hired men to find you. The charleys are sworn to arrest you. There is too much risk in going abroad."

She seemed to digest this news with a bit of surprise. "Then I shall have to concoct a better disguise."

"Can you not just stay out of harm's way?"

"You cannot tell me how long this will take, nor if I will ever be free. I've done nothing, and yet I am paying the price for everyone's stupidity! You have all played with my life as if I had no mind of my own. You, Olney, Rutherford and, yes, even my brother-in-law."

"I've told you I regret my part in that. If I could change it, I would. But I cannot turn back the clock. I have been arranging solutions to at least part of it."

She turned away from him and marched down the passageway to his study as if she were so angry she couldn't bear the sight of him. He followed, torn between anger and admiration.

Once inside the little room, she turned again. "Dear heavens. What have you been arranging now?"

He paused and took a deep breath. Lilly was not going to like this, but that was unavoidable. They could remedy it later, if need be. "This morning I went to my bishop and acquired a license to marry you."

Her eyes widened with disbelief. *"Marry?"*

"All we need now is your mother's consent. Hunter's would do as well. I've sent a message to him to meet us here as soon as he can arrange it. We could be married tomorrow morning."

"But…but…" she sputtered.

He rushed ahead, not wanting to hear her refusal. "I will be able to afford you a measure of protection Hunter would not. And I have resources Hunter would never use. I'm afraid it is your best chance to get out of this."

"It is not that I…I do not appreciate this great sacrifice you are making on my behalf, but have you stopped to consider what *I* might want?" Her voice dripped sarcasm.

"What you want is of little consequence at the moment. I have sent for Hunter and we shall work this out." He regretted the words almost the instant they were out. They were true, but they were not the way to win Lilly's consent.

"Never! I will never marry you for the sake of expediency."

"I do not care *why* you marry me, but marry me you will."

"Not unless you give me a good reason."

Damn! He hadn't expected her to be delighted about this, but he hadn't been prepared for her flat refusal. Would it make a difference if he confessed his love? Or would she merely turn up her nose and walk away? His other reasons, a part of them anyway, would have to suffice.

"Damn it, Lilly! No matter what you think of me and what I've done, I will not seduce an innocent and then abandon her!"

"You plead your conscience? This noble sacrifice of yours is no more than a way to soothe your conscience for last night?"

Knowles had appeared in the doorway and disappeared just as quickly. Devlin closed the door, hoping they would not be overheard. "Call it what you will, Lilly. Let me make this perfectly clear. I have no intention of fathering a bastard. That is not a matter for debate. If you are with child, it will be born in wedlock. No child of mine will be teased, taunted or shunned because he was baseborn."

Her mouth opened but she could not utter a sound. Good. Perhaps he could finish this before she caught her breath and attacked again.

"After I acquired the license, I found an estate agent. I have purchased a home in Mayfair, not far from Hunter's. I thought you would want to be close to your family."

"You…you…"

"You may choose the furnishings, of course, but I will interview the servants."

"You cannot be serious."

"Perfectly. I am painfully aware that I cannot bring a wife to live over a gin house, nor is it any way to raise a family."

Lilly looked down at her stomach as if it were something alien.

"I know this is not what you would have wanted, Lilly, and at the risk of making you angry again, I am sorry. But there is nothing we can do about it now except to minimize the damage."

There was a polite knock on the door and Knowles's voice carried through the crack. "Sir, the Messieurs Hunter are here to see you."

"Show them in, Knowles," he said, then pulled three chairs in front of his desk. "Please sit down, Lilly."

She sat in the middle chair, and he thought that was good strategy. Flanked by family, she would feel less vulnerable.

Lilly was still speechless. Married? Was Devlin mad? That was a high price to pay for one night of passion. Well, hers, at any rate. Perhaps Devlin hadn't felt anything at all. And a baby? A bastard? Was there anything the man had not thought of?

Andrew and James entered the study, their curiosity showing on their faces. She wondered if she looked half as bewildered as she felt. At a wave from Devlin, they took the seats on either side of her. Andrew reached out and took her hand to give it a reassuring squeeze. Would he still be kind when he learned what she'd done?

Devlin sat down behind the desk and took a deep breath. "Thank you for coming. I know this will be a shock to you, but I want to ask Miss Lillian's hand in marriage."

Jamie coughed and Andrew's eyebrows went up almost to his hairline. "Did I hear you correctly, Farrell? Marry?" he asked. "Lilly?"

Devlin nodded. "It is the only way out of this. Miss Lillian is my responsibility."

"While I agree you are responsible for Lilly being in this pickle, I fail to understand why you think marriage is necessary."

"I can offer her protection—"

"As can I."

"Ah, but I have no scruples. Do you doubt me?"

There was a long silence, and Andrew finally said, "Not in the least, Farrell. I know you will do whatever must be done to achieve your jail. If keeping Lilly safe is your jail, then I know you will die trying. But I do not think this is the sort of marriage…that is…"

"I know your objections. My reputation leaves something to be desired. And Miss Lillian could have done much better than me, had I not abducted her. You see, do you not, that I am responsible for her ruin, and thus I am responsible for her redemption."

Andrew nodded. "I appreciate the sentiment, but I hardly think marriage to you would redeem her."

Devlin winced and Lilly felt a twinge of sympathy for him, recalling how she had felt at Olney's parents' reaction to his choice. It was not a pleasant thing to be told you are not good enough.

"There are…other circumstances which could make marriage expedient."

She felt Andrew stiffen and his hand tightened around hers. "Explain, Farrell."

"I cannot explain how or why, but I found myself in a position… I seduced your sister-in-law."

Lilly gasped. How could he? Andrew came to his feet so quickly that his chair overturned. Jamie restrained him as he tried to move forward. "Damn you, Farrell," he snarled. "I would call you out if you hadn't saved Bella and Gina. I may anyway." He allowed Jamie to push him back into his righted chair and turned to look at her. "What say you, Lilly? Did he hurt you?"

Humiliation washed over her. How could she ever explain? But how could she let Devlin take the blame? "I have not so much as a bruise to show for it. He…he is being kind, Andrew. I must share his burden. I never once said no. I did not stop him when I could have. And I did not flee at the first opportunity. He kissed me first, but I think it would be difficult to determine who seduced whom."

Andrew's tension eased and Jamie managed a quiet chuckle. Devlin, on the other hand, looked astonished. "Lilly, you needn't do this. I am a man of…some experience, and you are—were—an innocent. The burden is entirely mine."

"Well, Lilly? Do you want to marry this bastard?"

Devlin blanched and Lilly suddenly realized the truth. He'd been enraged last night when she'd called him a bastard. Mere minutes ago, he'd vowed no child of his would be baseborn. And Andrew's words had wounded him.

"Call him anything but that, Andrew," she said in a quiet voice and saw a flash of understanding. "As for marriage, I have yet to hear an argument that would persuade me."

"If you are with child, Lilly?" Andrew's voice was gentle but compelling.

Unlacing Lilly

"I must have a little time. This—all of this—is so new to me. Tomorrow is too soon. I need a few days. Could I give my answer Monday, Andrew?"

"Of course. But I cannot, in good conscience, leave you here. Please collect your things. You will have to come home with me."

She thought of the danger to Bella and her family, and of the shame they would suffer to have her arrested on their doorstep. She glanced quickly at Devlin and realized he was watching her with something akin to consternation.

"I cannot go back, Andrew. I shall stay here."

Lilly retired to her room the moment Andrew and James took their leave. She did not want to argue with Devlin, nor did she want to face Knowles's disapproving eyes.

Knowles had anticipated her wishes, and she found a dinner tray on a side table. He had even taken the time to put a small vase containing three pink roses on the tray. Another apology? The dishes were covered to keep them warm, so she went to the dressing room to find her wrapper, intending to undress and prepare for bed. She would have her supper by the fire with a book for company.

A white box tied with blue ribbons had been placed on the chaise and she couldn't resist inspecting the card. She withdrew it from a tiny envelope and read the inscription. *To eliminate future problems, Devlin.* Curious, she plucked the ribbon and lifted the lid.

Resting in a nest of tissue was the most beautiful corset she had ever seen. Made of ivory silk and embroidered with pale pink, yellow and blue flowers, it had been crafted with exquisite care. The laces were made of silk cord and the boning was extremely fine.

And it laced in the front.

She smiled to think of Devlin choosing such a garment.

When had he done it? Between the bishop and the estate agent? It was completely inappropriate, of course, but so was Devlin.

She undressed, left her gown draped across the chaise and slipped on a nightgown and wrapper just before she heard a knock. Knowles come to take away the tray?

She hurried into the bedroom and called, "I haven't eaten yet, Knowles. I shall ring when I'm finished."

"It's me, Lilly."

Her heart thumped at the sound of Devlin's voice.

"Lilly?"

"I…I am not decent."

"I need to talk to you."

"Tomorrow."

"Now, Lilly. And you know I will not take no for an answer."

She stared at the door. Was there any point in trying to keep him out? She crossed to the door and threw the bolt. "Come in," she said, walking away.

The door opened and closed quietly, but Devlin did not speak. When she reached the side table, she turned to him. He looked haggard and tired. And still sinfully handsome. He was watching her, an odd expression on his face.

"What is it?"

"I just realized that if we marry…" He shook his head as if to clear it and came farther into the room. "There are some things you need to know."

"Please, I do not want an accounting of your sins or crimes. I think I will sleep better without that knowledge."

"I cannot make an apology for what I do not regret. I survived, Lilly. I did what I had to do."

She had a sudden vision of a young Devlin picking a pocket and running through a crowd to escape, as Ned had done today. Her heart ached for him. And for Ned. She gave him the tiniest of smiles. She had expected no less from him.

Devlin Farrell was not the sort of man to excuse his past. But then what could he have to tell her about?

He began pacing from the fireplace to the dressing room and back again, his hands clasped into fists. "It is about who I am."

"I have guessed that you were a love child, Devlin. You do not have to discuss it if it pains you."

"It pains me," he admitted. "And I must disavow you of the notion that I was a love child. My mother was raped."

She blinked. What could she say to such a dreadful admission? To grow up knowing he was a product of violence must have scarred him deeply. "I am sorry, Devlin. I hope she did not hold that against you."

He raked his fingers through his hair as he paced. "She was very dear to me. Gently born and reared. Her family fell upon hard times, and she was forced to find a position fitting for someone in her circumstances. She became a governess to a wealthy family. She was alone in the world, you see, and without protection."

Lilly wanted to stop him. His pain was almost too much for her, and she knew he had not told anyone else. But he was determined. She offered her wineglass from the dinner tray and he took it with a grateful nod, continuing his restless pacing.

"She was allowed to remain in her position for a time because she was an excellent teacher and a tireless worker. But the day came when the employer's wife discovered the governess was bearing her husband's bastard."

She bit her lower lip to keep from interrupting.

"Within hours of that discovery, she was thrown onto the street without being allowed to collect her belongings. My mother took work as a seamstress for a tailor. It was adequate until I was born, then, in the best of times, we barely scraped by. My mother's health began to fail. Consumption, I think. I remember her coughing frequently and hiding her handkerchief from me. When I was seven, she was dismissed because her hands had failed her. She could no longer sew the fine stitch the tailor's clients required."

Lilly stood and reached out for him, but he stepped away and shook his head.

"I am not done. You see, when she had sold everything she possessed to feed us, she took up another profession. I think you can guess which one, Lilly. I remember men coming and going, remember that some of them were kind, and others would beat my mother and strike me, as well. We lived in the meanest conditions, but she never failed in giving me my daily lessons and reminding me who I was.

"I think my mother knew when she was dying. It was winter, somewhere around Christmastide. She took me back to my father's house and begged crumbs. And begged for him to care for me. He laughed, Lilly. He and his heir, the same boy she had cared for and taught, stood in the stables where they'd made us wait, and laughed at us. That was the last time I spoke to him.

"My mother passed on a fortnight later. I was nine. For a time, the friends she had made in…the profession looked after me, gave me a place to sleep and a bit of bread. But I was in the way. No one wanted a small boy around. I was bad for business and was taken to a workhouse."

It was all Lilly could do to remain silent and to blink back her tears. She had always suspected that Devlin was of good stock, if not legitimate birth. But what he had endured was more than any nine-year-old should.

"Workhouses." He sneered. "That is a blasphemy. They generate poverty. They are governed by the worst sort of men and women. I was beaten insensible before I finally escaped on my third attempt.

"Thereafter, I lived on the streets, like Ned. I did whatever

I had to do to survive. And I'd do it again. But I'd had the benefit of an early education, and I knew what I had to do to get out of that squalor. I saved every penny that I did not have to use for food. I lived in doorways and alleys. I bathed in the Thames, and even stole my clothes. I could not wait to escape the city and find a better life."

He turned to her and she nearly cried at the stark, haunted look on his face. "But, in the end, I have stayed. This…" he gestured at the window "…is all I know of life. I've made fortunes, many times over, but I cannot escape what I am— not by denying it, and not by running away from it."

She stood, wanting to go to him, to comfort him, but his expression stopped her. He was not looking for her pity. Nor was he asking to be understood. He simply wanted her to know what sort of man he was.

"So you see, Lilly? For better or worse, I cannot escape my past. And here is the very worst of it." He drank the wine and threw the glass against the brick hearth. "I am Rutherford's bastard. Olney's brother."

Chapter Eighteen

Jamie and Devlin sat in a quiet corner of The Crown and Bear, watching the door. Devlin had sent a message out that he wanted to meet with the Gibbons brothers. The day had waned and it was dusk. Like cockroaches, the brothers probably did not come out until dark.

"That them?" Jamie asked, tilting his head toward the back door leading to the privy.

He nodded. That was them, indeed. Were there another two like them in London? The taller and older of the two, Richard, was dressed all in filthy black. He scanned the taproom and caught sight of Devlin, then nudged his brother, Arthur, and they ambled toward Devlin's table.

The two were an example of London's failure to care for its orphans. They'd lived on the streets, escaped every work-house and orphanage they'd been committed to, and had been in and out of gaol for their entire lives. Gossip had it that their mother had been a prostitute who had turned them out when they were barely old enough to toddle about. They'd grown up without social skills, morals or boundaries, and their behavior reflected that.

"Let me handle this, Jamie. I doubt they'd talk to a stranger."

"We've tried. They dodge us before we can get to them. I am impressed that all you had to do was put out a whisper and they come crawling out of the woodwork. One of the advantages of being the King of Whitechapel, eh?"

Devlin wished he'd never heard that term, but he supposed it was true. Whatever he wanted in Whitechapel, he got. He fixed the approaching brothers with a cold stare, knowing it was better to remind them that he was in charge than to allow them to think they were making the decisions.

"Eh, Farrell? Hears ye wants to talk to us."

Jamie brought his handkerchief to his nose and Devlin realized the smell of sewage clung to their clothes. He braced himself, unwilling to start the interview off with a perceived insult. The stench washed over him as the brothers sat in chairs across from him.

"Thank you for coming," he began, then realized the niceties were lost on the Gibbons brothers. "I need some information."

"We gots a lot o' that. What kind o' information?"

"I am looking for some old friends. Haven't seen them for a month or more. I hear they might be lying low in the rookeries."

"Lots o' people in the rookeries, Farrell. Most o' 'em don't wanna be found."

Devlin signaled Mick at the bar to bring tankards for the brothers. Perhaps a bit of ale would loosen their tongues. Though Arthur never spoke, Richard seemed able to read his expressions and interpreted for him. At the moment, he was hunched in his chair and glancing about, as if suspicious of everyone in the taproom. Guilty conscience, Devlin wondered, then remembered that the Gibbons brothers did not even have one conscience between the two of them.

When Mick put the tankards on the table and disappeared, Richard glanced at Jamie. "An' 'oo's this?"

If they knew Jamie was from the Home Office, they would never give them information. In fact, Devlin suspected they'd leave without finishing their ale. "A friend of mine. He's been helping me look."

Arthur grinned, exposing two rows of rotten teeth.

Richard nodded. "Artie says ye should o' come to us first instead o' wastin' yer money."

Devlin took a wad of banknotes from his waistcoat pocket and laid it on the table between them. "I've come to you now. If you've got something to tell me, that's yours." He inclined his head to indicate the money.

Arthur licked his lips and Richard's finger twitched. "Well, spill it then. 'Oo are the coves yer lookin' fer?"

"Gents," he said.

Richard laughed. "Gents in the rookeries? Hear that, Artie? Gor, that's a good one."

Devlin gave him an unamused stare.

Both brothers sobered. Richard tried again. "Say we was to know something. An' say we was bein' paid t' keep our mouths shut."

Arthur snickered at his brother's reference to his silence.

"Why would we tell ye anything?"

Devlin knew his reputation and was not above using it to his advantage. "So you could go on living another day?"

Richard's expression turned vicious. "That a threat, Farrell?"

"I'd prefer you to take it as a measure of my determination, but take it as you will. Have no doubt that I will eventually get the information I want, and have no doubt that those who help me will profit and those who don't…" He shrugged.

Arthur tugged Richard's sleeve and gave him a look coupled with one lifted eyebrow.

"Artie says we ought t' 'elp ye." He reached out and unfolded the wad of bills to take measure of the stack and gave a soft whistle. "These gents got names?"

"Some of them. If they all did, Gibbons, I wouldn't need you."

"Well, gi' me the ones you got."

"Henry Booth, Cyril Henley." Those were the men he would most like to find. Henley was likely the leader now and Booth would do anything Henley ordered.

Arthur's muddy brown eyes had gone blank and Richard pressed his lips together. Neither one of them spoke.

If Devlin were a betting man, he would lay odds that the Gibbons brothers were either in league with them or had been in the recent past. But he was not discouraged. Men like the Gibbons brothers knew nothing of loyalty. What they knew was fear and intimidation.

"The other men I'm looking for are their friends. Whoever is in league with them, Gibbons. All of them." He scooped up the wad of bills and held it up for them to see. "This much for each and every one of them."

Arthur emitted something like a delighted squeal and Richard glanced at him. "What do ye want? Just where they be? Or you wants us to bring 'em to ye?"

"Just where they are, Gibbons. And on the quiet. I do not want them knowing I'm looking for them. I want them where I can find them when I am ready."

"What ye gonna do?"

"That's none of your concern."

"Ye gonna tell 'em 'oo turned 'em in?"

Devlin glanced at Jamie, wondering if he knew the line of Devlin's thought. That, if the Gibbons brothers had been involved in procuring women for the rituals, there would be no way to protect them from the law or the rough justice of the rookeries.

"I can assure you they will learn nothing from me."

They drained their tankards and stood, wiping the ale from their chins on their sleeves. "When do ye need t' know?"

"The moment you have the information. And the sooner, the better."

Lilly glanced out her window to find that night had fallen. Knowles had brought her supper and had taken it away again. And still, she hadn't heard from Devlin. Hadn't seen him, in fact, since he'd made his startling admission last night.

Everything he'd revealed made such perfect sense that she wondered why she hadn't seen it before. His resemblance to Rutherford was not as apparent as Olney's, but there was something of the aristocrat in Devlin. Something in his bearing and pride. Something intangible, but obvious. A duke's son. She was not surprised at that much. He had the presence and authority of one born to the role, even if on the wrong side of the sheets.

And knowing his history, she could easily understand why he wanted revenge—no, *justice*—for his mother. And for the small defenseless child he had been. Her heart twisted every time she thought of him huddled in a doorway when the snow fell, or stealing stale crusts of bread no one else had wanted from trash heaps. And admiration when she thought of his single-minded determination in saving every spare cent to rise above the circumstances life had dealt him.

As she turned away from the window, she heard a familiar voice below. It was James Hunter. She stopped and went back to look down. James and Devlin were leaving The Crown and Bear, their strides purposeful and swift and, again, without a word to her.

A twinge of disappointment shot through her. She had hoped he would come home soon. She wanted to see him, to talk to him. She wanted to tell him that she understood, and that she did not think the less of him for it. She wanted to tell him that she would help, that she planned to go to Olney and tell him what a dreadful man his father was and that he was almost as bad. And she would threaten to tell everyone what they'd done to a defenseless woman and her child all those years ago.

Yes, she understood, and she would help him in any way she could. But first she would punish him. He needed to pay for using her as his instrument of revenge and, now, for shutting her away and ignoring her. Yes, he would pay for that. Oh, so sweetly. Perhaps tonight.

Devlin was surprised to find that Lord Marcus Wycliffe worked so late. He had always assumed the man had many more things to occupy his time than his duties at the Home Office.

Jamie performed the introductions and Wycliffe did not inform him that he and Devlin were already acquainted. Following his cue, Devlin played ignorance and took the offered seat.

"So, Mr. Farrell, Hunter informs me that you are assisting him in our attempts to bring down the Blood Wyvern Brotherhood."

"Tidy up the matter," Jamie corrected with a rueful smile.

Devlin proceeded cautiously. "I am asking a few questions on his behalf."

Jamie laughed. "A few questions, he says. I sat across the table from the Gibbons brothers earlier."

Wycliffe looked impressed. "Perhaps you can do *me* that favor one day, Farrell. I have a few questions of my own I'd like to ask that vermin."

"If I find they have had anything to do with procuring women for the Brotherhood's rituals, I will hand them to you on a silver platter."

"Just bring a posy to cover the stench."

Wycliffe grinned. "I have heard they have never, in their entire lives, bathed. I shall take your warning to heart, Hunter."

"As it now seems imminent that we shall be coming into custody of Henley, Booth, Elwood, Olney, Rutherford and the others, we thought we should put plans in place for the arrests." Jamie sat forward in his chair and rested his forearms on his knees. "We will be given their locations, but nothing else. I should think a pack of charleys rooting through the rookeries would send out an alarm. Have you any ideas?"

Wycliffe frowned and tapped his desk with his pen. "It isn't as if they are the king's men. They will not be in uniform. But we will need men we can trust. I have some favors I can call in. Hunter, your brothers, also Geoff Morgan, Harry Richardson and myself."

"Another day or two and we should have names and locations," Devlin said. "We will have to work fast then. Word of this sort of thing travels like wildfire through the rookeries. Secrets cannot be kept for long."

Wycliffe sighed and sat back in his chair. "Very well. I will say nothing to the watch until we are ready. Once I have your list, I can better organize the raid. I will need to prepare a statement to the public. This will cause a scandal if we catch members of the ton in our net."

Jamie gave him a mirthless laugh. "Prepare well, Wycliffe. There will be nothing *but* ton in your net."

He nodded and then took a deep breath. "Hunter, will you wait outside? I'd like a private word with Mr. Farrell."

Jamie's lips quirked in a sardonic smile but he stood and went to the door. "If either of you need me, I'll be close by."

When the door closed, Wycliffe gave him a puzzled look. "He doesn't know?"

"I did not think it was important."

"What? That you've been assisting me for years? Or that you are Rutherford's son?"

"Bastard," Devlin corrected. "And neither."

"Did you know the duke is ill? I've heard he has months left to him. Perhaps only weeks."

"I heard. But that makes no difference."

"I've also heard that Olney is a match for his father, in all ways. All ways, Farrell."

"I've heard that, too. I intend to stop them both."

Wycliffe looked aggrieved as he prepared to ask his next question. "Is it true, what I've heard whispered? That you are the one who abducted Miss Lillian O'Rourke?"

He nodded.

"I feared that when I learned that Olney's fiancée was missing. That was low, even for you, Farrell. I ought to haul you in, too. I could have you—"

"Don't work yourself into a lather, Wycliffe. It isn't as if I work *for* you, so you cannot fire me. I merely cooperate on certain cases."

"What are you going to do to correct the situation?"

"Marry her, if she'll have me."

To his credit, Wycliffe did not laugh at him. Instead, he seemed to consider the matter seriously before he spoke again. "Should she consent, you must make your parentage public. A duke's son—even a bastard son—has a certain standing in society. It would lift you above your current status."

Devlin laughed. "Do you think for a single moment that he would even acknowledge me? Or that I want that?"

"Perhaps not. But for Miss O'Rourke's sake, I would think you'd be willing to make that compromise."

He thought about that for a moment, but he could not escape his inevitable jail. "If we should find that Olney and Rutherford are involved with the Brotherhood, the cachet of the Rutherford name will not lift me any higher than I am at the moment. The scandal will finish the family."

Wycliffe considered his statement before he spoke again. "But if, for instance, you should discover that they were not involved in any actual sacrifice, and only attended the last ritual, it would be a matter of judgment…."

Was the man telling him to keep his mouth shut if he uncovered his father or brother's complicity in the Brotherhood? "Bloody hell, Wycliffe! This is what I've wanted the better part of my life. It would take a knife in my heart to stop me now."

Wycliffe gave him a sad smile. "I will leave it to your discretion."

Then there wouldn't be anything discreet about it.

Lilly wondered again how late Devlin would be. Did he ordinarily retire at dawn? Or did he retire whenever he felt the need for sleep? Knowles had retired hours ago, and he must know his master's habits.

There was so much she didn't know about Devlin. So much she wanted to learn. Whatever she knew about men was quite general, or had been told to her by her mother.

Guard your modesty, Lillian. It takes precious little to incite a man's lust—even a gentleman like your papa.

She smiled to herself, trying to imagine her staid and somber father as a lustful satyr ravishing her mother. That was too ridiculous to contemplate. Yet…

Yet she recalled Devlin as he'd been when they'd made love. Expert. Determined. Passionate. Would she have been able to stop him? She rather thought so. She thought Devlin's self-control was never very deep beneath the surface. He was a man who'd grown up guarding his secrets and denying his feelings. She had seen him deal with her brother-in-law and knew he could control his anger.

Dare she test her theory? Test Devlin? Was she willing to pay the consequences if she was wrong?

She heard the faint click of the door opening and closing, and the slide of the bolt. There was a long pause as she waited, then heard his measured strides coming down the corridor. His footsteps paused outside her door. She made a hasty decision—one she hoped she would not regret.

She hurried to the door and opened it just as Devlin turned away. "Did you want something, Mr. Farrell?"

He gave her a rueful smile. "A bit late for 'Mister,' is it not?"

She returned his smile. "Come in, Devlin. I have been waiting up to talk to you."

"I…I shouldn't. You are prepared for bed." He gestured at her pale blue wrapper.

"A bit late for modesty, is it not?"

"A lady," he said with a grin, "would not throw a man's words back at him."

"Lucky for me that I'm no lady." She was pleased that he recalled their exchange mere days ago. In the reverse, it seemed somehow naughtier. She turned away, leaving the door open for him.

Knowles had left a decanter of wine and glasses on the side table. She poured a healthy measure and took him the glass. A little spark traveled up her arm when their fingers made contact. She collected her wits and gestured at a comfortable chair beside a table and lamp.

He followed her directions and made himself comfortable. He was in shirtsleeves again and she realized he had left his coat on the table outside her door. "If this is about the things I told you last night, Lilly, let me assure you that they are all true and discussion will not yield more information or mitigating circumstances. Every word was all the bald truth."

She poured her own glass of wine and went to stand by the

fireplace. "I did not want to discuss it. I merely wanted to tell you how I feel about it."

His gaze dropped to the floor, as if he could not face her when she denounced him. Ah, but that was not her intention at all. "There are things we can choose in this life, Devlin. Who our parents are and the circumstances of our birth are not among them. I do not care in the least that Rutherford is your father or that Olney is your brother. I do not give a fig for the fact that you were born on the wrong side of the sheets."

His gaze lifted to hers.

"What I care about, Devlin Farrell, is how you have chosen to deal with me."

He nodded his understanding. "I know I hadn't the right to take you from the church. But, Lilly, if I could change it, I am not certain I would. I would apologize to you, but it would ring hollow. What I am sorry for is that I caused you distress, and that I have limited your choices by my behavior."

"Distress?" She arched an eyebrow at him as she took a reckless gulp of wine. She went back to the side table and filled her glass. She would need the fortification.

"Well, then. I suppose I should cause you a bit of distress, shouldn't I. Tit for tat."

"I—"

"That was not a question, Devlin. But, for the life of me, I cannot think what might cause you distress. Have you any ideas?"

"I… No."

Lilly tapped one finger against her cheek in pretended thoughtfulness. "Hmm."

He started to rise from his chair as if he would come to her. "Lilly—"

"No. Sit down, Devlin, and stay there. I do not want you distracting me. Do you think you can do that much for me?"

He eased back into the chair and she deemed his silence as consent. She plucked one end of the sash that secured her robe around her waist as she walked toward him, stopping just out of reach, and watched his expression as the gap widened to reveal what lay beneath. A muscle jumped along his jaw while his eyes darkened and grew heated.

"I wanted to thank you for your gift, Devlin. Very thoughtful of you."

She had laced her new corset over her sheerest silk chemise and was aware that the fabric hid nothing. Barely covered by the silk, the dusky areolae were subtly evident and the corset laced beneath them accentuated their size.

His breathing deepened and his tongue slipped along his lips.

"Thirsty?" she asked.

He nodded.

"Am I causing you distress?"

He nodded again.

"Good."

She let the wrapper slip down her arms, leaving her exposed. He started to rise again but she forced him back into the chair by placing her bare foot against his chest and giving a little push. She wagged one finger at him with a stern look.

He swallowed hard and his fingers twitched on the arms of the chair.

She hoped her courage would not fail her as she pulled the corset strings from where she'd tucked them in the V between her breasts, then untied the silk knot and let the strings dangle as she dropped her arms to her sides.

"Lilly, you cannot—"

"But I can. You want to touch me, do you not?"

He nodded.

"You want to unlace me, do you not?"

Again, he nodded.

She feigned an indifferent sigh. "And you are distressed? Oh, poor thing."

Chapter Nineteen

Devlin had been dreading what Lilly might say or do after the revelation of the circumstances of his birth. He'd been certain that she would reject him, and he had told himself that he could live with that as long as Lilly was happy. He'd been an idiot.

This Lilly—the slightly naughty Lilly, the coquette Lilly— would be impossible to give up. And yes, she was causing him the worst distress of his life. He wanted her. Wanted to touch her, to hold her, to kiss those pouting lips and bring those rosy nipples to erect little peaks that teased his tongue and set fire to his loins. He wanted to—

"Shall I show you how it works?" she asked.

Oh, God… He could not speak and nodded dumbly again. She had replaced the white silk cords with pink ones, making it easier to see the weave through the eyelets. She had done an intricate weave instead of a simple back-and-forth lacing. Slowly, one loop at a time, she proceeded with the undoing of *him.*

She fumbled with the laces for a moment and he realized that she was almost as tense as he. Ah, but he was drawn as taut as a bowstring, and she was merely shy.

But what game was this? What point did she hope to make?

That she could discomfit him? Cause him distress? Point taken. How much further would she go? Where would she stop?

She had been attending her laces and finally looked up at him again. A little smile, not as confident as she might want it to be, curved her lips. Her hair, as undone as she, fell over her shoulder and curled around her breasts like living blond tendrils. He was unaware that he'd groaned until she chuckled.

She walked around behind his chair and leaned over to whisper in his ear. "How distressed are you, Devlin? Are you in pain yet?"

Her breath in his ear, moist and hot, caused him to shudder. He couldn't be certain what sort of pain she was referring to, but he was near to doubling over with the pain of his arousal. "Yes," he admitted.

"Good," she said. Still behind, she reached around him and undid his cravat. Thank God Knowles had only tied a simple knot this morning. One tapering fingernail traced a line down his neck to the button that fastened his shirt. She slipped her hand inside and rested her palm flat against his chest.

"I can feel your heartbeat, Devlin. Is it racing? Or does it usually beat so fast?"

"Only when I am…distressed," he admitted, hoping she'd stop and praying she wouldn't.

"Good," she said again, and with each pronouncement of that word, he loved her a little bit more.

For all her unpracticed moves and tentative touches, she was the most erotic woman he'd ever known. From the accomplished whores who'd taught him what a woman likes to the coy courtesans who'd ignited his passion and his imagination, none had ever aroused him as much as Lilly O'Rourke.

She came back around in front of him, and he was pleased to see the flush of passion on her cheeks and the way her eyes had grown soft and deep. Sweet Lilly was not untouched by her own ploy. She plucked at her corset strings again, loosening one more row of laces, then fumbled when she drew the strings through the eyelet.

"Allow me," he offered.

"Would it cause you distress?"

He barely hesitated, the lie coming without premeditation. "Yes."

"Liar."

A dimple deepened in her cheek as she tried to hold back a laugh. He was fascinated by that look, and by the warm feeling it always evoked in him. He remained motionless while she went to the side table and poured more wine. She turned to face him as she took a drink. Something in his face must have startled her because her hand shook and a drip of sweet red wine fell to her chest, a single bead of it trickling a slow path downward toward the chemise.

Ah, there it was! His breaking point. He stood and crossed to her in three easy strides. She did not retreat but held her ground with a challenge—one he was eager to accept.

He bent her backward over his arm and lapped at the wine before tracing the path of it upward. But he did not stop there. He licked downward again, following the course the droplet would have taken, nudging her chemise lower with his chin. At last he captured one enticing bud between his teeth and gave a gentle tug.

She moaned and went limp. He fought the urge to toss her upon the bed and take her swiftly. She had begun this torturous game, and he would damn well finish it. But Lilly's game was one of gentle teasing and he would answer in kind.

He took her to the cheval mirror, stood behind her and slipped his hands around her waist. Slowly, he moved them upward to the laces beneath her breasts. The chemise he'd nudged lower no longer shielded her modesty. The rosy crescents peeked above the fabric and made him nearly wild with lust. He took a deep breath and began the slow methodical unlacing of Lilly O'Rourke.

He drew each lace through one eyelet at a time, drawing the moment out. Lilly watched him, making no move to cover herself or escape his handling. When, finally, the last lace was freed, she leaned back against him and met his gaze in the mirror as he cupped her breasts.

"Do you want me?"

He nodded.

"Good." She sighed, turned in his arms and put hers around his neck. "I think I'd die if you didn't."

"Then you'll live forever," he murmured into her hair.

He lifted her and carried her to the bed, trying to cool his ardor. He wouldn't make the mistakes he'd made last time.

She fumbled with his shirt, tugging the tails out of his breeches and pushing it over his head, sliding her palms over his flanks in a frantic hurry. He placed her on the coverlet and helped her, even more eager to feel her flesh against his. He kicked off his shoes and his breeches were easily discarded, then his drawers and stockings.

Lilly had been helping him but she was still clad in her chemise. His patience, tested to the end, snapped. He tore the fragile fabric from neck to hem and pushed it off her arms. He paused, wondering if he had frightened her with his urgency, but she merely laughed.

"I believe I only have one chemise remaining, Devlin."

"Good," he said, nuzzling her neck before he pushed her back against the pillows.

She was like wildfire beneath him, twisting and burning out of control. Her every touch inflamed him and drove him closer to the edge, but he let himself be guided by her reactions, by her urgings and sighs. Prepared to go slowly this time, to attend to her every desire, her every unspoken wish, he was kissing his way down her stomach when her voice stopped him and she tugged at his hair.

"Devlin, please! I need you *now.*"

She was perfect!

He rose above her and pressed forward gently, but she wrapped her legs around him and lifted to him. He delved deeper and she went with him, taking all of him and matching him thrust for thrust, moan for moan. She was like a fist of velvet and fire around him, unlike anything he'd ever known before.

She cried out her release with a soft surprised scream as he spent himself inside her.

Lilly was a goddess. His goddess.

Though she woke alone again, Lilly had a clear memory of Devlin kissing her and slipping from her bed to go to his own. Somehow, she did not think that would fool Knowles, though his face had been impassive when he'd brought her breakfast tray.

She'd dressed in her best morning gown of sprigged muslin, a summer confection of multicolors on a cream background, and decided to look for her host. Knowles had mentioned that he had not left for the day, and she wondered if he was waiting to talk to her. She hoped he had found a convincing argument for her to marry him.

When she reached his study, she heard voices and paused. Devlin was speaking, then another male voice she did not recognize. She wondered if she should interrupt him or simply find Knowles and ask him to tell Devlin that she would wait for him in the library. If his business was private, he would not welcome an interruption.

She had turned away but heard a name that stopped her where she stood. *Cora O'Rourke.* Her deceased sister? But what could Devlin have to do with that? Against her own principles, she turned back toward the door.

"…think whoever is involved may have fixed his attention on the O'Rourke girls."

"I had not thought of that," Devlin's voice replied. "Cora dead, Miss Eugenia and Miss Isabella abducted to be the next sacrifices but for our interference? I will contact Hunter immediately and advise him to keep close watch on them."

"Wasn't there another girl?"

"You know there was, Jack. You drove the coach."

"Ah, yes. Miss Lillian." "Jack" chuckled. "Have we any reason to be concerned for her?"

There was a slight pause before Devlin answered, as if he were considering the matter. "None. I will lock her in her room if necessary."

A long sigh followed that opinion, then, "That is not what some of your 'lads' are hearing. They've been bringing me news of disappearances. D'you recall Buxom Betty? She used to loiter in the taproom at The Bell and Whistle? No one has seen her in more than a week."

"Bloody hell," Devlin snarled.

Lilly gulped. She'd thought that ugliness was done with. The mere idea that someone might be lying in wait for one of her sisters made her nauseous. She would have to warn them at once.

"As for Olney," Jack's voice continued, "we've had the devil of a time finding anything on him. Have a lead on Rutherford, though, and I will follow that to its conclusion."

So then, Devlin's attempt to discredit or disgrace his father and half brother had not ended with her. Devlin was nothing if not a very determined man.

And then a niggling doubt tickled the back of her mind. Was seducing her, keeping her close by, just another ploy of Devlin's to hurt the family? Was he still using her?

No. He had made a clean breast of it with her family. He was protecting her from being arrested and sent to gaol. He had proposed marriage. Would he do all that just to spite Rutherford?

"…I think the Blood Wyvern Brotherhood is more concerned with hiding from the law than with finding new sacrifices. But warn the girls, eh? They should be aware of what is afoot in the rookeries."

"Aye. Meantime, I've learned where Booth is hiding, and one or two others. But Henley has eluded me. He's a canny one."

"The most dangerous, I've heard. Have you had any luck finding proof that could be used for a conviction?"

She heard a chair scrape on the wooden floor as someone stood.

"Nothing. I think you can abandon hope of that, Dev. Henley would never leave loose strings like that. If there was proof, it would have been found weeks ago. And that is why I am worried about the O'Rourke girls. If they could identify any of them…well, it could be very dangerous for them."

"I've got the lads on that…."

Their voices faded as Lilly spun and fled down the passageway to her room.

There was no time to waste if she were to meet Gina and Bella. Lilly would have to leave at once. She twisted her hair into a knot and pulled her straw bonnet over it, making certain it covered any trace of blond strands. Although the day was warm, she added a light shawl over her shoulders to mask her shape. Surely now there would be nothing to give her away.

She snatched up her reticule and hurried to the stairway door. If Devlin caught her, he would put an end to her plan. She could not risk that. Her sisters' lives could be at stake.

She ran and did not slow down until she was only three streets away from Andrew Hunter's home. She paused to catch her breath in the park where Devlin had first kissed her. Sooner or later, her sisters would be along.

She sat on a bench, planning her next move. If Gina and Bella did not come, she would have to go through the mews and the garden in back of the house.

Though she was keeping her head down, she was aware of someone taking a seat on the bench beside her. Then a gentle nudge to her arm.

A hushed, secretive voice said, "Are you meeting someone here, Miss Lillian?"

Olney! An uneasy chill raced up Lilly's spine. She risked a peek beneath the rim of her bonnet. "How did you know?"

"Your gown, m'dear. You wore that one morning when I called upon you."

Drat! "Are you going to call for the charleys?"

He laughed, a gentle sound reminiscent of the Olney who had courted her so many weeks ago. "No, my dear. I have been coming here every day since I know your sisters walk here at this time. I have been hoping to encounter you."

"Why?"

"To apologize, Miss Lillian. I acted like a fool. I was angry and distraught. I had hoped we could put it all behind us, and then you lied about the jewels, and it tweaked me wrong."

"I… It wasn't a lie. Exactly. You see, Mr. Farrell had gone back to fetch them, and he had not arrived back yet. I was so certain he would be back any moment…"

Olney nodded. "I gather that to be the case. I believe I collided with him on my way out. So then, the jewels have been returned?"

She lowered her head again, knowing how illogical her explanation would seem. "No. Someone had taken them by the time he returned. He is searching for them now, but I cannot promise they will ever be found. Please, Olney, talk to your father. Ask him if there is a compromise we could reach. Some way to make amends and put this all behind us."

He reached out to take her hand and give it a comforting squeeze. "That is what I want, too, my dear. I think Father is beginning to come around. I think, too, if you were to speak to him, it would help persuade him."

If there was even a small chance of that… Olney read her hesitation and pressed his advantage. "Tomorrow? Meet me tomorrow and I will take you to him. If we could straighten this mess out, Miss Lillian, we could still marry. As far as society knows, we changed our plans at the last minute out of respect for the dead queen. We could go forward again in a few weeks, and no one would be the wiser."

She could never marry him now, but she could not tell him that. She could do nothing, in fact, that would upset this new and delicate truce. They must settle the matter of the jewels first, and then the matter of their engagement.

He squeezed her hand again. "My bastard brother only took you out of spite, Miss Lilly. But in spite of that, I am still willing to marry you. There would be no impediment to our vows."

None but her consent. None but that Devlin had spoilt her for any other man's touch. Only that he was all and more than she had ever wanted.

"Did you know he came to see us?" He smiled when she looked up at him, astonished. "He asked us to withdraw the charges. Said he'd bring the jewels back as soon as we did. And he told us he'd had knowledge of you. Gloated that he'd ruined you for me."

She gasped. How could he?

"But here come your sisters, Miss Lillian. We mustn't let them see us talking until we have settled matters, eh?" He stood and lifted her hand to his lips. "Tomorrow. I shall be here at four o'clock. Do not disappoint me, m'dear. We shall make my father understand that none of this is your fault."

And with that last pronouncement, he was gone. By the time Lilly collected her wits, Gina and Bella had recognized her and were coming toward her.

Bella's eyes filled with tears. "Lilly! Oh, it is so good to see you, but you shouldn't have come. Andrew warned us we could be followed."

"Come." Gina pulled her to her feet. "We shall walk. Bella and I were on our way to the modiste. If we keep moving, perhaps they will not suspect anything."

Her sisters flanked her, led her from the park and entered the busy foot traffic on the street.

"I've come to warn you," she told them. "I overheard Mr. Farrell talking to someone. They were discussing those awful men who killed our Cora—some sort of brotherhood. Some of them escaped and are hiding in town."

Gina's footsteps faltered, and she squeezed Bella's arm. "What did they say?"

"I think that they are trying to find them all so they can bring them to justice. And they are worried that a woman has disappeared. Then there was something about a Mr. Henley and trying to find proof. I am afraid that if you can identify any of them, the court may ask you to testify, Gina."

A nearly panicked look spread over her face and Lilly realized the depth of her fear. Anything that could frighten the ordinarily intrepid Eugenia must be very bad, indeed.

"I only recognized a few," Gina said. "Lord Humphries, a man named Throckmorton… They, and the rest, were wearing robes. I did not even recognize Andrew until he pushed his hood back. Oh, I cannot believe all this is coming back. I want to go home, to Belfast."

"Mama will not budge until this scandal with Lilly is

settled." Bella slipped her arm around Gina in an attempt to comfort her, then stopped and turned around. "But I think it would be safer if none of us go abroad until this is over."

Lilly wondered again what had happened that night in July. Certainly more than she had been told. "I…I am trying to work things out with Olney and the duke, and Mr. Farrell is still searching for the Rutherford Sapphires. Surely all we need is a few more days to settle matters.

"Gina, please tell me what happened that night," Lilly said. "Perhaps I could help you if I knew."

"I cannot tell you anything, Lilly. I had been drugged. I do not…remember more until the last, when the opium began to wear off."

"Would you recognize Mr. Henley if you saw him?"

A violent shudder shook Gina's delicate frame. "I will never forget his face. Or his…voice. It haunts me every night in my dreams."

"Lilly, please," Bella entreated. "Gina is not up to this. It is still too fresh."

Ah, it was these men, then—this Blood Wyvern Brotherhood—who had killed Cora and ruined her family. Whatever had been done to Gina was worse than anything ever done to Lilly. Mr. Farrell had been callous to her feelings in the beginning, but as kind to her as she'd allowed him to be. And later…later he'd been everything she could want.

She gave both her sisters quick hugs. She'd come to warn them, and she'd done that. Now it was time to find a way out of this quagmire. She'd been undecided about meeting Olney and his father tomorrow, but now she knew she would have to face them to end the scandal. "Go home. Keep safe. Tomorrow should see an end to my scandal and you can go back to Belfast, Gina."

Chapter Twenty

Lilly was nearly back to The Crown and Bear when Ned caught up to her and gave her a cheery smile. "G'day, Miss Lilly. Yer lookin' fine today. Got a blush on yer cheeks an' everything. Me ma used to say it's a sure sign a woman's in love."

She laughed and ruffled his shaggy hair. "Or it could be a sign that it is summer and hot in the city."

He gave her an impish grin. "I seen the way Mr. Farrell looks at ye. I think 'e likes ye, miss. We'd like t' see 'im 'appy, y'know."

"We?"

"The lads an' me."

"What lads?"

"Look around, miss. Me an' my mates. Gutter rats, they calls us."

She glanced around the square and noted a few stray boys, some barely eight years old, others twelve or so. Ned's mates. "And you want to see Mr. Farrell happy?"

"'E looks out fer us, 'e does. Sees we got a square meal every day. A place to sleep in the winter. No slimy flash 'ouse, neither, but a proper cot and blanket."

"He does?"

"Aye. Pays fer it 'imself, 'e does. 'E pays a gent 'oo teaches us our numbers an' letters and ciphers. An' if any of us gets 'urt, 'e takes care of it. 'E's as close to a da as any of us has."

She smiled. Her heart had ached when Devlin had spoken of his early years, of sleeping in doorways and digging crusts of bread from other people's garbage. But he had remembered, and he had changed the little he could. Her heart swelled with tenderness for him.

"Aye, and the doxies, too."

Doxies? "Do you mean women?"

"Aye. Strumpets. Drabs. Y'know. Women what—"

"Yes!" She held up one hand to halt him before he could explain further. "He cares for them, too?"

"Not the same, Miss Lilly. Only those what wants t' leave the trade, so to speak. Or wants t' go 'ome t' the shires."

Because of his mother.

"They learns a real trade, not just liftin' their skirts. Somethin' what could get 'em hired. It's what 'e does, miss."

"What?"

"It's what 'e does. There's plenty o' men in the rookeries what never do anything fer anyone. Not Mr. Farrell."

A lump formed in Lilly's throat. She had loved Devlin from the moment he had carried her home from the gypsy camp. From the precise instant that she realized he had, indeed, rescued her from a disastrous marriage when he carried her from that church. The man was aggravating, arrogant, autocratic and secretive. But he was also generous, kind and charitable.

He rose from his beginnings and became a better man than his "betters," because the true measure of a man is not in the circumstances of his birth, but in his character and deeds. Devlin Farrell was the best man she'd ever known.

"Wait 'ere, miss! I think that's one o' the gents Mr. Farrell wants."

She turned to see a blond man weaving his way through he crowd, glancing over his shoulder as he went. Yes, he ooked like a man who was hiding from something. Or someone. She watched the top of Ned's shaggy head as he gave chase. She could not see exactly what happened, but either the man stumbled or Ned bumped into him. She heard a faint apology in Ned's puckish voice and then saw his head bob away as the man continued on his course.

A moment later, Ned was beside her again. He brandished a small leather-bound book. "Can you read this, miss?"

She took the volume from him and opened the cover. Written in a fancy script were the letters *BD, LH*. That told her nothing. She opened to a random page and scanned the lines. Andrew's name popped out at her, and Henley's. There were others, but she did not take the time to read. This was enough to tell her that the man whose pocket Ned had just picked was one of the men Devlin was looking for.

"Good work, Ned! Mr. Farrell will want to see this. Come along so you can give it to him."

"I'll catch up to 'im later, miss. I got to 'ide. When a gent finds out 'e's been picked, 'e calls the charleys."

"Not this one, Ned. He is hiding from them, too."

He grinned but she could see that he didn't entirely believe her. In his experience, he was about to be chased. He pushed the journal back at her. "You takes it. Mr. Farrell was goin' t' give me a reward, though."

Lilly opened her reticule, pushed the journal inside and gave him the only thing she had—a five-pound note. His eyes grew round and he pushed it inside his shirt. "I never 'ad so much at one time, miss."

"I shall see that Mr. Farrell knows you found this. I am certain he'll want to thank you."

He beamed, turned on his heel and was gone.

* * *

Devlin was waiting for her when she arrived back at The Crown and Bear. He'd been pacing between the foyer to the sitting room long enough that there were scuff marks from his boots on the gleaming wood floors. Poor Knowles would spend hours polishing the marks out.

He gripped her shoulders to hold her immobile. "Where have you been? Did I not tell you to stay inside?"

She untied her bonnet. "I seem to recall something of the sort."

"I was worried about you, Lilly. Every charley in London is looking for you. Will I have to set a guard on the door?"

She held her temper because she could read the concern in his eyes. And because she knew he was right. "I promise that I will not go out again unless it is absolutely necessary." And if it meant finding a way to reconcile with Rutherford, the meeting with Olney tomorrow would be necessary. Her head began to throb.

He released her, looking slightly abashed for his anger. " shall hold you to that. If anything happened to you…"

She dropped her reticule and bonnet on the entry table "Yes, I know. How would you ever explain it to my sisters And Andrew would demand answers. I did not mean to put you in an untenable position, Devlin, but I chafe at being shut away. And I hope you will not think ill of me, but when I came looking for you this morning, I overheard you talking to someone who said that Gina and Bella might be in danger."

"And you went to warn them?"

"Yes. But I was very cautious, and I met them in the park They went home straightaway, and so did I." Her conscience troubled her a bit for skimming over her meeting with Olney but she knew he would forbid her to meet him again.

He sighed and turned toward the sitting room. "Lilly, I sen

someone to warn Andrew Hunter the moment Jack left. You needn't worry that I would let such a thing escape me."

She followed him, taking the hairpin out of the severe knot on top of her head. "I suppose I should have thought of that, but the O'Rourke women are not accustomed to someone taking care to their safety. Since Papa died, we have learned to fend for ourselves."

"No more, Lilly. If you could learn to trust me, I would see to all your needs. I would keep you safe and provide everything you could want."

Her hair tumbled down her back, and she dropped the hairpin on a nearby table. "That is very kind of you, Devlin, but I am not your problem."

"Have you come to a decision regarding my proposal?"

Yes! Oh, yes! "Give me a reason, Devlin. A single reason. One that has nothing to do with you abducting me, or feeling responsible for my predicament."

His eyes looked stark and he turned away from her. "What do you expect me to say that I haven't already said? I'm the duke's by-blow, Lilly. I was reared on the streets of Whitechapel. I have stolen and cheated for most of my natural life. My friends are among the most hated and feared men in England. I live above a gin house. I have little to offer you, but I offer it, nonetheless."

He was wrong. He was twice the man she had ever expected to marry. He could have escaped Whitechapel and started a better life anew but he had stayed, and Whitechapel was a better place because of that. He was changing lives for the better, and he had carried on his charity in the shadows, not seeking acknowledgment or thanks. And she wanted him more than she'd ever wanted anything in her entire life. But not on his terms. On hers. If he could not say the words she needed to hear, she would let him go. Because Devlin deserved someone he loved.

"I need to think, Devlin. And, if you should think of any persuasive reason in the meanwhile, please advise me of it." She turned and left him standing there, a puzzled expression on his face.

Devlin sat back in his chair and watched the other men in Wycliffe's office—Andrew and Jamie Hunter, Jack Higgins and Wycliffe himself. He was not accustomed to being included in strategy on this side of the law. All his work for Wycliffe had been confidential and done as a favor.

Jamie stood and went to the cupboard where Wycliffe kept his whiskey. "The Gibbons brothers found me this afternoon. They've located Booth and Henley in a warren off Petticoat Lane. If you ask me, they knew it all along. Just wanted to make it look as if they made an effort to come up with the information." He poured himself a small amount and held the bottle up for others. When they all shook their heads, he carried it with him to Wycliffe's desk and put it down.

"Where are they now?" Wycliffe asked.

"The Gibbons brothers? I gave them some cash and told them to get out of town for a fortnight."

Higgins grunted. "Why? In their own way, they are as bad as the Brotherhood."

"If Henley catches wind of this before we can put our plan in action, the brothers would be dead and the Brotherhood would be gone."

Silence met this assessment. They were likely all thinking that London would be a better place without the Gibbons brothers. Devlin knew it for a fact, but now was not the time to remind them of that.

Jamie wrote an address on a piece of paper and pushed it across the desk to Wycliffe. "That's where they are. According to the brothers, aside from Henley and Booth, there are at least six of them clustered together in the same tenement."

"That was easier than I thought. It was a good idea to put the Gibbonses on this, Farrell."

Devlin shrugged. Had there been any other way to get the information quickly, he wouldn't have dealt with them. He knew from long experience that there was a price for dealing with the devil, and he prayed that information had not come too dear. It was only a matter of time before Richard and Arthur would turn up to claim a favor in return.

It was Jack's turn to report and he took a deep breath. "There are rumblings of a resurgence of the Brotherhood. Nothing certain yet, but a disappearance or two. Could be nothing to it. Could be the beginning of something new. I do not think we can afford to sit on this for long."

Wycliffe combed his fingers through his hair and sighed. "We cannot afford to sit on it, but there is nothing we can do without evidence. Is there anything we can tie to them? Any proof at all?"

"Not yet. No bodies have surfaced, but if they've been clever, they never will."

"Henley, I believe, is more canny than Lord Humphries was. Henley did not have the brains to think up the Brotherhood scheme, but he is certainly capable of keeping it going and even eliminating the mistakes of the past. Humphries got sloppy. Henley won't."

Devlin agreed. "The lads are reporting the same things— one or two missing tavern girls, but little else. I think they'd have heard if something was afoot."

Wycliffe folded the address and put the scrap of paper in his waistcoat pocket. "And the other matter, Farrell?"

"I put Freddie Carter on it since the Home Office was involved anyway. He reported that he had a lead northeast—

a jeweler in Colchester." Colchester was the nearest town to his cottage, but Wycliffe did not need to know that. Devlin had every intention of keeping his haven secret. "I think it is logical to assume that any thief would want to unburden himself of stolen goods as quickly as possible. The jeweler was suspicious, however, and the thief ran off. Impossible, now, to tell if those were the Rutherford Sapphires."

"God only knows where they may surface."

"*If* they surface," Devlin finished.

It occurred to Devlin that Colchester was almost too close to his cottage. What thief would risk running into his mark? Or selling to a jeweler who might have knowledge of them? No, the thief would have to know better. Know they were safe in trying to sell the gems. And that could only be—

"Proof," Wycliffe pronounced. "All this is for naught if we cannot come up with proof. We can arrest them, lock them up in Newgate, but we cannot prove a case against them and will not be able to hold them. Do you think Miss Eugenia O'Rourke could be persuaded to testify?"

Jamie shook his head and finished his whiskey. "She is still a bit distraught over the events that night. I would hate to press her, Wycliffe. 'Twill ruin her in society, despite that she is not to blame for any of this."

"She may have to testify anyway. With no other proof, she is all we have." He stood and went to a cabinet to withdraw a file. "We cannot afford to wait any longer. Each day that passes is another day they may bolt England altogether. Another day that could cost another woman her life.

"Hunter, tomorrow night, when you receive word from me, take your brother and the charleys to Petticoat Lane. Use force—whatever you must, but bring them in. I will handle Lord Elwood. He will take the arrest easier from me. Farrell, you may choose. Stay home and keep out of it, or take care of your own business."

Devlin knew Wycliffe was giving him the discretion to arrest his father and half brother, let them go or keep out of it entirely. The choice was his. "I will inform you tomorrow," he said as he stood.

Intending to look in on Knowles and Lilly, then retreat to his office downstairs, Devlin let himself into his apartments. The clock in the sitting room chimed twelve, and he realized he'd been gone longer than he intended. As he walked down the passageway, a voice stopped him.

"Devlin?"

He retraced his steps to the sitting room. Had Lilly waited up for him? How…domestic. And how interesting that the thought gave him a warm feeling in his center.

She was sitting in a comfortable chair, holding a book and looking quite peaceful, as if she'd been prepared to wait until dawn if necessary. "You needed something?"

"I forgot to mention that I encountered young Ned this afternoon. He gave me something to deliver to you, but I forgot it when you…began interrogating me."

He smiled. "It was hardly an interrogation, Lilly."

She stood and brought him a small brown leather-bound volume that had been resting on the table. "Where did Ned come by this?"

"He picked a pocket. He said the man looked like one you described."

He opened the cover and found an inscription on the facing page. *BD, LH.* Bryon Daschel, Lord Humphries. His heartbeat accelerated. He looked up at Lilly and could tell by the expression on her face that she had seen the contents. Lord. He would have spared her that if he could. "How much did you read, Lilly?"

"The first three pages. That's all I had the stomach for. I

collect he was the founder of the group that killed Cora and injured Gina. He was an evil man, this Lord Humphries."

He nodded. "As bad as anything that ever came out of Whitechapel."

"Well, you have it now, and I've discharged my duty to Ned. If you will excuse me, I will retire."

Bittersweet disappointment washed through him. This awkwardness between them was new. Just last night she had given herself to him heart and soul, and tonight she was nearly a polite stranger. He reached out for her as she passed him, and she stopped with an inquisitive arch of an eyebrow.

"Thank you, Lilly" was all he could manage.

She looked down at his hand on her arm and a delicate shiver went through her. "I cannot stay here any longer, Devlin. You know that, do you not?"

"Tomorrow, Lilly, we will settle this."

He watched her disappear down the passageway and then took Humphries' diary to his study, turned up the wick on a lamp and sat down with paper and pen.

Some time later, he had made sense of it. He had compiled a list of names, dates, places and deeds. It was enough to turn the stomach of a charnel-house keeper and he was glad Lilly had stopped reading. The accounting of the ritual that had ended her sister's life was lurid and disturbing. Humphries had dedicated a page in his journal to each participant, detailing the extent of their participation. This book in the founder's own handwriting was all Wycliffe needed to bring an end to the case once and for all.

Why had Henley kept the damning evidence? Blackmail, perhaps? Had he been extorting money from the members of the Brotherhood? If so, Henley was living on borrowed time. These men would not pay hush money without reprisals.

And now, at *his* fingertips, was the means to destroy his

enemies. His mother had not been Rutherford's only rape. And Olney, though he had been less involved than most, was far from innocent. He'd been a fairly new initiate and had not been entrusted to the procuring of victims or the disposing of them.

Devlin was glad, now, that his father had not raised him.

After a long hesitation, he tore two pages from the book and closed it. He hadn't decided, yet, what to do with them. Then he penned a quick note to Wycliffe and wrapped it around the diary. Tomorrow he would deliver it to Wycliffe's office, then pick up Ned and bring him here. Devlin knew Ned's technique, and the lad would not be safe if Henley remembered the boy who had bumped into him before the diary went missing. Yes, Henley was likely in a panic by now.

He stood and stretched, wondering if Lilly would still be awake. He wanted her to know that the threat to her would be over by tomorrow night. He wanted her to know that he had kept his promise. By tomorrow, they would settle this, and their future.

He barely hesitated at her door and when he tested the knob, it turned. She had not locked him out.

"Lilly?" She did not move and he was disappointed. He had wanted to share what he had learned with her.

He went forward, hopeful that she would waken. She had woven her hair in a prim little braid. Her cheeks were flushed and one hand, the fingers curled toward her palm, rested on the pillow beside her. Had she been reaching for him in her sleep?

The sweep of her dark lashes fell upon her cheeks and her lips parted in a soft sigh. He was roused by the vision. He wanted her. Would always want her. Unable to stop himself, he leaned over and traced the curve of her cheek with one finger.

She stirred, and the hand that had rested upon the pillow found his. She turned her face toward their hands and kissed his palm before bringing it back to her cheek and smiling, her eyes still closed.

Lilly was in that netherworld between sleeping and waking, where all things were unreal and held no substance. Where honesty was the only thing that mattered.

His viscera twisted with the strength of his reaction. He knew in that moment that he would do anything for her. Anything.

"I love you, Lilly O'Rourke," he whispered, saying the words aloud that he had held in his heart for so long, afraid of rejection and scorn.

Devlin knew it was a risk entering the Home Office in the middle of the day. If he was recognized, his usefulness to Wycliffe would be over. Not that he cared much about that. But the diary was too valuable to entrust to anyone else.

Wycliffe's door was open and he looked around the panel and found him alone. He closed the door behind him and Wycliffe looked up.

"What…" He came around his desk and passed Devlin to lock the door. "What possessed you—"

He tossed the diary on Wycliffe's desk and took a seat while Wycliffe returned to his chair and untied the string. "What is this?"

"Everything you need."

Devlin sat quietly while Wycliffe read his summary and then leafed through the book to verify certain facts. When he looked up again, his face was a mixture of disgust and elation.

"Where did you get this?"

"One of the lads picked it off a 'gent' in the market yesterday afternoon. He described Henley."

"You are right. This is everything we've been praying for. Everything we need. With this as evidence, 'twill be like Humphries is testifying from beyond. It's all here." Wycliffe paused at the rough edges still remaining from the torn pages. "Well, almost all."

Devlin grinned but said nothing.

Wycliffe sat back in his chair. "If there were missing pages, do you think they might turn up again?"

"Possibly. Possibly not. But there would be no more threat."

"Then tonight we go forward. Tonight justice will prevail, and these men—" he held up the sheet of paper "—will be arrested."

Chapter Twenty-One

Lilly hoped Olney would not be late. She was anxious to discuss solutions and then go back to The Crown and Bear. She'd had to leave before Devlin had returned from whatever errands had taken him away so early this morning, and she wanted to talk to him.

Secretly, quietly, in the middle of the night, she had heard the one argument that would gain her consent to marriage. *I love you, Lilly O'Rourke.* It couldn't have been a dream. If Devlin still wanted her, she was his.

The park was crowded in the warm afternoon. Children were playing under their governesses' watchful care, ladies were enjoying a leisurely stroll and gentlemen tipped their hats to them as they passed. Lilly was, in fact, certain she was being watched and fighting a dreadful feeling that something would happen to ruin her meeting.

Suddenly Olney was beside her, taking her hand. "Come, m'dear. My coach is waiting."

She stood and noted Olney's excited face. She had only seen him so agitated when he'd gone to ask his father for permission to marry her and she hoped this did not portend a repeat of that. She never should have let him believe reconciliation would be possible.

He took her arm and led her toward the street and his waiting coach. He handed her up, then climbed in behind her and knocked on the roof. The coach started off at a brisk pace and she was relieved there would be no further delays.

"I am so pleased you came," Olney said. "Everything has been prepared for you."

"Prepared? Whatever for?"

"Er, tea, m'dear."

"Very considerate of you, but I cannot stay long, Olney. I must be getting back."

"Back where? Where, precisely, have you been staying whilst the charleys have been tearing up the town for you?"

"With…with a friend. I am certain you will understand that I cannot give you a name. They have protected me at considerable risk to themselves."

"Come, you can tell me, m'dear. I would not do anything that would cause you harm. Surely you know that by now."

But what came to her mind was that Olney had believed the worst of her and tried to push her to her knees in her brother-in-law's library. She shook the memory from her head and proceeded cautiously. "What difference does it make now, Olney? I am here, and we are going to see your parents."

"Not my parents, Miss Lillian. My father. 'Twould never do to let the duchess see you. She would send you packing before we could utter a single word."

She glanced out the window and noted that the coach was not headed toward Rutherford House. "Where are we going?"

"We have a small cottage a bit out of town. You will be quite comfortable there."

A frisson of fear shot up Lilly's spine. Something was

dreadfully wrong here. She reached for the door handle but Olney pulled her back.

"Tch-tch," he mocked. "Can't have you taking a tumble, can we?" His grip tightened around her arm.

"—but then the gent puts 'er in a coach an' they was gone. I couldn't chase on foot, Mr. Farrell, but I tried to keep my eye on 'er, like you said."

Devlin stared at Ned, trying not to show his own alarm. The boy was more disheveled than usual and had worked himself into quite a state. "Calm down, Ned. Take a deep breath and tell me everything you can about what you saw."

Ned took a swallow from the cup of tea Knowles had brought. "It were a big coach. Black. An' it had a gent's crest on the door."

"Can you describe it for me?"

"Had a cross an' two horses. An' a shield an' sword. That's all I remember."

It was enough. Rutherford. Lilly had met either Olney or his father and had gone away with them. Jealousy tweaked him and forced him to ask, "Willingly? Did she go willingly, Ned?"

"'Peared to. 'E took 'er arm, but she didn't try to get away."

"Was it a young man or an old man who took her away?"

"Like you, Mr. Farrell."

Olney. "What direction did they go?"

"Toward Paddington, sir."

There was nothing out there but roads leading out of town. Where in God's name would Olney take her? The Rutherford estate was in Essex—the wrong direction. He went to his study door and shouted, "Knowles!"

The valet came so quickly he must have been lurking close by. "Sir?"

"Miss Lillian is missing. Young Ned here says that he saw

Olney put her in a carriage and take her away. Northeast of town. Do they have any holding up there?"

A flash of alarm passed through the valet's eyes. "I cannot say what property they have now, sir, but they used to have a rather large cottage in St. John's Woods. The duke used to take his, ah, indiscretions there. I believe Olney had begun using it, too, before I was discharged, sir."

I cannot stay here any longer, Devlin. You know that, do you not?

No. She could not—she *would* not—go willingly with Olney. Not after giving herself to him so completely. And yet his demons rose to taunt him. He was baseborn, beneath her. He was tainted by his past, unable to give her the things she deserved—respectability, security, consequence in society.

Devlin buried his disillusionment. Whether she wanted him or not, she would be making a mistake to go with Olney. Now, with what he knew about his half brother, he knew that with dead certainty. Lilly needed rescuing again.

"Knowles, I will need directions to that cottage." He turned to Ned. "Stay here, lad. I will take care of it. Knowles will fix your supper and find you a place to sleep upstairs near him. I don't want you wandering about until tomorrow. Understand?"

He nodded and followed Knowles from the study. Devlin stood, folded the two pages he'd ripped from Humphries' diary and tucked them in his waistcoat pocket. He slipped a pocket pistol in his jacket and a knife in his boot, and headed for the door.

As if to frustrate him further, a loud banging started just as he reached for the knob. He opened the door and found Durriken standing there, a thunderous look on his face and Drina in tow. He was not surprised to see his friends—in fact he had been expecting them—but he cursed the timing.

"Sorry, Durriken. I have business to be about. Come in and wait, if you wish. God willing, I will be back in a few hours."

"Alas, this will not wait, old friend. It will only take a minute." He pushed forward, leaving Devlin no choice but to lead them to his study and offer them a glass of the deep red Madeira that Durriken loved so well. Drina hung back, staring at the floor and looking miserable.

When they were settled, he asked, "Now, what is this about?"

"I have come to humbly beg your pardon for my wretched kinsmen—" he turned and looked squarely at Drina "—and women."

Devlin did not even raise an eyebrow when Durriken withdrew a sparkling necklace and earrings from his deep pockets. The Rutherford Sapphires, of course.

"This one—" Durriken gestured at Drina "—took them from your cottage."

She looked up then, tears welling in her eyes. "I wanted to say goodbye to Florica," she said. "But you were gone. I went up the stairs to see if she had left me anything, and I found those on her table."

"Enough!" Durriken shouted. "You did not think she gave them to you. Not even you are so foolish, Drina."

"No, not that Florica would have given me such beauty, but that they meant so little to her that she could leave them behind. If she did not want them, I did."

Devlin had suspected something of this sort since learning that a man had tried to sell them in the village. "Why did you not return them to me when I asked the next day?"

Again, Durriken answered for her. "She begged the man who wishes to marry her to sell them," he snarled between gritted teeth. "Brishen had departed for the village before you returned. The girl was frightened that you would punish her, eh? She should have feared me."

He examined the jewels. They were all intact and none the worse for wear. He added them to the cache in his pockets.

"How did you find out?"

"Brishen told me. He feared the *gajo* would follow him back to the camp and wanted us to leave. We are on our way to France. God willing, we shall return next spring. We do not steal from our own, Devlin, and you are one of our own."

"I understand and forgive my brothers," Devlin said. "And I forgive my little sister, too. Next time, Drina, tell the truth. It will go easier with you."

She nodded and a small smile began to form on her lips, the first Devlin had seen since their arrival.

It occurred to him that if Drina had returned them sooner, he would never have had Lilly, even for so little time. Never been able to pretend that she would always be waiting for him at night, always a breath away. "And thank you, my friends, for not returning them too soon."

The coach ride to St. John's Woods did not take long but it was dark by the time they arrived at the address Knowles had provided. Devlin studied the house as he stepped down and straightened his jacket. He was prepared to be denied admittance, but that had never stopped him before.

The lane was quiet and only a single light illuminated the entry. He knocked and a moment later, a faintly disreputable butler answered the door. "Sir?"

"I am here to see Rutherford or Olney. Either will do."

"I shall inquire if they are receiving." And the door closed in Devlin's face.

No. Not this time. He applied his boot to the door. Two solid thumps, and it was open. This was becoming a habit with him. The butler's eyes grew round and fear showed on his face.

"You may retire for the evening," he said with a mocking

smile, and the butler hurried away. Devlin doubted he'd see him again.

Light spilled into the corridor from a room to the left of the foyer. "What is it, Compton?"

Devlin pushed the door open wider and stepped in. "Compton has retired. I let myself in."

Rutherford coughed and Olney leaped to his feet from the overstuffed chair he'd been lounging in. "How did you find us?"

He shrugged. "The point is, I did." He glanced around the room, spotted a sideboard with a decanter and glasses and went to pour himself a glass. "We have a few items to discuss," he said over his shoulder.

"See here—" Rutherford began.

"I'd advise you to hear me out before you begin issuing threats or ultimatums. It's deuced hard to eat one's own words, and I wouldn't want you to choke. *Before* I'm done, that is."

He took a sip of his wine and went to look out the window, both to be certain his coach was still there and to determine if anyone might be joining them. Reassured, he turned back to his father and brother.

"First, I want to know where Lillian O'Rourke is."

Olney's eyes shifted to the corridor. "How would we know?"

"Do not play games with me, Olney. I was not asking if she was here, merely which room you are keeping her in."

Rutherford looked confounded. "How do you know such things?"

"You've had several days to have me investigated, have you not? Do you mean to tell me that you have not been advised that I know a great deal about everyone? And that I can acquire any information I want?"

The first grudging gleam of respect lit Rutherford's face. He coughed again and dabbed at his eyes with a handkerchief. "Very well. I know who you are now. What I want to know is what you want from me. Money? Recognition? I do not think so, Farrell. Do you really think I'd claim a king of criminals?"

"I have enough money to see me through a few lifetimes. As for your recognition—no. You are not a father I would be proud to claim. I do not want people knowing that I share blood with an old reprobate and his scoundrel son."

"Then?"

"I want Miss O'Rourke. Bring her to me."

Rutherford laughed. "All this for a chit? What a waste, Farrell. Are you so stupid that you cannot think of better extortion than a whore?"

Devlin's blood boiled. Whore? He tightened his jaw until he could control his words. "Miss O'Rourke," he repeated.

"Very well, we have her," he admitted. "Olney wants his turn."

He turned to his brother. "If you touch her—"

"What makes you think I haven't? Didn't I tell you what a practiced slut she is?"

"You lied."

"How can you be sure?"

Devlin merely grinned. Olney took the meaning, and his face turned livid with anger. He started for Devlin, but something warned him back—likely Devlin's reputation.

He removed the jewels from his jacket pocket and tossed them on the sideboard as if they were trash. "Here are the fabled gems."

Rutherford stood and snatched them up with a greedy leer. Once he had them in his grasp, he laughed. "Given up your bargaining card, have you not, pup? Why should we give you Miss O'Rourke now?"

"You mistake me. That wasn't my bargaining card. I simply did not want them. Tasteless and gaudy. Too ostentatious for my liking. No, I have something a bit more powerful than that."

They laughed, so certain they had the upper hand now. Devlin couldn't help a small chuckle of his own before he asked, "Where were you on July thirteenth?"

Olney turned white. Rutherford began coughing again and Devlin wondered if he'd be able to catch his breath. "Take your time," he invited. "I am certain it will come to you."

"If…if you know enough to ask the question, then you know damned well where we were," his father finally managed.

Devlin nodded to confirm this assumption.

Olney took a hesitant step forward. "How?"

"I was there. I came with Andrew Hunter."

Father and son digested this news before Rutherford played his trump card. "Your word against ours, Farrell. And you know which of us the courts will believe."

"Ah, but I have proof."

"There is no proof." Olney straightened his spine, more sure of himself now. "If there were, we would know it by now."

"I have it," Devlin said. "And *that,* gentlemen, is my bargaining card."

Rutherford narrowed his eyes, an ugly sneer forming on his pallid face. "You are bluffing, pup."

"Humphries kept a diary."

Both men gasped at Devlin's revelation.

"I know, for instance, that Olney attended the last three rituals. And that he had not achieved enough status to participate in the ritual. And Humphries mentioned that you were involved in the planning of several, Rutherford. I know, too, that you participated in rape. My mother was not the first, I gather, but I can guarantee that you have raped your last woman."

"Others were more involved than—"

"That does not pardon you, Rutherford. Those men are being arrested at this very moment. I believe Lord Wycliffe will be knocking on Elwood's door momentarily. No doubt the scandal will ruin him."

Rutherford fell back into his chair, shaken by this news. "He will be coming for us next."

"He would, but I ripped out the pages of that diary that mention your names and crimes. So there is one tiny glimmer of hope," Devlin offered. "One small chance to save yourselves."

"Miss O'Rourke," Olney guessed.

Devlin hesitated. This was the moment he'd waited twenty bleak years for. He had saved for it, planned for it. He held their fate in his hands. He could destroy them utterly, or he could spare them. There was no doubt that they deserved the worst the courts could deal them. Indeed, the chance of losing both fortune and title at the end of a rope was a breath away. His breath.

And none of it meant anything without Lilly.

For Lilly, then.

"Miss O'Rourke," he confirmed.

"Get her," Rutherford ordered his son.

Olney went to the door.

Devlin pulled the pistol from his jacket pocket and pointed at Rutherford. "And do not think to come to the rescue, Olney. I am a crack shot at any distance, and your father is too big a target to miss."

Olney's glare was enough to tell Devlin that the idea, at least, had occurred to him.

"Now," he said when Olney had disappeared, "here are the rest of my terms. You will withdraw all charges against Miss Lillian. You and your son will never whisper so much as a single word against her. At each and every encounter, you will both treat her with respect and consideration. Furthermore, you will indicate to the ton that the fault for the interrupted nuptials was all yours."

Rutherford nodded his consent, but Devlin was not finished yet. "And you, *Father,* will go nowhere but your house and your club. Consider it a form of jail if you wish but, should you manage to find the vigor, I must be assured that you will not despoil another woman. Do you understand?"

"But that is absurd!"

He shrugged. "I hear you haven't long to live anyway. I think you should be spending your remaining time in making whatever amends are possible—anonymous restitution to the victims' families might be a good start. And time on your knees in prayer, of course. I would not want to meet my maker with *your* sins on my soul.

"As for junior, well, I shall be keeping a very close eye on my brother. I gather from Humphries' diary that he had not crossed the very murky line you crossed years ago. There may yet be hope for him. Though, should he stray far from the straight and narrow path, or should either of you damage Miss O'Rourke in any way, a page or two might arrive on Wycliffe's desk…."

If Rutherford's complexion was any indication, he was moments from apoplexy.

"Come now. It isn't all that bad. All either of you have to do is mend your ways."

"You swear by those terms?" Rutherford asked.

"I do. And then all you will need to worry about is your associates. I cannot keep your friends, or those members of the Brotherhood who may be trying to bargain for their lives, from talking. If you've been discreet, and continue to be discreet, you have no need to worry."

Lilly burst through the door and flew into Devlin's arms. She looked frightened but uninjured. He kept his pistol pointed at Rutherford's chest until Olney appeared, unarmed and defeated.

"Have they hurt you, Lilly? In any way?"

"No. But I think…" Her arms tightened around him.

He knew what she thought, and she was likely correct. He gave Olney and Rutherford his darkest scowl. "I can only guess what you planned for Miss O'Rourke, but it will never happen. Never. Your friends will not be arriving."

"Here, now. Who said—"

"Enjoy the remainder of your evening," he said over his shoulder. He lifted Lilly in his arms as he had in the church and carried her to the door.

Lilly, the saucy wench, was thinking the same thing. She sighed and whispered in his ear. "Thank you for rescuing me from Olney again, Devlin. I hope this will be the last time."

He smiled, knowing he'd rescue Lilly his whole life, if that was what it took to keep her safe. And his. Always his.

Epilogue

"He has managed to surprise us all, Lillian," Mama said, looking around the lavishly appointed sitting room.

"Hmm?" Lilly could not keep her eyes off Devlin. Across the room, in a circle of his new family, he turned to catch her gaze, a crooked smile on his handsome face—as if he were the cat that swallowed the canary. He raised his glass of French champagne to her and drank a silent tribute. But when he licked his lips and winked, her knees went weak. Oh, she hoped her family would leave soon.

"Giving his bride a house as her wedding gift," Mama explained. "And such an extravagant house! I had to content myself with pearls for my wedding gift."

"Yes, it is very nice, is it not? His other home would not have been appropriate for a married man, he said. But I would have lived with him anywhere," she said, still watching her husband.

Gina sipped her champagne and watched the men, too, a

wistful look on her face. "Yes, but it would not have been fitting considering his new status, now that he is generally known as a Manlay—Rutherford's acknowledged natural son."

"Rutherford acknowledged him? I had not heard this news."

Bella smiled. "Rather canny of him, I thought. 'Tis a good way for him to assure himself that Devlin will keep whatever family secrets he carries. Now, for your husband to disgrace the Rutherford name would be to disgrace his own name."

"His name is Farrell."

"Regardless, he is a duke's son, and that will open doors hitherto closed to him. Coupled with his link to the Hunter family, he will be entering new circles."

A new level of acceptance? No more to be known as the King of Whitechapel? She was not certain she cared a whit for that. But she cared for Devlin, and if it would make him happy, she would take any name he chose.

Mama sniffed. "Whether you care or not, Lillian, I am well pleased by this turn of events. There is no disgrace in marrying a duke's son, even one born on the wrong side of the sheets. Though it would have been better—"

"Enough, Mama. I have no doubt I married the right brother." She watched as Andrew, Jamie, Charlie and Lord Lockwood shook Devlin's hand and came toward them in preparation for leaving.

"I suppose," Mama allowed. "After all, Olney had not purchased you such a grand house."

"House?" Devlin asked, having caught only the last of the conversation as the men joined them.

"Heavens, yes! Quite impressive. Why, just look at the grand staircase. Magnificent!" Mama sighed happily.

Lilly slid a sideways glance at Devlin. "Oh, I don't know, Mama. All that up and down, up and down."

Devlin laughed and gave her a look that warned her she was about to pay for her teasing. "I shall be pleased to assist you with that, Mrs. Farrell."

* * * * *

Chapter 1

October
New York City

Nicole Masters was sitting cross-legged on her sofa while a cold autumn rain peppered the windows of her fourth-floor apartment. She was poking at the ice cream in her bowl and trying not to be in a mood.

Six weeks ago, a simple trip to her neighborhood pharmacy had turned into a nightmare. She'd walked into the middle of a robbery. She never even saw the man who shot her in the head and left her for dead. She'd survived, but some of her senses had not. She was dealing with short-term memory loss and a tendency to stagger. Even though she'd been told the problems were most likely temporary, she waged a daily battle with depression.

Her parents had been killed in a car wreck when she was twenty-one. And except for a few friends—and most recently her boyfriend, Dominic Tucci, who lived in the apartment right above hers, she was alone. Her doctor kept reminding her that she should be grateful to be alive, and on one level she knew he was right. But he wasn't living in her shoes.

If she'd been anywhere else but at that pharmacy when the

robbery happened, she wouldn't have died twice on the way to the hospital. Instead of being grateful that she'd survived, she couldn't stop thinking of what she'd lost.

But that wasn't the end of her troubles. On top of everything else, something strange was happening inside her head. She'd begun to hear odd things: sounds, not voices—at least, she didn't think it was voices. It was more like the distant noise of rapids—a rush of wind and water inside her head that, when it came, blocked out everything around her. It didn't happen often, but when it did, it was frightening, and it was driving her crazy.

The blank moments, which is what she called them, even had a rhythm. First there came that sound, then a cold sweat, then panic with no reason. Part of her feared it was the beginning of an emotional breakdown. And part of her feared it wasn't—that it was going to turn out to be a permanent souvenir of her resurrection.

Frustrated with herself and the situation as it stood, she upped the sound on the TV remote. But instead of *Wheel of Fortune,* an announcer broke in with a special bulletin.

"This just in. Police are on the scene of a kidnapping that occurred only hours ago at The Dakota. Molly Dane, the six-year-old daughter of one of Hollywood's blockbuster stars, Lyla Dane, was taken by force from the family apartment. At this time they have yet to receive a ransom demand. The housekeeper was seriously injured during the abduction, and is, at the present time, in surgery. Police are hoping to be able to talk to her once she regains consciousness. In the meantime, we are going now to a press conference with Lyla Dane."

Horrified, Nicole stilled as the cameras went live to where the actress was speaking before a bank of microphones. The shock and terror in Lyla Dane's voice were physically painful to watch. But even though Nicole kept upping the volume, the sound continued to fade.

Just when she was beginning to think something was wrong with her set, the broadcast suddenly switched from the Dane press conference to what appeared to be footage of the kidnapping, beginning with footage from inside the apartment.

When the front door suddenly flew back against the wall and four men rushed in, Nicole gasped. Horrified, she quickly realized that this must have been caught on a security camera inside the Dane apartment.

As Nicole continued to watch, a small Asian woman, who she guessed was the maid, rushed forward in an effort to keep them out. When one of the men hit her in the face with his gun, Nicole moaned. The violence was too reminiscent of what she'd lived through. Sick to her stomach, she fisted her hands against her belly, wishing it was over, but unable to tear her gaze away.

When the maid dropped to the carpet, the same man followed with a vicious kick to the little woman's midsection that lifted her off the floor.

"Oh, my God," Nicole said. When blood began to pool beneath the maid's head, she started to cry.

As the tape played on, the four men split up in different directions. The camera caught one running down a long marble hallway, then disappearing into a room. Moments later he reappeared, carrying a little girl, who Nicole assumed was Molly Dane. The child was wearing a pair of red pants and a white turtleneck sweater, and her hair was partially blocking her abductor's face as he carried her down the hall. She was kicking and screaming in his arms, and when he slapped her, it elicited an agonized scream that brought the other three running. Nicole watched in horror as one of them ran up and put his hand over Molly's face. Seconds later, she went limp.

One moment they were in the foyer, then they were gone.

Nicole jumped to her feet, then staggered drunkenly. The bowl of ice cream she'd absentmindedly placed in her lap shattered at her feet, splattering glass and melting ice cream everywhere.

The picture on the screen abruptly switched from the kidnapping to what Nicole assumed was a rerun of Lyla Dane's plea for her daughter's safe return, but she was numb.

Before she could think what to do next, the doorbell rang. Startled by the unexpected sound, she shakily swiped at the tears and took a step forward. She didn't feel the glass shards piercing her feet until she took the second step. At that point, sharp pains shot through her foot. She gasped, then looked down in confusion. Her legs looked as if she'd been running through mud, and she was standing in broken glass and ice cream, while a thin ribbon of blood seeped out from beneath her toes.

"Oh, no," Nicole mumbled, then stifled a second moan of pain.

The doorbell rang again. She shivered, then clutched her head in confusion.

"Just a minute!" she yelled, then tried to sidestep the rest of the debris as she hobbled to the door.

When she looked through the peephole in the door, she didn't know whether to be relieved or regretful.

It was Dominic, and as usual, she was a mess.

Nicole smiled a little self-consciously as she opened the door to let him in. "I just don't know what's happening to me. I think I'm losing my mind."

"Hey, don't talk about my woman like that."

Nicole rode the surge of delight his words brought. "So I'm still your woman?"

Dominic lowered his head.

Their lips met.

The kiss proceeded.
Slowly.
Thoroughly.

* * * * *

Be sure to look for the
AFTERSHOCK *anthology next month,*
as well as other exciting paranormal stories
from Silhouette Nocturne.
Available in October wherever books are sold.

n o c t u r n e ™

NEW YORK TIMES BESTSELLING AUTHOR

SHARON SALA

JANIS REAMES HUDSON
DEBRA COWAN

AFTERSHOCK

Three women are brought to the brink of death...
only to discover the aftershock of their trauma has
left them with unexpected and unwelcome gifts of
paranormal powers. Now each woman must learn to
accept her newfound abilities while fighting for life,
love and second chances....

Available October wherever books are sold.

Harlequin® Historical
Historical Romantic Adventure!

HALLOWE'EN HUSBANDS

With three fantastic stories by

Lisa Plumley
Denise Lynn
Christine Merrill

Don't miss these unforgettable stories about three women who experience the mysterious happenings of Allhallows Eve and come to discover that finding true love on this eerie day is not so scary after all.

Look for
HALLOWE'EN HUSBANDS

Available October
wherever books are sold.

REQUEST YOUR FREE BOOKS!

Harlequin® Historical
Historical Romantic Adventure!

™

2 FREE NOVELS PLUS 2 FREE GIFTS!

YES! Please send me 2 FREE Harlequin® Historical novels and my 2 FREE gifts (gifts are worth about $10). After receiving them, if I don't wish to receive any more books, I can return the shipping statement marked "cancel". If I don't cancel, I will receive 6 brand-new novels every month and be billed just $4.94 per book in the U.S. or $5.49 per book in Canada, plus 25¢ shipping and handling per book and applicable taxes, if any*. That's a savings of 20% off the cover price! I understand that accepting the 2 free books and gifts places me under no obligation to buy anything. I can always return a shipment and cancel at any time. Even if I never buy another book, the two free books and gifts are mine to keep forever.

246 HDN ERUM 349 HDN ERUA

Name	(PLEASE PRINT)
Address	Apt. #
City	State/Prov.	Zip/Postal Code

Signature (if under 18, a parent or guardian must sign)

Mail to the **Harlequin Reader Service:**
IN U.S.A.: P.O. Box 1867, Buffalo, NY 14240-1867
IN CANADA: P.O. Box 609, Fort Erie, Ontario L2A 5X3

Not valid to current subscribers of Harlequin Historical books.

Want to try two free books from another line?
Call 1-800-873-8635 or visit www.morefreebooks.com.

* Terms and prices subject to change without notice. N.Y. residents add applicable sales tax. Canadian residents will be charged applicable provincial taxes and GST. Offer not valid in Quebec. This offer is limited to one order per household. All orders subject to approval. Credit or debit balances in a customer's account(s) may be offset by any other outstanding balance owed by or to the customer. Please allow 4 to 6 weeks for delivery. Offer available while quantities last.

Your Privacy: Harlequin Books is committed to protecting your privacy. Our Privacy Policy is available online at www.eHarlequin.com or upon request from the Reader Service. From time to time we make our lists of customers available to reputable third parties who may have a product or service of interest to you. If you would prefer we not share your name and address, please check here. ☐

HH08R

Silhouette®

SPECIAL EDITION™

**FROM *NEW YORK TIMES*
BESTSELLING AUTHOR**

LINDA LAEL MILLER

A STONE CREEK CHRISTMAS

Veterinarian Olivia O'Ballivan finds the animals
in Stone Creek playing Cupid between her and
Tanner Quinn. Even Tanner's daughter, Sophie,
is eager to play matchmaker. With everyone
conspiring against them and the holiday season
fast approaching, Tanner and Olivia may just get
everything they want for Christmas after all!

*Available December 2008
wherever books are sold.*

COMING NEXT MONTH FROM

HARLEQUIN®
HISTORICAL

- **THE MAGIC OF CHRISTMAS**
  by **Carolyn Davidson, Victoria Bylin and Cheryl St.John**
  (Western)
  Three festive stories with all the seasonal warmth of the West—
  guaranteed to keep you snug from the cold this Yuletide!

- **SCANDALIZING THE TON**
  by **Diane Gaston**
  (Regency)
  Lady Lydia Wexin has been abandoned by her family and friends,
  and creditors hound her. Her husband's scandalous death has left her
  impoverished, and the gossipmongering press is whipped into a frenzy
  of speculation when it becomes clear the widow is with child. Who is
  the father? Only one man knows: Adrian Pomroy, Viscount Cavanley...

- **HALLOWE'EN HUSBANDS**
  by **Lisa Plumley, Denise Lynn, Christine Merrill**
  (Western/Medieval/Regency)
  All is not as it seems for three lucky ladies on All Hallows' Eve. The
  last thing they expect from the mystery of the night is a betrothal!

- **THE DARK VISCOUNT**
  by **Deborah Simmons**
  (Regency)
  A mysterious gothic mansion haunts Bartholomew, Viscount Townsend,
  but it is also the new home of childhood friend
  Sydony Marchant. The youthful bond they once shared is lost—will one
  stolen kiss be enough to rekindle that intimacy and help them unravel
  the shadows of the past?

HHCNM0908